THE
KNOT

THE
KNOT

TIM WYNNE-JONES

McClelland and Stewart

The Canadian Publishers
McClelland and Stewart Limited
25 Hollinger Road, Toronto M4B 3G2

Canadian Cataloguing in Publication Data

Wynne-Jones, Tim.
   The Knot

ISBN 0-7710-9051-X

I. Title

PS8595.Y66K66   C813'.54   C82-094728-8
PR9199.3.W96K66

Printed and bound in Canada
by T. H. Best Company Limited

Grateful acknowledgement is made to the Ontario Arts Council for its assistance.

Lines from Edward Albee are from *A Delicate Balance* (New York: Atheneum, 1966).

Lines from C.S. Lewis taken from *That Hideous Strength* (New York: The Macmillan Company, 1947).

For Amanda West Lewis

Prologue

R. Rum Crawford was on the roof when District Supervisor Colin McIlwane stopped at his door. McIlwane knocked smartly, militarily, having rung the doorbell several times without apparent result. Doorbells were low on Crawford's priority list; so were visitors. Sprawled on the nether side of the roof Crawford was not at first aware of McIlwane's presence below. He was busily caulking around a newly installed skylight when he noticed the Supervisor's distinctive car – a dangerously blue Gremlin with imitation wood panels – parked on the street. A man is marked by such possessions. Crawford himself drove a brown '74 Plymouth Duster in which the previous owner had left hanging a scented pair of fuzzy dice. Crawford had not removed them; they weren't his style but they were the car's.

Ratatatat.

Check-up time again. Since Crawford's accident, Colin McIlwane had come by regularly but never yet unannounced. He was an old and solicitous friend. The last check-up had been a month earlier. They had sat together in the open stands watching the Argonauts in a driving rain. Crawford had lasted three quarters. The Argonauts had lost. Crawford wasn't much in the way of company; not since the accident, anyway.

From where Crawford now lay he could see no more of his visitor than a thick shoulder, swathed in bilious green water-repellent fabric, which swayed in and out of view below the eaves. McIlwane, sensing Crawford's presence, waited with the patience of a Jehovah's Witness, tapping a large foot lightly. Crawford slid back out of view and rolled over on his back. Resting his head on folded arms he looked up into the October bright clouds. Nine months, was it really so long? The house was nowhere near completion. It was a funny old thing and on the wrong side of the tracks to ever be truly valuable. But it was home. When the medical officer had given him leave, he had thrown himself into its renovation, and was rapidly going through a life's savings in the process. Crawford aimed his caulking gun at the sun, which winked momentarily from behind the cloud curtain. A whistle sounded from the candy factory up the street.

"Crawford?" McIlwane called between cupped hands.

Crawford slithered further out of view. He didn't want solicitous company. He didn't want *any* company. He wanted to work on his house, shore up his defences. From where he lay he could turn his head and see boys in white aprons, smeared with chocolate like dried blood, come out of the factory into the daylight for a smoke. Above them a tall chimney spewed chocolate and coconut fumes into the thick city air. Every so often the effluvium from the chimney was anise-scented.

Crawford lived on Baseball Park Road, on the outskirts of Cabbagetown. There was no park anymore and no baseball. In an old panoramic photo once he had seen the park. It had stretched north from Queen Street all the way to the borders of Cabbagetown but now the outfield was a wasteland of railroad tracks. Crawford was the only full-time resident on the block. Across from him there was a row of deserted but not always empty houses boasting a tenancy of cats and stray humans who arrived in the city via the railroad corridor, slipping out of drag freight in the middle of the night. They seldom bothered him or he them.

He watched McIlwane finally retreat to his car, stop, and then write something in a small pad, looking for all the world like a traffic cop. He returned to leave the note and then departed. The blue Gremlin shuddered into animation and, pulling a U-turn, wiggled off down the road. Crawford's relief at his departure was tinged with sadness. He immediately regretted his childish game of hide and seek. His reticence was the real wound. The bullet had long since been removed but it had left a hole in him. His head fell back on his arms, he closed his eyes. There was the dead man's face with its dead eyes which did not reflect the light shone in them. Crawford snapped his own eyes open again and was momentarily dazzled by the sun. McIlwane didn't like him to refer to what had happened as an accident but then what had it been? Had the whole episode been contrived? Had he deserved to be shot? What he had done could hardly be called investigative prowess. He had shuffled into a warehouse and into a madman's line of fire. He had been decorated and granted an extended leave of absence to forget the whole thing. But he couldn't quite. And it was that which brought McIlwane back for his regular check-ups, usually under the guise of some cheerful outing.

The sun slipped back into an envelope of clouds and Crawford checked his skylight. Then straddling the peak of the roof he slid down its steep side, reptile fashion, caulking gun still in hand. Tossing it to the ground he heaved himself out and over the eaves, landing heavily but on his feet and on the porch, facing the front door where Colin had stood minutes earlier. His note was stuffed in the mailbox, a small white invasion of Crawford's privacy. What diversion had Colin come up with now? Why hadn't he phoned first? With a strange sense of foreboding, Crawford retrieved the note.

Part One

"...he 'discovered in his
mind an inflammation
swollen and deformed –
his memory.'"
C.S. Lewis

1

It had all started innocently enough with an idea but ideas had a way of running amok in Crunkscully's mind. It wasn't that he had lost his memory but he did have a habit of losing access to it; memories were there, all right.

Crunkscully arrived home to the unmistakable aroma of baked tuna. Not a remarkable aroma but a worrisome one considering his room had neither stove nor hotplate. The source of the smell was soon discovered. Sisyphus had vomited on the heat vent. Sisyphus was, otherwise, conspicuously absent. Having cleaned up the hardened mess, Crunkscully sat down in his armchair breathing heavily from the exertion. After a moment he heaved himself up again and gazed out of the window. Fall cool air seeped in around its rotten frame and the glass wobbled in and out with a slow rhythm which made it seem like the room was breathing. For all that, he could not open the window; several generations of paint resisted his attempt. If she had escaped that way then she had done so as a ghost on the room's breath, and ghosts left something behind. Something more substantial than vomit.

He looked down at the littered patch of yard thirty feet below, expecting to see among the beer bottles and cigarette cartons a cat's flattened corpse. A newspaper stirred momentarily animate; a shadow sidled along the fence.

Crunkscully's eyesight was not very good. Without thick

spectacles the world was a blur and with them it was rendered strangely limpid, as if submerged. He wiped both bottle-glass lenses on his tie and placed the heavy glasses on his nose. No cat. Beyond the rotten green fence in the alley stood Frank, the house superintendent, waxing his car. The car was gold and very clean. Aside from him, the alley was deserted. Crunkscully turned back from the window to his room.

He had known when he had brought her here she was an old cat, despite her slimness and the strength of her vocal cords. She liked to jump. She pitted herself against dizzying heights: the rack in the closet, the transom over the door, and shelves which only she could see on the room's bare walls. These mad displays were conducted with dismaying regularity accompanied by her distinctly Siamese yowl, shrill and scolding. She wanted to escape, to go home, and he had hoped she might lead him there. But when he had tied a string around her neck, she didn't lead him anywhere in particular and complained mightily. He was sure she was one of Connie's. Now all that was left of her was a smell. He called softly: "Sisyphus." There was no answer. Sisyphus wasn't really her name anyway.

If the room was bare without her it had not been much better with her. After three weeks of occupancy it still had the bleakness about it of the want ad; it was a "rm furn," little else. The furnishings were vestigial, serviceable at best; an iron bed, a night table, a garbage can of school-surplus grey, and a metal chair of recent vintage and doubtful construction. There was also an easy chair, more comforting than comfortable, and a dresser. The dresser was rather grand. It was oak with a tall mirror and looked as if it had been in place for a century. It would probably still be there when the old house finally caved in; hovering majestically above the ruins. The walls were of no particular colour. There were blemishes where pictures once had hung. Above the bed hung the blemish of a cross which reminded Crunkscully of hospital. It was like a memory of hospital that could not be removed; a painful memory. He missed the simplicity of hospital. The excitement of the outside world was enervating at times.

In the whole room only the dresser showed signs of occupancy for it had, like a magnet, accumulated what personal remnants Crunkscully still possessed. For him, the dresser was like a shrine. Its surface was cluttered primarily with tape cassettes, a portable recorder, and a veritable confetti of notes scribbled on torn bits of paper, some of which, more important than the rest, were Scotch taped to the mirror's edge.

Taped on the oak frame of the mirror was a newspaper clipping. A man and a woman and a cat smiled at the camera. Connie had remarried, someone named Bernard K. Muraskin. In the picture she stood with him on the steps of their renovated townhouse. Connie was smiling the most and holding the cat, which squirmed. Bernard was stroking the cat and squinting. The story accompanying the picture was glib society-page chatter. Crunkscully had circled the caption with a felt marker. "Connie, K. and cat pose for posterity. A son is away at school." He had underlined "A son is away at school" three times.

It seemed the Muraskins had been in town for just a few days, but Connie had made quite a to-do of what a fine city Toronto was. For Bernard K. the city held one major interest – the Hermes Corporation over which he had fought a rather strenuous battle for control. The details of the battle did not besmirch the society page. Rather, the article was about their homes in London, Zurich, and Jamaica, and their "landing pad" in quaint little Cabbagetown for those times when Bernard K. had to guide Hermes through a crisis. Connie liked Toronto for the trees, according to the article.

Connie had so changed that Crunkscully scarcely recognized her. Her hair was darker than he recalled and frothy with curls. She looked altogether too young, not the Connie he remembered at all; but he didn't trust his memory.

Crunkscully picked up the walking stick that leaned against the dresser's side. That too was a memento from the past. There

15

had been a time when he fell over backwards a lot. The spell had passed. There were so many spells.

�֎

Number 14 Elmsley Court might have sounded to some an attractive address but it was a less than desirable home. It could be characterized by a complete absence of grandeur, not only in its crumbling façade but in the life which pervaded it. Despite its immense, gloomy presence the house was far from indestructible: bricks had been known to fall from the chimney, windows had, on occasion, slipped from weathered putty moorings and steps, now and then, disintegrated under too heavy a tread. It was a desiccated Victorian monster inhabited by a variety of lost souls with whom, after three weeks, Crunkscully held only a nodding acquaintance.

In the corridor outside his room one of those souls hobbled past. He could tell from the gait that it was the woman in room 9 who had confronted him on his first night there. In a drunken stupor, and with a salacious wink, she had admitted to being Adolf Hitler; *the* Adolf Hitler. Most of the time her name was Olga. As far as Crunkscully could tell she never left the house except now and then when the day was warm, and then only to walk around in circles in the scruffy front yard. She might have seen Sisyphus and this fact presented him with a dilemma. He found it difficult to talk to people and he avoided confrontations with strangers but if Olga had seen his cat then confront her he must. He opened the door the slimmest of cracks. In a tremulous whisper he asked: "Have you seen my cat?"

By now the woman had passed his door. She stopped and turned around with a kind of delirious grin, as if he had said something very kind or had offered her a prize.

"My cat?" he tried valiantly again.

Her grin drooped somewhat and then it faded entirely. Her eyes were glazed like scalded eggs. She was scratching a sore on her lower lip. "I didn't take no cat." She scowled.

"Excuse me," Crunkscully apologized hurriedly and shut the door.

This did not deter Olga. In her addled brain she stood accused. Defiantly she raised her voice. Louder it grew, and more abrasive, and her verbal attack more obscene and progressively obscure.

Crunkscully hated scenes. He hated attention of any kind; attention invariably confused him. If Olga kept on long enough, as she showed every sign of doing, someone else would come, and then someone else, until a crowd had gathered at his door. He could see it now; a veritable lynching mob. They would bring their lawn chairs and beer and wait patiently for him to open up. The image was horrifying, so, plucking up his courage, he resolved to face the enraged harridan.

As soon as he opened the door her tirade stopped dead. She beamed up at him. "I've been thinking!" she announced proudly. "It were probably them kids."

Crunkscully was too perplexed by her sudden shift in mood to respond. Then, down the corridor, a door squeaked open and a fat brown face appeared. Olga clasped her hands to her breast for all the world like an uglified Mary Pickford and then waved at the face which hung like a moon in the twilight of the hall.

"Them kids been 'round again?" asked the moon.

"That's right, Chas," said Olga.

"It really doesn't matter," muttered Crunkscully, and he pulled his head back through the crack like a threatened turtle.

Olga jammed her foot in the doorway. She had on orange high heels and green socks. "Oh, it's okay. Chas can tell you all about 'em," she said enthusiastically.

The moon rose on thick rounded shoulders until his body almost filled the hall. He walked very slowly. Even close up his face was like a moon. It was pockmarked and in its stillness was like ancient eroded rock. His lips hardly moved when he spoke and because Olga's did when she listened the two appeared to Crunkscully to be ventriloquist and dummy.

"Come in here on a dare, little buggers." Chas spoke as if his mouth was filled with gravel. "Turn everything upside down and make off with your radio. Is that what they got – your radio? You might tell Frank, but what's he gonna do? They can get in this place half a dozen ways."

Before Crunkscully could speak Olga jumped in excitedly, pointing at Chas.

"He's Ojibway."

Crunkscully managed an awkward smile. Chas nodded and continued with his diatribe.

"One day I catch some of dem Regent Park smart-ass brats and have 'em for lunch." Olga cackled. "You and me, eh, Olga? We eat 'em all up." The idea seemed to please the Indian. He looked almost as if he was going to smile if only the act were not so painful.

Olga grabbed Crunkscully's arm. "Shot on both sides," she proclaimed.

It always happened like that. Crunkscully was quite certain his brain was melting. The conversation had seemed to make some kind of clumsy sense and then out of the blue "shot on both sides!"

Chas had grabbed his hand now and was pumping his arm up and down.

"And don't let me catch you callin' me Charles. I hate the goddamned king. The name is Chas. Chas Shot On Both Sides." Now his stiff face cracked around the edges, revealing a cavernous mouth full of eroded teeth.

Not knowing what else to say and feeling too weak in the knees to retreat, Crunkscully said his name. "Crunkscully."

Chas seemed puzzled. "What kinda name is that?"

"It's my name," said Crunkscully without much conviction.

"Say that again," said Olga.

"Crunkscully...it's my name."

Olga ruminated for a moment and then her face lit up. "I know that voice!" she exclaimed. Then she rubbed at one of the flowers on her print dress as if it was a stain.

Crunkscully's mind wandered. What kids? he thought. Was Ross one of them? Could Ross have broken into his room and stolen Sisyphus back? And what about Sisyphus? But he said nothing.

Olga was clinging to Chas's large arm and the Indian was staring straight down into her glazed eyes. "Eat 'em up Olga, won't we?"

With obvious delight, she nodded, smiling insanely.

The rendezvous had quickened into romance, the relationship had progressed to new depths of intimacy. No longer aware of Crunkscully's presence Chas and Olga wheeled around in the hallway in a stuttering clockwork and made their way down the dimly lit passage to Chas's room. As they departed Crunkscully overheard Olga say: "Who's he think he is anyway, accusing me of stealing his cat!"

"Who's he think he is anyway," muttered Crunkscully, back in the safety of his room. The confrontation had exhausted him.

Standing before his dresser he wrote out a note to himself: "Find Sisyphus." As an afterthought he added: "Sisyphus is a cat."

2

"His mind is like a desert, an arid place, but capable of blooming suddenly. Memories, like seeds, lie near the surface there, in hard kernels waiting for a passing storm to release them, to live again, however briefly. Somewhere in his imagination a storm is brewing all the time. Right now. Any minute."

His memory spoke to him from the tape in the third person present. For reasons he no longer remembered he must have made that decision when he had first undertaken the project of recording his thoughts and dreams. Now the voice no longer seemed his own. It was so confident, so articulate. Perhaps in truth it was not his voice at all, but rather a voice that had once been his own. It was a rich voice, like coffee with cream. Other disembodied voices came and went: doctors in a hurry, amused nurses, and a curious Mister Fowle who identified himself as a roommate. But not Connie. A nurse had told him she had moved to Vancouver.

The coffee-and-cream voice reminded him of who he was and to the best of its ability who he had been. It remembered jokes and anecdotes. It described to him how he felt and tried to explain to him what was going on. It recited passages, straight out of medical journals, delineating the progression of his disease, and it consoled him when the knowledge seemed particularly grim. His brain was degenerating. His own memory had turned against him and this adopted memory had become his closest friend. He had even thought to explain to himself for posterity what he was doing: "It is a time capsule. When his own memory fails the way he knows it must, when it fades away to nothing in time, then he can play himself back." It was a good idea, assuming he remembered the tapes. He had twelve of them so far. Mr. Fowle had called them his disciples.

Crunkscully fast-forwarded the present cassette. "Crunkscully hates attention. He couldn't pay it in school or stand at it in the army." There was an amused chuckle. A woman's voice asked him about the army but, in fact, he'd never been in the army; he was merely entertaining. "Welcome to the twilight ward," the voice continued, "where reality is a thing of the past." Nobody laughed. The performance continued and then ended abruptly. But it wasn't the performance that had ended, it was his memory of it. Sometimes he erased things he didn't want to hear anymore. It was a convenient kind of memory.

Much of it, he knew, was no more than confabulation. He replaced what was forgotten with imagined experiences. He couldn't always tell truth from fiction. His life was full of holes. He filled them in, he re-invented his life. It reoccurred to him in no particular order, a narrative of detached incidents, episodes, like bits of coloured glass in the bottom of a kaleidoscope tumbling into ever-changing patterns.

Side one ended. He turned it over. Side two began; a concerto by Vaughan Williams for oboe and strings. He had written down the title of the piece and then had crossed it out. Nonetheless there it was, plaintive, beautiful music that transported him somewhere full of bright air. Halcyon days. He had a number of tapes of music, bits and pieces between other entries. In this way music had become part of his memory, its strands were interwoven with what he could remember of himself. He pressed the earplug further into his ear and, holding it there, he closed his eyes.

If he had once been garrulous he had learned or chosen to live a more private life. And if it seemed to him listening to the tapes that he had once been a gregarious sort he shunned company now.

In hospital, other patients had helped to pass the time and entertaining gave him something to do; he had to do something! Despite the indications on the tapes, hospital – the memory of hospital – remained a great empty expanse of waiting. Now, his strangely impersonal memory and his music were his most cherished companions.

The music suddenly stopped mid-scherzo. His voice interrupted the recording with all the urgency of a radio bulletin: "He has a strange new relationship with his memory; his memory haunts him. It has made a commando raid on his senses. His memory demands to be all there is, all there has been, and all there ever will be."

The message ended and the taped voice breathed heavily for a moment into Crunkscully's ear. He breathed heavily in resonance with it. He remembered a room within a room. Lights and dials.

There were moments he would rather not remember but which forced themselves upon him. In those moments the kaleidoscopic vision suddenly burst and sharp splinters clattered down the tunnel which connected him with his past, seeming to pierce the membrane of his sight with their intensity. There was one particularly bright and sharp sliver which often tumbled too agonizingly into focus. Ross. A nurse had told him he had no son but it was the same nurse who had told him Connie lived in Vancouver.

His son was Ross. That name was etched too deeply in his memory to be dislodged by a disorderliness of mind. Connected with that name like the tail of a comet was some vague but dreadful memory, rendered especially dreadful in its vagueness. No one could tell him about Ross – not what he wanted to hear – but Ross lived in him compellingly. He came to him in a dream. Crunkscully would feel the sensation of sinking down into his bedclothes, slipping down still further clear through his nightshirt into sleep-like water until he was entirely engulfed in the dream. The circumstances varied but the central image was always the same and it all took place at the bottom of the sea.

There was a beautiful white perambulator with a blue hood and high bright silver wheels. Crunkscully hovered near the pram, but never close enough to see inside and not wanting to. Then suddenly the pram would start to drift towards him, pushed by some irresistible current. He always would try to swim away but without success and when he looked down his feet would be buried in the sand and his legs bound by seaweed. In his desperate attempt to get away he would churn up the water and in his exertion he would soon be surrounded by streaming columns of air bubbles which obliterated his vision of the pram drifting closer and closer towards him. Then suddenly he would stop breathing; the last of the bubbles would float upwards to the surface and as it burst into the air he would always waken. No matter how desperately he had struggled not to look into the pram or see what was or wasn't there the dream always frustrated him and left him heartsick. The vision was fraught with guilt. He had a son, or he had *had* a son. It was a mystery.

As soon as he had seen Connie's picture in the paper he had resolved to find the truth. He had an idea which he kept on a cassette labelled: "The Idea." He would leave the hospital and find the house in the picture. The picture was his only clue; he had no address but the one in the paper – "Cabbagetown." He discovered Muraskin's number was not listed in the phonebook.

He examined the picture closely for clues. The house was sandblasted brick and there was a stained-glass window above the front door. There was iron railing on either side of the front steps. Beside the porch grew an unruly forsythia and under the front window a flower box brimmed with geraniums. The address was hidden. It would be on the wall behind Muraskin's shoulder or on the door behind Connie's frothy head. For hours Crunkscully had stared at the shoulder, the head, trying to find the numbers in the whorls of half-tone dots.

Cabbagetown was a strange hybrid of a community in the

urban core of Toronto. It wasn't more than a mile square. The streets were narrow and tree-lined, and the architecture Victorian in style, if not uniformly in vintage. Whatever else it was, it was old and quaint and well-situated. It had become a slum when the middle class had fled to the suburbs but now it was undergoing a renaissance as a new middle class flooded back into the city's heart. The houses, grand or ramshackle, row or detached, were being resuscitated. The results were mixed; some fine homes were artfully reclaimed to a serviceable beauty, grander homes refurbished to something of their erstwhile splendour, and some less noble shacks given a glamour far exceeding their original value. Propped and stayed, their faces lifted like vain dowagers, the ersatz competed with the splendid, and pretension sidled up to good taste hoping to be mistaken by the uninformed. Cabbagetown wasn't merely housing, it was something of a movement spearheaded by the historically minded, the community spirited and, not least of all, the speculatively shrewd.

On every street could be found masons and carpenters and glaziers swarming like busy beetles over the rotting carcasses. And like the mythic scarab they found new life within the decay. From empty lots sprang luxury flats and townhouses. Amidst the hurly-burly, the poor watched from their shabby porches what was, they thought, their indigenous land reclaimed from the oblivion of Skid Row, and which was now suddenly threatening them on every side. It was a neighbourhood in flux; welfare and well fed living side by side. A dance company had taken over the local church and the neighbourhood store boasted track lighting and sold Perrier water and king crab. Handsome folk shared the sidewalk willy-nilly with winos and panhandlers. It was a microcosm of the city; a cell in all its stages of vitality and decay.

If Cabbagetown was compact it was dense and the house in the clipping, or its clone, could be found on every block of every street with depressing regularity. To Crunkscully's torment no façade could have been more typically Cabbagetown than the one he sought. Fall had made his task still more difficult for it had stripped the flowering bushes and reduced everything to a dreary sameness. All the window boxes were empty; bulbs carefully stored away in dark basements. In the twisted pretty lanes Crunkscully mounted his campaign of redemption, looking for that one particular well-groomed façade behind which Connie and Bernard K. smiled and squinted and a Siamese cat, possibly Sisyphus, squirmed, and from which Ross left for school. Of the holes in Crunkscully's memory none was more regrettable than the absence of a scale of time. The hospital records set him at forty-five and his stay at the hospital at three years. But he could not remember how long before that Ross might have been born and therefore he could only guess at his present age. He nurtured the idea of a young boy, an adolescent. He looked at young boys in the street, he looked at himself in the mirror and Connie in the clipping, and from that he tried to imagine a son. It wasn't much to go on. Some days he got very depressed. To combat depression, he developed a kind of morning worship. Every morning he reviewed his notes and tapes. The clear, confident voice reminded him that the mission was not hopeless – it was the centrepiece of his daily office – a litany: "Ross is alive," said the voice calmly. "Crunkscully didn't kill him."

3

Stink rapped sharply on the Harringtons' front door. He did not expect an answer. He knocked again. A woman walked by on the sidewalk with a borzoi on close harness. Stink turned to watch her pass. Two doors down a real estate lady with very blonde hair was showing a house to a young couple. Stink watched them nod their heads in tandem as she pointed out features of the house, too absorbed to notice a boy on a porch two doors away. He turned back to the door.

When the lady and her dog had rounded the corner and the house hunters had been led indoors, Stink hopped lightly over the low fence which separated the Harringtons' house from its neighbour. Between the houses was a narrow gap leading to a pocket-sized back yard. There was a low doorway set in the porch, the door was weathered and warped and gave way with a shove. He ducked down three stairs to a tiny alcove in which the residents parked their bicycles. Manoeuvring himself around the bikes, Stink pushed tentatively on the door to the basement. It was bolted but not securely; the wood was punk. He heaved a shoulder at the door and the bolt gave. In the basement ahead a dryer hummed and a belt or small change clanged noisily in the metal drum. There were no other sounds. No human sounds.

Jane Harrington's studio was at the back of the house on the second floor. A white baby grand stood before a dazzling wall of glass. Another wall of shelves held records, tapes, and stereo equipment; a third wall framed pictures of Jane Harrington with other celebrities. There was only one thing Stink wanted from the room and he found it in a sturdy aluminum suitcase. Honora Sheehan had described the case to him. Inside there were seven microphones set in velour compartments and, under a false floor, seven cords. The microphones and their corresponding cords were each a different colour to match the variety in the recording star's wardrobe.

Arlo had made a point of telling him to take the one which was gold plate. It was by far the flashiest but Stink lifted one in matte black from its compartment. It was all black, from its round mouthpiece to its snub base. It had the weight and metal coolness of a gun. He caressed it unconsciously for a moment, the way one does such an object, and then returned it to its case, slipping the plate gold one into his jacket pocket. It seemed ludicrous taking only one but it made little difference to Stink what or how many of them he took. He did as he was told.

A buzzer sounded, startling Stink. He listened. There was no further sound, no sound at all. Dimly he recalled the distant clang of the dryer and realized that it had stopped. How strange that a buzzer should have announced the end of a drying cycle to an empty house. The house seemed impenetrably quiet.

Stink sat at the piano and struck a note. There was no musicality to the act. It was like hurling a sound at the silence and hearing it, almost watching it, soak up the sound. He started the metronome, stopped it. He wandered through a door into a bathroom where red lingerie hung on a line above the bathtub. Stink padded noiselessly from the bathroom into a narrow corridor leading to a bedroom and through the bedroom to a study redolent with pipe smoke. The walls were covered in some dusky fabric and there were diplomas and books everywhere. Dominating a dark corner stood a brown leather wing-back chair. Stink sat, gingerly at first, and then, unable to resist, he slid into the comforting lap. Like Goldilocks, or her dishevelled shadow, he closed his eyes. All noise seemed to subside as if the leather wings were guards beating back sound from his ears.

The voices, the ones which ordered him around, could not reach him here. Their commands were soaked up by the room's weighty stillness. There was, to Stink's way of thinking, nowhere as peaceful as an empty house. His own place was often empty, he seldom crossed paths with his aunt, but there was the distraction of familiarity and the pall of unhappiness. The quiet of a strange house was delicious; the danger of his occupation only made the tranquillity more compelling.

Stink was an imaginative boy; he existed in his head, and his corporeal self sprung from his mind like the awkward ganglion of a spider plant in a suspended flower pot. But despite the almost constantly febrile state of his imagination it did not run to worldly matters. He had been breaking into houses since he was ten but it was not until he had met Arlo that he had ever thought to rob the houses into which he forced his entry. Robbery spoiled the exquisite contentment of his escape and getting rid of the merchandise afterwards only complicated matters. Arlo handled that end of things, and he had managed to convince his partner that complication was a necessary by-product of growing up. Stink accepted this vague explanation fatalistically. Nothing in his short life had led him to believe that growing up would be anything more or less than increasingly complex.

Now, at thirteen, he was a master Crib-Cracker, as Gob called it, and life had become almost unbearably complex. With Gob his life had become quite incomprehensible. Gob was like growing up gone mad. Gob was as inescapable as age except for rare moments like this one in a strange and empty house. Gob ruled over all the voices that clamoured for Stink's attention. His domination was despotic. He demanded there be games – wreaks and wrinkles. A wreak because it didn't make money but left a bad smell. A wrinkle because it was the kind of prank that gave the rich wrinkles. Making the rich unhappy amounted to a religion in Gob's mind and was a sport with which he had inculcated his youthful followers. In one sense the Knot was an army involved in a kind of holy war. It was only one side of the gang; the amusing side.

Gob demanded that Stink spy and shadow and in return there was money and gifts and the promise of a revolution. Revolution was the nearest thing to continuity in Stink's life. His father had talked about a revolution but had died before it came.

Outside there was the sound of a car door shutting. The solid thud broke the stillness of Stink's solitude like a glass shattering. He had not really been asleep – unless sleep was a drug distilled from quietness. Peering through the drapes he saw it was only the house-hunting couple. They were leaving. But while Stink watched, another car arrived and the real estate lady with the excessively blonde hair rewound her song and dance. Stink could afford to linger a minute longer. He allowed the room to close its dark, warm arms around him.

In the hall downstairs a grandfather clock struck the hour. It was time to leave. He stopped in the hall and saw himself in the antique face of the clock. Reflected there he looked the phantom he felt himself to be – a ghost stranded between ethers. With his fright of hair and his features suspended where a face might normally have been, he made quite an impression on those who did see him.

He left by the front door. The street was empty.

✤

In a park in front of the cathedral on Queen Street, Stink waited for Arlo to bring the sacrificial victim, the mark.

It would be some pink-cheeked gull in a shiny shirt and pressed jeans; a boy fat on sundaes; smelling clean – of soap and Lifesavers. They were all the same to Stink. They all wore braces to make their teeth grow straight and long. They had all fallen in love with Arlo and they all wanted to join the gang.

Arlo wore silver talismen around his neck, and his tawny hair long. When he smiled the ends of his mouth turned up as if pulled by invisible strings.

He had always been confident. At age eleven, when Stink had first met him, Arlo had been into voodoo which he practised in an abandoned garage attic. Particularly gullible classmates were charmed or scared out of their allowances for the privilege of having witchdoctor Arlo stick pins in the likenesses of hated sisters or teachers. In the candlelight Arlo encouraged the sharing of secrets and boys being what they are invariably bragged of domestic treasures. That's where Stink came in. While Arlo manipulated people Stink manipulated locks. It had been a lucrative enough arrangement. And then Gob came along.

The sun was hot, westering and casting fat shadows. Stink sat down heavily on a park bench. Shabby pigeons sacheted just beyond the range of his pointed black shoes. He hugged the canvas bag of loot closer to him.

He and Arlo had arranged in advance that there would be several items, one of which would be considerably valuable but not enough to make the mark wary. Accordingly, Stink had gathered a pocket calculator, a man's signet ring, a low-priced SLR camera, and Jane Harrington's gold-plated microphone.

It was a game. The mark would attempt to deposit the loot, item by item, at the pawnshops lining Church Street, returning the payment to Arlo after each successful trip. Then the mark would be given something truly expensive and uncommon, in this case the microphone, and the trap would be sprung. As soon as he produced the instrument, the pawnee would slip into the back office on a pretence and make a call. A police car would arrive almost instantaneously – there was always one in the neighbourhood – and the dupe would be led away blathering ineffectually. He would be let off with a reprimand, but his parents would be frantic and embarrassed, wondering where they had failed. Life would be miserable for a while.

The take was never significant. It was the game that was important and the planning behind it. Finding just the right merchandise and just the right boy to be the disposable fence. It honed the respective talents of the Knot, for Gob wanted his boys and girls in good condition and in a state of readiness. "Taking the gull to the candystore" was one of Gob's favourite wrinkles.

On busy Queen Street a trolley disgorged a plain brown crowd into the sunshine and among the derelicts and bag ladies Stink saw Arlo with his latest mark in tow.

The boy was so in Arlo's thrall that he had to be guided through the traffic at the intersection. The two boys approached him and Stink tightened his grip on the handle of the canvas bag at his side.

"This is Nonny," said Arlo thwacking the boy on the back affectionately. "Nonny wants to join the gang."

Arlo sounded like a game-show host introducing the latest contestant. Stink made an effort to smile and an effort not to puke. The game was on.

on the top of a Sterno can. *Those* were the bad old days." He chuckled. "Hit a bad patch." His palm indicated a skid.

"Me too," mumbled Crunkscully.

"Canned heat?"

"I don't remember."

Crunkscully fidgeted. "There was a small room," he said, "with all sorts of controls but no window; well...there was a window but only into another room."

Frank squinted and looked thoughtful.

"'Spect so," he said. "Crunkscully. Now what kind of a name is that?"

It was a familiar question.

"My name," he said.

"Oh, I'm not prying," said Frank. "I don't really care who you are. I just meant what nationality is a name like that?"

Crunkscully hadn't given it much thought. "Irish?" he said insecurely.

"Hmmm, wish you weren't Irish," said Frank with characteristic candour. "Not that I've got anything against the Micks, mind you, but you see, we've got one already. Tommy Connacher." He held up his fists in front of his face with one finger up for Tommy. Four more fingers popped up as he recited the lodgers' names.

"Olga is a Czech, Chas is one of your 'indigenous peoples,' Werner Boost is a German, and my old buddy, Monsieur Calmette, is a Frenchman. Now my name is Francis Reginald Qualtrough, if you can believe it, and I'm a Brit. If you were from somewhere else we'd have ourselves a regular League of Nations."

Crunkscully nodded his head gravely, as if he understood the dilemma. "Swedish."

"What?"

"I've decided that my name is Swedish."

Frank threw his arms back and laughed. He slapped his knee. "Good for you!" he said.

Crunkscully smiled, glad to oblige.

34

Frank shook his head and became thoughtful. "Crunkscully," he said. "I never heard a name like that but I sorta feel I know you. But I couldn't, could I, you being from out of town?"

Crunkscully gave the matter serious consideration and then shrugged his shoulders.

Frank looked thoughtful again. "It takes all kinds, doesn't it? Some people got it and some people don't. Now take me, for instance. I had it all, money, looks, and brains." At this point he snorted. "Boy, I blew it! Drank myself into a hole. Canned heat, vanilla extract, Aqua Velva. And I gotta stomach the size of a pea to prove it. What about you, Crunkscully?" Crunkscully chewed his lip and leaned back against the door. Frank, sensing his diffidence, spoke up. "Jeez, listen to me! You must think I'm the R.C.M. and P. or something. Hell, I didn't mean to pry. You aren't mad, are you?"

"Oh, no," said Crunkscully.

"That's good. I'm a blabbermouth, don't mind me."

Crunkscully dug his hands into his pockets. He was enjoying himself. He felt he should say something. "It's okay," he said at last. "It's just I don't remember much."

Frank considered this and then his face brightened.

"Well, you've come to the right house," he said emphatically. "I call this place Neverland."

"I think I was somebody too," said Crunkscully. "I think I was the mayor but that couldn't be, could it?"

Once again Frank's ready laugh filled the small grey room. He stopped suddenly. "Have you seen my Golden Hawk?" he asked.

"I...I don't think so," said Crunkscully, getting an awkward feeling in his stomach. "But I lost my cat," he added hopefully. Frank didn't seem to have heard him.

"That car is a dream, Scully – do you mind if I call you that? Someone offered me ten thousand dollars for it only last spring but I couldn't go through with the deal. A Studebaker Golden Hawk Gran Turismo. Every bolt is the original, what it was born with. You hear a lot about planned obsolescence, and I believe it – ask Werner Boost some time about planned obsolescence.

But now and then the plant makes a mistake and off the line there rolls that one in a million. The one that got away. You know, this'll sound a bit queer to you, maybe, but that car is like a son to me."

"Like a son," said Crunkscully dreamily.

"Like a son," repeated Frank and his voice quivered. "Some day, Scully, I'll take you for a ride. A ride on the wings of a hawk."

Fascinated, Crunkscully watched as Frank, still "enthroned," transported himself so that he was behind the wheel of his car. He seemed to be driving some impossible dream and it was only when he reached down to shift gears that the imaginary stand-in evaporated. For a moment Frank looked sad. "The gear shift is gone," he explained. "It's a little tricky to drive it without the knob there. I was going to buy a new one but it seemed wrong, somehow; like buying an artificial leg."

"Where did it get to?"

"Kids!" said Frank.

"Kids," parroted Crunkscully. Again kids.

"Hellions, that's what they are! This place is an easy target for them. We're sitting ducks. And, damn them, they attack! They're like rats, swarms of 'em. You don't believe me? Wait until Hallowe'en."

Crunkscully was not pleased with the proposition but Frank's voice changed all of a sudden. "Mind you, they ain't been so bad lately, come to think of it. Maybe Werner's right." The realization seemed to throw Frank into consternation. "Anyway, Cabbage-town has its fair share of them," he said at last. He was thoughtful for a moment and then asked: "Have you got a couple of bucks, Scully?"

"Sure," said Crunkscully, a little taken aback. He reached into his pants pocket.

"Nah, I don't want it," said Frank, waving his hands in protestation. "We're all getting together for dinner tonight and you're welcome. Don't see you in the kitchen much. Anyway, Tommy'll want some money for the booze, Werner is donating the meat, which he stole, and I'm throwing in the rest. I'm also the chef," he said, blowing on his fingernails and buffing them vigorously on his chest.

"Thank you," Crunkscully said.

Frank smiled, then his smile faded and he shook his head. "Who the hell would want to steal a gear-shift knob?" he said, and left the room.

Returning to his room, Crunkscully sat in his armchair, lost in thought. Quite lost.

5

Riverdale Park stretches along the eastern boundary of Cabbage-town, overlooking, indeed spilling into, the Don Valley. The lands to the north of the park form the enormous Toronto Necropolis and a laneway separates the cemetery from the park's zoo, which skips down the steep hillside in a series of miniature pastures and duck ponds. The laneway curves off around the perimeter of the cemetery, to nowhere in particular. The park's single resident is the zoo keeper. A gravel pathway tumbles down below the zoo keeper's house through the zoo, past pig, sheep, and goat pens, to a reservoir heavily shaded by stout willows. The reservoir is fenced and locked at night.

In the middle of the reservoir stands an island ringed with bullrushes and dense with underbrush. The little island is reached by a narrow pedestrian bridge. The island boasts an elaborate stone shed with a steep copper roof. The shed is like a miniature jail, twenty foot square, sturdy, and with windows fitted with metal grids. Inside, benches have been built into the walls, but the shed is otherwise empty. It had once been a lions' den when the zoo kept wild things.

The Park Authority has changed the locks on the shed's door several times, fearing it was being used by rubbies as a shelter. The Park Authority did not know that on the infrequent nights the Knot assembled there, no rubby would have got within a thousand yards of the shed.

Tonight was one such occasion, and everywhere in the park were stationed the junior members of the gang, on guard duty; "playing Bo Peep," Gob called it.

Stink had arrived for the meeting early. He was always early, and consequently always waiting. His punctuality was inspired by fear not ambition. The shed was draughty and damp but he wore only a T-shirt, threadbare jeans, and his pointed black shoes. On his T-shirt, in faded glitter, was the name of a rock band: "Woke Up Screaming." It could as easily have been a confession.

Somewhere in the dark shed a backed up gutter dripped water against stone. Outside, cars occasionally passed on the nearby Bayview Extension, and beyond that and the railroad tracks and the sluggish Don, a brown worm of a river, a steady stream of traffic on the expressway coiled southward from the suburbs for a night on the town.

When the others started at last to arrive they greeted him by his name or as the Hood-pick or Sly Boots, and he identified them by rank or name or by some characteristic nickname, as was the gang's custom. One, Benno Kashiki, was the Drunken Tinker or Spindleshanks; another, Hank VanderLoon, was called the Froglander. There were girls too: The Daughters of the Earth and The Shadows, Honora, Agnes, and Queenie Sheehan. The head girl was Kiki Druitt, whose rank was the Demander for Glimmer of Fires. Gob sometimes called her the Coffee Shop; that was a joke, making a coffee shop out of a woman, "in and out without paying."

The shed was filled with hushed chatter and smoke. Someone practised kung-fu moves, someone filed her nails, someone else drummed nervously at loose change and hummed a pop tune, but not in tune. Heavy blankets had been hung across the windows and pocket flashlights played about the space, spotlighting bits of flesh and leather and graffiti against hard, grey stone. Stink manoeuvred his lank frame into the least crowded corner and waited. Before his eyes, faces lit up suddenly in cigarette-lighter flares and then were blown out.

Arlo arrived late, for dramatic effect – but then Arlo could get away with such games. There was a commotion because he wore a helmet with a battery-operated siren and a red beacon on the top. It was merely a child's toy, noisy and foolish. It was difficult to tell how seriously Arlo took anything other than himself.

The commotion was at least partly due, however, to the girl Arlo brought with him to fill the vacancy of Kinching Coe in the gang's inner sanctum. She would have been selected by Gob, sight unseen, based on the reports of his lieutenants. Tonight she would meet her master for the first time. Her predecessor had proven disloyal. Nobody but Captain Hakum knew quite what had become of her, and he was mute on the subject. Hakum was Gob's third in command. His rank was Angler; his role, hit man.

The new girl received the attention of an alien being as she made her way into the shed. From his corner Stink watched her in the ubiquitous light. She was as slim-hipped as a boy and her sex was further disguised by an overlarge leather jacket. Her hair was short, black once dyed red, and straight like his. Below a dark fringe, which ended at her eyebrows, high-boned cheeks accentuated her triangular face. Large eyes and lips threatened this geometry.

When the interest in the new arrival died down, she slipped through the smoke and jostle to Stink's corner. She smiled at him, and Stink, without knowing quite how, smiled back. Several muscles in his face smarted with the novelty of the expression.

And then Gob arrived.

Stink heard the sharp intake of breath as the neophyte recognized the blind old invalid who paraded the streets of Cabbagetown in his outlandish wheelchair. A wheelchair decked with placards on aluminum wings, giving the impression of a mangy bottom-heavy tri-plane. The wings were clipped at night. It was the initial perquisite of joining the Knot to learn that Gob was not blind after all, nor was he a fool. He played at being mad, and it was a role he performed with alarming acuity.

Gob sat for a moment in the doorway before wheeling into the shed and pulling the door to behind him. Thin flashlight beams played across his face, never alighting there, granting only fleeting glimpses. His cranium seemed too large for his neck, but there was a lot to carry in that bone-box, as he called it, and as he took every opportunity to remind his youthful crew.

In the weak illumination his skin was yellow, waxy in texture, and his eyes were far too small under a massive hairy brow. They peered like darkling creatures from a cave. The skin on his forehead was broad and smooth but fell into rubbery creases around the lower extremities of his face. What he had of hair was the colour of sand close to the tide, wet and plastered to his knobbly skull, and collected in sticky curls along his collar. He smiled, the way a man smiles when he reveals a secret. His teeth, even dimly lit as now, were astonishingly white against his yellow skin. He had a name for them: his "crashing cheats."

Gob renamed the world, re-itemized it. He spoke in Billingsgate, Pedlar's French, Flash lingo, but never when there was anything important to say; only for effect. This shared language created a bond within the group but like any currency it also served to establish leadership. Gob controlled the purse strings. Cabbagetown was his Begler Bec, and he was its Begler Beglic; he was the Knot's Fanger and they were his Afterlings and Scrogglings. The man at the top – at the very top – was the Grand Vizier, alluded to but never seen. It was the Grand Vizier who bankrolled the Knot. He paid for information, and the gang, under Gob's supervision, had become the eyes and ears of the burgeoning little community of Cabbagetown. They also patrolled the area and kept it free of competing agents. What minor heists Gob allowed them were for amusement only.

Gob was a great teacher and the Knot represented his master class. There was little that went on in Cabbagetown which they didn't know about. First they learned to see through Gob's eyes and gradually they learned to perceive through Gob's senses. They were like his blood pumped into the arteries of Cabbagetown and back through the veins, carrying all manner of dirt to the heart. The secret of the program was a simple one: no one was above suspicion and nothing was unimportant. Gob would listen patiently to the most trivial report from one of his Scrogglings and then expiate on possible ramifications. He tucked away in his bone-box anything which would be useful to his own purposes, to his holy war.

He wheeled further into the shed and pulled from his overcoat a mammoth breakman's flashlight. He shone the hot white spot around the room. He clicked his tongue as the faces turned from the light. "Wednesday's children," he said reprovingly, "looking both ways for Sunday." This too was ritual, the customary dressing down. "The whole lot of you squint like a bag of nails," he barked, and to indicate his superiority he stared into the torch, held at arm's length, like a samurai or a fire eater.

At these moments Stink snuck back into himself. He found his way again to his most recent sanctuary, the Harringtons' study. The traces of pipe smoke still curled in his nostrils. He forced his way back into the enclosing warmth of the wing-back chair until he could hear clear through Gob's ranting. The dripping gutter became a ticking grandfather's clock in the quiet of an empty house. Dimly he heard Gob name the new girl Teri, as if he had just then invented the name. The old man shone the flashlight directly in her face but she did not flinch. Stink watched her large brown pupils contract to nothing against the lamp's gaze. Then abruptly the beam was snapped away.

Then Gob fished a length of string from his greatcoat and this too was like magic. Through the open front of his coat could be seen the tattered hems of at least one other jacket, a cardigan, a waistcoat, and more than one shirt.

The deed done, the string was handed, along with the flashlight, to Earnie, a tall black stick of a boy: The Ruffler, Gob's second in command. By means of a hook at either end Earnie hung the flashlight from the rafters. It swayed momentarily, casting an assortment of weird shadows on the walls and floor.

Gob folded his hands placidly in his lap, like some harmless old codger, though if one looked closely at the large hands, they were deeply rutted and coarsely veined. He held his knees together tightly in a practised caricature of modesty. He looked about and frowned. Vernon Pilchard was missing! He eyed those in the room whom he believed to be friends of the truant, but no one volunteered an explanation. Gob sighed wearily. He was not at all pleased with Vernon's absence. Somewhere in the room a boy beat his fingers in a staccato rhythm against the change in his pocket. Gob began to champ, and his eyes seemed to shine even more brightly from their fleshy caves, like bats about to fly into the room. His thick fingers played an agitated game in his lap. Then suddenly he smiled.

Someone stirred. Someone else stretched. The suspense lifted. To Stink it was like waking from a dream into a room full of people waking from the same dream. The meeting had at last begun in earnest.

With great panache, Arlo recounted the demise of Nonny, his latest mark, embroidering the story for an eager audience. To Stink's great relief, he was not called upon to report since Arlo described his part in the operation far more thoroughly than Stink could have done himself. Honora Sheehan had on a previous occasion described the Harringtons' house, she was after all their babysitter. Gob encouraged such community involvement.

There followed a variety of reports. It seems Alderman Hurley's wife had a new lover, the Roses on Sackville a new stereo, and Diana of Mont Clifton (a prize-winning bulldog bitch) a new litter. There was only one report, however, which really seemed to spark Gob's imagination. It came from Wagtail Barkley who worked as kitchen help in an exclusive restaurant called Simon's, on Carlton. The owner, Simon Tisler, was a very wealthy man, as was his son who made frequent appearances at the restaurant and invariably took a small key-operated elevator up to the second floor. Wagtail had not found any other way of getting up to the second-storey rooms to check the place out, but he had seen from outside that the windows were barred. Simon Jr. was a notorious playboy and often took women to his loft, Wagtail had noticed. Gob decided that Kiki would try to establish just how catholic the playboy's tastes might be. Kiki was not beautiful but was, at fifteen, sexually inspired and inspiring. Before joining forces with Gob she had been a prostitute for three years. Each member of the Knot had his or her special talent.

Finally it was time for the distribution of pay packets. Gob dug the little brown envelopes out of a number of different pockets and called out the names by rank. When he was finished there was left only Vernon Pilchard's pay. Gob curled his big fist around the packet and squeezed until the veins in his hand looked as if they would burst. When he opened his fist the packet was gone.

❖

It was Stink's turn to lock up. As the last to leave, he had also to obliterate the footsteps on the dirt floor, which he would accomplish with a wooden board. But before carrying out these duties he sat for some moments in the dark thinking of the new girl. She had sat so close. Reaching along the bench with tentative fingers he thought he could touch her. The bench was still warm where she had sat, or he imagined it was. Keeping his hand on that warm place he leaned back against the stone wall and closed his eyes. It was all so very complicated.

6

Colin McIlwane returned to Baseball Park Road but this time he made a point of phoning ahead. Crawford was ready for him.

The note the supervisor had stuffed in his mailbox had been innocent enough. "I've got something for you!" He was coming back, ostensibly to explain what that something was, but with kid gloves in place. There was the delicacy of Crawford's mental health to consider. Crawford had been changeable – "tetchy," McIlwane called it – since the events of the previous January which had resulted in his leave of absence. This tetchiness had flared up at his last review in July. Crawford had been flippant; a far worse crime in the police force than out and out anger, he had come to learn. It had been a distinctly foolish line of questioning which had brought it on, but McIlwane had made it clear afterwards that such displays did nothing for Crawford's future on the force. McIlwane was keeping his eye on Crawford.

"I've got something for you!" did not mean a football game. Crawford had perceived the innuendo in the note. It was a kind of challenge and he was prepared to deflect that challenge at all costs.

Crawford's and McIlwane's friendship went back in time. Crawford's first promotion from the beat had been to the Youth Bureau where McIlwane had briefly served as his divisional commander before being promoted to district supervisor. In that position McIlwane was responsible for co-ordinating bureau activities for all the divisions in District 5 of the city's east end, which embraced Cabbagetown. It was an advisory position and, as such, it allowed him to act as an intermediary between Youth Bureau workers and their immediate superior, in Crawford's case, the decidedly unenlightened Maltby Wheeler, "The Horse Sergeant." Off the record, Wheeler had only one suggestion for juvenile delinquents – the whip. It was an attitude which brought him into direct confrontation with his more liberal youth workers. With artful diplomacy McIlwane had intervened on numerous occasions. He had saved Crawford his job once before.

When McIlwane knocked it was shortly before 8:00 P.M., and Crawford answered the door in a blue apron upon which was written "Another Perfect Mess."

He cleared a chair in the living room and the supervisor plunked his large frame into it, sending up a cloud of sawdust in the process. Crawford perched uneasily on the arm of a settee; something of his mother's in need of repair. The two men exchanged pleasantries, and McIlwane started to fidget. He pulled a screwdriver from under his rump and handed it to his host. Crawford grinned nervously like a Cheshire cat; an impression created by an unruly moustache which bristled from either side of his nose. He was, otherwise, a particularly lean and sunken-chested cat. A stray.

From the kitchen a timer beckoned, and Crawford shot to his feet. He excused himself and left the room, dropping the screwdriver haphazardly en route in an overladen tool chest.

McIlwane watched it roll to the floor, and resisted the temptation to pick it up. He lit a cigarette instead, and looked around the room. He shuddered; disorder upset him. There was a breakfast tray on a steamer trunk. A *National Geographic* open on a dusty coffee table. In a shadowy corner stood a fig tree, choking in plaster dust, and on the one entirely finished wall there was a smattering of strange wall decorations all of which Crawford had picked up in the Orient. One appealed to McIlwane and he had questioned Crawford about it on a previous visit. It was a crazy map made by Trobriand Islanders of bamboo sticks knotted in significant array. The knots represented islands, the bamboo currents, or so Crawford claimed. Apparently Trobrianders could find their way through their treacherous archipelago with such a device in hand. Beside it there was a painted silk fan, two garish masks, and an Indonesian shadow puppet with a long neck jutting out from the shoulders, and a very straight nose. Crawford had told him that such features were considered heroic in Indonesian culture. McIlwane stared at the gangly creature. Funny what people considered heroic, he mused, and puffed on his cigarette. He and his wife lived in a neat suburban split-level. He could not imagine what it must be like to live alone with only masks and improbable maps for company. Neither could he picture living in a construction site for months on end.

Crawford had no second floor, only lofts fore and aft. Above, the ceiling joists were exposed and, looking up, McIlwane had the impression of being in the ribbed belly of a corsetted Victorian whale. It must be a desolate existence, he thought.

Crawford returned at last wearing a strangely supercilious grin which made McIlwane wary, but delight soon replaced wariness as McIlwane's gaze fell on the tray his host was carrying. There were huge slabs of steaming pie, a silver jug of cream, frosted almond pretzels and assorted tarts. There were also steins of beer and two thick-glass thimbles of bourbon. McIlwane quickly put out his cigarette in an ash tray, which looked remarkably like a shrunken head. It was, he learned, and Crawford described at length the market in Surabaja where he had purchased it, while his large friend helped himself to a piece of pie.

McIlwane had an appetite to match his sizeable frame and Crawford had gone to great lengths to excite his senior's palate with these gustatory delights in the hope that he would forget all about his plans for Crawford, whatever they were, in the oblivion of alimental satiety.

For nearly an hour the two men indulged in the kind of conversation suitable to the ingestion of sweets, but gradually Crawford began to suspect that the diversion could not go on much longer. McIlwane was happily sated, but he was beginning to include in their chit-chat news from the office. Just gossip at first, but Crawford could feel the conversation slipping inexorably towards the topic he least wanted to discuss. He hated to see all his distractionary tactics wasted, and began to recount another anecdote from his days on the Hong Kong police force. He could tell that McIlwane wasn't really listening.

Leaning across the tray set before him, and reaching for another tart, McIlwane finally came to the point of his visit. "I think I've got something for you, Rum," he said without looking up.

Crawford's spirits drooped. The note in the mailbox had said as much, and he had spent most of the day thinking up a suitable rejoinder. "Why?" he said, and watched McIlwane knock over the silver cream jug.

"You needn't worry. It's just a little snooping around. Nothing heavy." McIlwane busied himself mopping up the spilled cream with a paper napkin.

"Yes, but why me?" said Crawford. "I'm not a cop anymore." McIlwane frowned. Crawford corrected himself: "Not right now, I mean. Not officially."

"Oh, I know that," McIlwane said, pleased that the ice had been broken. "I've arranged for the investigation to be officially unofficial, so to speak. Assuming that you're interested, of course. I can't *make* you take the job. It's completely up to you." Crawford nodded and suddenly abandoned all pretence of playfulness.

"What if I'm still scared shitless."

"Of being shot?"

"That and – "

"Shooting someone," Colin interrupted. "Rum, that's just plain healthy. You know that as well as I do. Every cop should be a little scared of shooting a man."

"What about shooting a dead man?" It was strange to hear himself say it. He had avoided any mention of it in his report. McIlwane looked confused, so Crawford tried to explain. "What if a corpse has his gun trained on you; how are you supposed to feel then?" He had raised his voice but it suddenly dropped away to nothing.

McIlwane did not answer. He didn't want to pry. Whatever delusions Crawford lived with, no matter how curious, they were not his concern right at the moment, unless Crawford wanted to share them. He didn't seem to anymore.

"It's just a bad memory, Rum. Let it go." Crawford didn't answer but the tension in his shoulders lessened a little and his features relaxed until he could smile, enough that his old friend decided to continue. "Maybe you don't want to think about this right now, but there are some things you should know. You've had a rough time. Most of your superiors understand, but there are some who think differently; think you're being molly-coddled." McIlwane paused to pick his words. Crawford waited. "Let's just say there is talk. The implication is some nice, safe, office job, up the ladder, out of the line of fire. You do have a university education, after all, and you've done more than your part on the street."

Crawford stirred uneasily. "I don't like office work."

"I know."

Crawford downed his shot of bourbon. McIlwane continued. "It would be nice to go before your review board again in November with some positive indication of your abiding interest in detective work, don't you think?"

Crawford was nibbling nervously on the end of his moustache. "So, you've cooked up some little piece of detection that'll give me a chance to prove myself."

"Not really."

Crawford raised his voice: "You know what I feel about that macho horseshit. It's supposed to be a job, not a contest."

"I couldn't agree more." McIlwane wouldn't rise to the bait. "I'm not suggesting you have to prove anything to anyone except *you*. I'm looking for 'willingness to co-operate,' quote unquote."

"But who says I want to *co-operate*?"

McIlwane could not answer that nor did he plan on arguing with Crawford. He turned his attention to the tart he had been eyeing some moments earlier. It was the last one. He picked it up very carefully, as if it were booby trapped, and then suddenly he popped it in his mouth whole and dusted off his fingers.

Crawford stared at McIlwane whose cheeks had puffed out to accommodate the snack. It was hard to take the man too seriously. He grinned in spite of himself. "I don't know what you have in mind but it's blackmail, Colin. Benign blackmail."

Colin swallowed. "It won't be stressful, Rum. You'll be nothing more than a glorified fink. I need information. Hell, I don't even know exactly what I'm looking for. I want you to shuffle around Cabbagetown – the old-clothes routine – with your eyes and ears open."

"What's the 'officially unofficial' business supposed to mean?" Crawford asked.

McIlwane looked pleased. "It means everybody knows and nobody is responsible. I've already convinced the powers that be it would be good occupational therapy, and no more dangerous than an easter-egg hunt. If and when you find anything, a real investigation will be set up through the usual channels. Officially you're still on leave. In fact you'll be operating in a kind of limbo."

"I can't think of anything more frightening than officially sanctioned limbo," said Crawford.

"It's not a make-work project," said McIlwane, reading his thoughts. "I didn't manufacture the whole thing to humour you or to simply impress your review board. The fact is, I can't get anyone interested in a little theory I've been developing – not interested enough to open it up for investigation. This way I kill two birds with one stone: I get a crack detective on my case and you get a chance to show what a co-operative fellow you can be, in a pinch." Crawford sighed and slouched back in the settee. If anything, it looked to McIlwane like unhappy resignation, but he was an optimist. He lit a cigarette. "I take it you're interested."

"I hate it," came the reply. "What am I supposed to be interested in?"

McIlwane smiled. "I'm not going to tell you, not on a full stomach. There's a mess of data I want you to see first. All I wanted tonight was to tempt you down to headquarters. I will say this much: your background in the Youth Bureau may be helpful, and your intimate knowledge of Cabbagetown will also come in handy considering the – how should I say – heterodox nature of this neighbourhood." McIlwane's face wrinkled into an even broader smile. He was the used-car salesman who had successfully prevented a customer from looking under the hood.

Crawford grew sullen. McIlwane supposed he was doing him a favour but it was the kind of favour a dentist does when he drills a bad tooth.

"Okay," Crawford said at last. "I'll come and look." McIlwane made to stand up and Crawford added quickly: "But I can't come tomorrow; I've got guys coming in to help pour concrete in the basement." It didn't sound very convincing. "It might take a while, a week maybe." Crawford got to his feet. "But I guess since it's not really a case there's no big rush."

McIlwane grunted and struggled up from his chair.

Crawford handed him his raincoat, which he had hung on a nail by the door. He was suddenly amused. "It's kind of a not case for a nut case, isn't it?"

McIlwane raised an eyebrow but otherwise did not respond. He flicked his cigarette out the open front door. It was left at that.

Crawford leaned against the door jamb and watched the Gremlin carry McIlwane away. The night air was heavy with chocolate from the factory up the street. The sky was like dark chocolate unsweetened by stars.

It had been foolish to imagine he could distract McIlwane from his intentions. He had stalled him but that was all. He turned to look at the plates on the tray, now empty but for crumbs. Colin had eaten clear through the ambush.

7

"Ready, Scully?" Frank didn't wait for an answer but shuffled down the hall to the room of Chas Shot On Both Sides, where he knocked on the door. His slippers made a flip-flop sound on the bare wood floor.

Crunkscully was trying to remember how to tie a Windsor knot in a green tie he had bought that afternoon to mark the occasion. He cleared a space on the mirror and looked at himself between the memoranda and the newspaper clipping.

Sometimes, just for an instant, when he looked at his reflection he thought he recognized himself. As if he might have seen that face before; maybe in a newspaper clipping. In a clipping he would have been sure to have kept his hair brushed. It was tousled now, like a nest, the colour of dead grass, straw threaded with the odd strand of gold. His eyes were pale blue but the settings were muddied; bloodshot from irregular sleep and with a yellowish tinge. His complexion too was sallow and his face gaunt, but the overall effect was not unhandsome, rather distinguished in an insecure way. It was a weary face, difficult to pin an age on. He couldn't for the life of him see a child's face, or a young man's face in the mirror, but still, he felt sure he had seen the face somewhere before. A muscle twitched in his forehead – that was new.

His tie was at last secured and he slipped on his jacket. With one last attempt to slick down his hair he left the room. He descended to the dinner party below, feeling like an ingenue at her coming out. An ingenue in motley.

"Hi, Scully," said Frank waving a wooden spoon by way of a greeting. Ash fell from Frank's cigarette into the pot he was stirring and he tried to spoon it out.

Olga turned to Crunkscully as he entered the large noisy commonroom. She seemed to be suffering the same problem Crunkscully had himself of not quite being able to place his face. Then suddenly her eyes lit up crazily.

"D'ja find yer cat?" she asked.

"No, thank you," said Crunkscully with a little bow. He was more nervous than he had expected.

Olga had on her lapel a name tag which read "Hi, I'm — Welcome aboard!"

"I don't expect you'll see it ever again," she said with a sigh of regret.

"I didn't know you had a cat," said Frank.

"He *had* a cat," corrected Olga.

"It's gone," said Crunkscully.

"That's too bad," said Frank. "Never had a cat here. Dog once. Some budgies – they got cancer. Can you believe it? Bird cancer." He had fished out the last of the ash onto the stove top and now he leaned against the counter with a look of regret on his face. It only lasted a few seconds and then he raised and lowered his shoulders with a sigh. "You could lose anything in this house," he said.

"Like my radio," said Chas.

"Like my gear-shift knob," countered Frank.

"Then, do you think it was stolen?" Crunkscully asked.

"Maybe so, maybe not. It's a big house; the doors are never locked. I tried once but everyone kept losing their keys – a waste of time. Neverland, like I said." He winked. "Sorry, though. I mean about your cat."

Olga had returned to talking in a drunken hush to Chas who seemed lost in reveries. Crunkscully sat at the chair next to hers at the long table. Her accent had thickened under the influence of alcohol as had her tongue. She was trying to explain to Chas how it had been Poland who really started the Second World War.

Across the table from her sat Tommy Connacher. He seemed out of place in a house of relics, for he could not have been more than twenty-five. He had a shock of red hair and was, at present, staring across the table at Olga. It looked as though he were trying to levitate the woman, so intense was his gaze. His eyes were hard and blue and shone out from under a bristle of red eyebrow. He acknowledged Crunkscully's presence briefly with the same glare, as if Crunkscully was next in line to be raised, and then he returned his attention to Olga and her story. In her story she was explaining how miserable the Winter Offensive had been. Tommy looked startled. "Goddamn war!" he said bitterly. His hands were wrapped tightly around a beer bottle, the companion to six more lined up in front of him, empty.

Remembering what Frank had said, Crunkscully gingerly placed a one-dollar bill on the table in front of him. Tommy seemed not to notice it but to Crunkscully's amazement, Olga's hand shot out and grabbed the bill. She had shoved it down her bodice before Crunkscully could do a thing.

"Bonjour, Monsieur Cwunkscully. So we meet at wast." This hale greeting came from Monsieur Calmette who was sitting on a ragged davenport by the window. He was not really very fat but his limbs were so short that he appeared roly-poly. His feet dangled above the floor and were shod in very new running shoes. His features also were short and round; his nose was little more than a bump; his mouth a mouse hole. He was grinning profusely at the moment. "We have a bet on the Sehwies," he said. "Me and Wehneh. He says the Piwates, I say the Angels. What do you say, Cwunkscully?"

Against the wall, perched hazardously on a pile of newspapers on a hassock was a tiny television. The leaning television of Pisa. Crunkscully looked there now for some clue to the enigmatic question. The screen was smeared, and the channel ghosting. Crunkscully could only vaguely remember having ever watched a baseball game but never one with two pitchers pitching at once. He squinted to make out the action. Two balls flew across the plate, two batters struck out. "I don't know who I'd pick," said Crunkscully quietly.

Calmette didn't seem to hear over the noise in the room. Frank had turned on a radio to a country music station and Chas had pulled a harmonica from his work shirt to play along. He bent over, engulfing the tiny instrument with his huge hands and lips and his long black hair fell forward like a curtain across his face. To Crunkscully's surprise the accompaniment was tuneful. Melancholic.

Olga turned her attention to Tommy's serious, troubled face. Her hands had strayed to cover his fists which still clutched the beer bottle so tightly it seemed it might burst. This made Crunkscully decidedly uncomfortable and he turned his gaze to Frank. Frank was liberally dousing the bubbling ingredients in the pot with a red Chateau de something-or-other from which he took liberal swigs.

"You look fine," he said to Crunkscully when he saw him look his way. "This here, in case you're wondering, is beef bourgignon," he added inconsequentially. "Something I picked up overseas in WW two. I make it pretty spicy on account of my tastebuds being out of whack. Sterno!" he said, winking. "I call it my Top-o'-the-Stove Bourgignon, on account of the oven." He kicked it furiously to illustrate its state of disrepair. "You're from out West, aren't ya?"

Crunkscully was caught off guard by the question. He must have told Frank that when he arrived. He nodded and Frank nodded as if they had reached an agreement.

Tommy suddenly turned on Crunkscully with a look of rage. "Did you ever meet a guy named Eddy the Midwife?"

Crunkscully thought he hadn't and although he didn't ask Tommy why he wanted to know the reason was volunteered.

"Coz if I ever see him again I'll rip his fucking face off!"

Just then someone hit a home run and the tiny television exploded with applause as did Werner Boost, who'd been sitting quietly up until now beside Monsieur Calmette. "Yah, yah, yah," he said. He bounced up and down on the davenport until it appeared that M. Calmette might roll right off. Boost was a big man shaped like a pear. He was almost bald with a lick of hair like a stem. His face was blotchy and his nose was red suggesting that his circulation was not up to dealing with his sluggish frame. When he smiled his eyes like little pips disappeared in thick folds of flesh. He was smiling now; the Pirates were out ahead.

Crunkscully peered past Werner and out the window. On Elmsley Street an old cripple with dark glasses wheeled himself by in a wheelchair which supported a shaky scaffolding of metal links and all manner of banners and placards. Crunkscully had seen him before; the placards decried the past and prophesied the future. It was a kind of floating autobiography flapping above the cripple's oversized head.

"I hear Vancouver is really something," said Frank.

Crunkscully watched the cripple wheel out of vision.

Werner Boost suddenly became interested in the newcomer, now that his bet on the game seemed more secure. "Vhat makes a smaht fellow like you move from a reech place like Wancouver to a dump like zis een zee fall?"

To Crunkscully it was a very complicated question, and while he considered an answer old Calmette poked Boost in the side. "Is this going to be one of youah jokes?" asked Calmette almost ecstatic at the prospect. Boost glared at him and Calmette shook with silent giggles.

"My son," said Crunkscully. He averted his eyes to watch a beer commercial on the television. The game returned. Across the room Monsieur Calmette shouted above the racket of baseball and a turgid country love song.

"Fwankie has a son in Afwica, don't you Fwank?"

Crunkscully looked at Frank with surprise. Frank's cheeks had coloured slightly and he seemed to be smiling self-consciously.

"What's he do there?" asked Tommy urgently.

"He wuns the place!" said Monsieur Calmette with a twinkle

in his eye. The little man then erupted into gales of laughter. Frank stirred the big pot of stew vigorously.

"Any particular place?" asked Crunkscully.

"Nah," said Frank without looking up from his task. "The whole place."

Everyone laughed, even Tommy who let out a high-pitched whinny which was dangerously close to the sound of a siren. Crunkscully winced.

Chas had retired to the corner near the radio. He laughed very softly, distantly, and to no one's surprise he had tears in his great doe eyes. "You see much of your kid?"

Crunkscully felt distinctly uncomfortable.

"Not enough," he answered ambiguously.

"I know what you mean," said Frank. "Really I got three sons. Two in Africa, if you can believe it, and one out back in the alley." He winked and Crunkscully, after a moment, winked back.

Olga rejoined the conversation. Her voice was sullen and scarcely intelligible. "Children don't care. You bring them into the world. You change their diapers sometime. You bring them up and then they dump you like a potato. They don't want to see you, they even hate you when you never did nothing for them."

"I hate my old man!" slurred Tommy Connacher.

In a moment the whole mood had changed. Everyone, even Calmette, looked morose, all conversation had languished, and Chas was sobbing openly, his body heaving with the effort.

"I've enjoyed about as much of this as I can stand," said Frank, shrugging his shoulders. "Talk about kids or folks always does that. But what else is there when you get right down to it?" The desperate atmosphere of gloom lasted another moment and then, remarkably, everyone was cheerful again.

So far Crunkscully had refrained from drinking but now he helped himself to a bottle of beer from a refrigerator which seemed to hold little else. This was a cue for Calmette.

"It's dwink," said Calmette. "It's aweways the same, ain't it, Fwank? Fwank knows."

Frank took up the cue enthusiastically. "When you're sober

you can't remember what you did when you was drunk and when you're drunk all you can remember are things that happened to you when you was drunk. So you end up being drunk all the time to avoid thinking about it."

"That Fwank," said Calmette. "He's a wegular Socwatees!"

"Maybe that's where you lost your memory, Scully – in the bottle." Frank talked about memory as if it were an article, a piece of jewellery.

"I don't think so," said Crunkscully. In a room, he thought, with dials and buttons and someone on the other side of a glass counting the time off on raised fingers: three, two, one....

The baseball game was over and the set was off. So was the radio, and Chas was talking solemnly to Werner Boost. Everyone was at the table and Frank with a cigarette clamped between his lips was dishing out stew onto massive piles of noodles.

Crunkscully had the strangest feeling someone had asked him about Ross but he wasn't sure what he had been asked. Fear drove him to unusual lengths of temerity. "He's away at school," he said in a whisper.

"What did you say?" asked Calmette, handing him a laden plate.

With trepidation he repeated himself.

"And the best place fawh them," said Calmette.

"Fucking school!" muttered Tommy. He was salting his meal recklessly.

And so the conversation turned to school and education, something no one seemed to know much about. The dearth of actual first-hand knowledge gave rise to a long and involved debate on what each of them assumed school was like or what they had heard.

Werner Boost was quite sure that the public school system was run by the Mafia. He also remembered that as a child he could recite backwards *The Cranes of Abicus* by Schiller. He hadn't gone any further with his formal education, however, because it was obviously a waste of time. Werner was writing a book entitled *The Roman Invasion of Canada*. He had been writing it for fourteen years and had written in excess of three thousand pages. It was a treatise on the Mafia, a subject on which he considered himself the pre-eminent authority. The Mafia had first come to Canada with Christopher Columbus, he explained, and they had not looked back since.

Opinion on whether he was, in fact, right was sharply split with Tommy Connacher as his chief opponent. Tommy knew the *real* story but he wasn't saying. This made Werner's poor nose glow like a beacon with indignation. His German accent grew thicker until it was all slurs and clicking. Throughout it all Frank kept smiling and every now and then he winked at Crunkscully, which made Crunkscully feel as if he was in on a joke, though he wasn't sure what joke. Werner went on to his theory about organized crime involving the kids in the area. Half the kids in Cabbagetown were the illegitimate offspring of Mafia families, he said. He was at that moment investigating the theory. Tommy argued contemptuously that the Mafia didn't waste its time on such small beer, and further asserted that he could get a job with "the Man" if and when he wanted. The roars of derision this inspired did nothing to cool his hideous temper.

Crunkscully began to feel tired and walked out on what was turning into a heated argument. He stood for a few moments on the front porch with his arms wrapped around himself against the cold. He saw two teenagers dart down the alleyway across the street, pursued by nothing that he could see. The wind pushed the leaves around. If it was not in fact raining the wind was shaking two days' rain from the skeletal horse chestnuts lining the street. Over on Parliament Street a car squealed from a stoplight and somewhere he could hear the frantic wail of an ambulance although it was too far away to produce more than a shiver of recognition. Though he was tired and cold he felt better than he had felt in a while. The beer had been good. It seemed he had been suffering a headache which vanished as he drank. He had not upset the stew or broken anything and for the first time in a long time he had the strange feeling of belonging. He would find Ross in such a neighbourhood. Not in Vancouver. Maybe the hospital was in Vancouver – it was difficult to say. Ross would visit him at number 14 and meet his new-found friends. With this pleasant thought in his mind he climbed the stairs to his room. Behind him in the commonroom equanimity had been restored as the roomers huddled around the little television to watch the 10:00 news. Crunkscully stopped on the darkened stairway for a moment and listened to the modulated voice of the announcer recounting the day's events. Like his own taped voice it seemed secure. It was emotionless. Chas was playing his harmonica; a sad and lilting accompaniment.

❖

Crunkscully awoke the next morning early and refreshed. It was still not light and he lay in his bed for several moments looking wide-eyed into the darkness. Every now and then his thoughts arrayed themselves with lucidity and this was one of those precious times. When he got up he dressed in the recently acquired shirt and tie, tying the Windsor without difficulty this time. He then went about his morning offices of sorting through the accumulation of notes he had written to himself and strewn on the dresser top. His mind clear, he determined to put his shrine in order. The dresser top was the retrieval centre of a complex little system of thought. It was important not to let it slip into the same state of disorganization as his brain.

The scribbled notes ranged in subject matter from the mundane to the profound. In the slashes and scrawls which should have been looped ascenders, and in the burps which represented clumps of vowels, but looked, in their horizontal insistence, more like the graphic printout of a rapidly fading heart, Crunkscully revealed the urgency with which his ideas were conceived and committed to paper. Some of the messages he could scarcely decipher but like some primitive shorthand they summoned up images. There was one that simply reminded him to buy milk for Sisyphus, and another recommended Trifluoroperazine whenever he was agitated or confused. He crumpled both of them and dropped them in the wastebasket. Some were duplications of one another and carefully he edited them, disposing of the excess copies. Last night before he had gone to bed he had written out the names of his fellow roomers, over and over, and now he placed this list on the mirror and fixed it there with Scotch tape. If he could no longer store memory in his brain he must at least try to accumulate it.

When his notes were neatly reordered and his tapes had been dusted and stacked, he took from the dresser a large map and spread it out on the bed. It was a street map of considerable scale: every inch equalled two hundred feet. He couldn't remember from where the idea had come but the map had been obtained from the Municipal Topographical Surveys Office at City Hall. It had been an ordeal, a test of endurance for Crunkscully's shaky confidence. There had been furtive phone calls and countless repetitions of his enquiry as one department transferred him to another. Then there had been City Hall itself with its two wings and countless floors of offices; everything conspired to confound him. On that day three weeks earlier his gloomy sense of persecution had reached new heights, and he had, at one point, become quite certain that the whole thing was a trick; that City Hall was merely a façade, behind the doors of which lurked nurses to welcome his return. And something had gone wrong that day. City Hall had made him uneasy in an unidentifiable way. He had cried at one point outside the men's washroom on the third floor, and had eventually stumbled home with his trophy, exhausted and infinitely older than when he had set out.

The map had been a stroke of brilliance, the only strategy he could wage against the vast numbers of houses in Cabbagetown and their uncanny sameness of architecture. The map showed the outline of all the houses and he could tick off with a red magic marker all those which did not match the house in the newspaper clipping. The houses that were similar he ticked in green. It was a simple routine, and Crunkscully could handle routine moderately well.

When Crunkscully finally made his way downstairs, the

commonroom was empty but for Monsieur Calmette. He was sitting in his place on the davenport, his hair dishevelled from sleep, and still wearing his pajamas over which was a red dressing gown. From his plump little feet dangled fuzzy slippers. He was balancing his breakfast on his lap and watching a children's program on the television. His plate was heaped high with leftovers from last night's stew. His face scrunched up in a smile when Crunkscully appeared. "Have some coffee," he said. "It's on the wange."

Crunkscully had been anxious to get started but he felt an obligation to his new-found friend and deferred. The coffee tasted good and it was very hot. He held it securely in both his hands.

Calmette watched his program, turning occasionally to smile encouragingly, but without further conversation.

Crunkscully sipped the hot black elixir. He noticed something on the wall. It was a flicker of light. At first he thought it was a creature and with his impaired vision he couldn't tell if it was coming from the wall or reflected on it. It was light without shadow, moving like a hummingbird, quivering in one place for a moment and then darting away. It captivated him. He hurriedly cleaned his glasses on his tie. It was still there – bright and animate. The creature of light buoyed his spirits. He looked over at Calmette to see whether he too had seen it.

Calmette was grinning furiously and his eyes were wide with expectation. His knife was poised before him and its surface shimmered with the same light which danced across the walls and ceiling. "Tinkah Bell," he said in a hush.

8

His insubstantiality both real and imagined made Stink a natural
spy. He was not particularly ingenious or even uncanny. He was
a shadow, and could lose himself in a man's footsteps. He could
follow anyone – anyone that is, except Gob. One summer evening
he had tried and Gob had trapped him in a blind alley, with a
warning. "These winkapeeps are like needles of tempered steel,"
he had whispered in Stink's ear. "They can pierce a Scroggling's
skull and see his thoughts festering there." Stink had needed no
second warning. From that day he had endeavoured not to so
much as think in his master's presence.

Vernon Pilchard would have been wise to have learned the
same lesson. Vernon had been a loner. He had resisted joining
forces with the Knot as long as he could but Gob had won him
over at last, by force, and not entirely, or so it seemed. Gob had
long since detected Vernon's questionable loyalty. He had even
predicted the boy would revert to his solo career. When Vernon
missed the last meeting there was really no doubt in Gob's mind,
and Stink had been put on the boy's trail.

This day he followed Vernon to a house at the end of a quiet
street and watched him break in through a basement window.
From the moment he slid through that window and out of
Stink's sight, he slipped from Gob's grace. His membership in
the Knot ceased.

In the event that Stink did catch Vernon up to his old tricks,

Gob had provided him with a phone number and instructions. So, without wasting another moment Stink found a phone booth and dutifully made the call. To his shock, the number was that of the police station. Hardly able to believe his ears, he stammered and hung up. He stood for a moment in a cold sweat. Gob's idea of justice, his sense of humour and of proportion, were all beyond Stink's imagination. To deliberately contact the police seemed such an outrageous risk. And yet one did not question Gob's commands. He dialled the number again.

"There is a break-in at 1 Amiel Crescent." He said just that and hung up, remaining where he was to watch the results of his call.

Moments later, a yellow patrol car rushed past the phone booth and up Amiel Crescent. Across the top of the intersection a block away another passed almost simultaneously. Stink felt stranded somehow, like something in a bottle hurled from a boat and left bobbing in the wake. Suddenly he sensed that he *was* being watched. He swung around and there was a man standing behind the booth, staring in at him through thick spectacles, which made his eyes pop out from his head. Stink panicked. He had been trapped – caged – like Vernon. He clawed at the door and scrambled from the booth. The man meanwhile had circled it and was there when Stink sprang from it like a jack-in-the-box. He stumbled back drunkenly as Stink darted past him.

Later, when Stink could think clearly again, he realized he knew the man. He was the tramp who stumbled around the neighbourhood with an enormous map. Now he was someone else to worry about. Someone else to watch. Someone to report to Gob. There was no telling who he might be in reality, or what he wanted in Cabbagetown. No one was above suspicion or to be judged harmless at face value. The tramp would find out soon enough into whose territory he had stumbled.

9

Part of Crawford's problem was that he had never really decided to become a policeman. With a meaningless arts degree from a provincial university, he had answered an ad in the newspaper to serve as a policeman in Hong Kong. He had applied for an adventure not a job. Chinamen weren't very big, he remembered thinking. He had been stupid, not simply naive, he remembered ruefully, but three years in Hong Kong had cured some of that. He had suffered his first great love affair there – "yellow fever." He had collected a few trinkets on his holidays and in the line of duty he had crawled under open box-cars stinking of fish, with rats nibbling on his fingers, to watch drugs exchanged on the docks at night. He had come back less narrow-minded but with no talents but those of a cop, and a cop he became. He had graduated from the Youth Bureau to investigative work. For a few months he had been a detective and then the force dropped the title in favour of investigative sergeant. It always seemed to Crawford a particularly Toronto kind of thing to do. He was made an undercover agent; an old-clothes man. It fit him to a tee.

He had been swallowed whole by his profession and then suddenly, nine months ago, spit up again. He wasn't at all sure he was ready to climb back into the monster's mouth.

But McIlwane was right to challenge him now. Without any of the details he recognized a golden opportunity complete with trainer wheels; shuffling around – Crawford was a past master.

He did let the week pass without responding. McIlwane didn't phone; he didn't need to. Finally on Sunday Crawford decided to take the plunge. It rained that night. The autumn sky poured out its heart and Crawford's newly installed skylight didn't leak. It seemed a good sign.

The next morning, Crawford, dressed in mufti – jeans, a Chinese workshirt, and a very old, very comfortable, pair of black Wallabees – caught the trolley on Queen Street at 8:15. He had done it for years but he hadn't done it for months. He was not defended against the jostling for position, the acid hit in the nostrils of fresh deodorant. He had forgotten the unfocussed, vacuous eyes, the sullen lips waiting for the wake-up kiss of coffee. McIlwane was trying to tempt him back to this? A fat man coughed horribly in his ear and Crawford decided to walk; the drizzle would be comparatively comforting. As McIlwane had temporarily been seconded to serve on a task force operating out of the Jarvis Street headquarters, it was there that Crawford headed.

When he arrived he had to ask directions several times. At last he found McIlwane, who greeted him pleasantly enough, if without display. Crawford had expected no more.

He was led to a custard-yellow room with a floor of battleship linoleum the colour of dried turd. The room was bare but for a conference table and one homely filing cabinet. McIlwane livened up the drab setting in a plaid tie. His sizeable frame was sheathed in gabardine, rivalling in brilliance his blue car. There was nothing subfusc about the man on this soggy Monday morning except perhaps his demeanour. He seemed disgruntled. The task force was a temporary affair and he had no office. Consequently he carried his office around with him in a huge black briefcase out of which he now produced several thick wads of computer printout and a scad of notes scribbled on yellow foolscap.

Having assembled his data in an efficient array before himself, McIlwane coughed politely and folded his hands. It was an unconscious ritual learned from years of giving briefs. His presentation began with the formality of a series of questions to most of which he knew the answers. "You were in the fifty-first precinct, weren't you?"

"I grew up there," corrected Crawford.

"What kind of crimes were you up against on a day-to-day basis?"

Crawford nibbled on his styrofoam coffee cup as he recalled his early patrol duties. "Vagrancy, drunken and disorderly, wife beating, child beating, husband beating, assault – more verbal than anything else, lots of break and entry, petty larceny...." The list was complete enough.

McIlwane nodded and unwound the skein of his interrogative presentation another inch. "And the kids in the neighbourhood – what were they like then, what were they into?"

Crawford laughed. "Kids were our stock in trade. There were more arrests in fifty-one than any division in town, or at least more contacts. Cabbagetown was rough in those days. There were a lot of thugs; street wise but not so bright. Crime...let's see. Dope springs to mind. The bike gangs still hung out in the area and they had cornered the synthetic market, acid, etcetera. We made a lot of spot checks and confiscated a lot of drugs and weapons. There was juvenile prostitution and rape, much of it family stuff. You know, Daddy not letting his girl out on a date unless she bent over the upstairs railing for him first.

"There were cars stolen but mostly for joy rides. Shop lifting, robbery – mostly muggings, purse snatching, property damage, and increasing vandalism when the swells started moving into the area. The local kids loved having fancy stone lawn ornaments to smash – "

McIlwane cut him off, satisfied with the answer. "Okay, it's been twelve years since you worked that part of town, but as a resident what do you think the crime profile might be now?"

Crawford tasted the coffee, made a face, and went back to nibbling the cup's rim. McIlwane was taking him around the course, introducing him to the jumps, marking off the steps for him. It was comforting; had he been more straightforward Crawford might have balked.

"The area is changing," he said. "The demography – is that the word? There is a lot less riff-raff and a lot more conspicuous wealth which creates a certain amount of tension; envy, among the lower-income families who hadn't known they were poor until they landed rich neighbours. There's still an active itinerant population holed up in some of the old boarding houses – "

"So what about the crime scene?" asked McIlwane.

Crawford thought a moment.

"I suppose there's less flagrant violence. The bikers are gone so no gang warfare, at least I'm not aware of any. The streets are well lit and busy so there is less mugging. Mind you, there's a network of alleys and laneways – I knew them as a kid – so there's probably quite a bit of skulking around; back door jobs, wilful property damage, hibachis and lawn chairs missing, that kind of thing. In the way of big crime I'd say that the honey has probably attracted some fat flies. There's probably a number of big thefts – there have been," he said recalling headlines over the past year. "But I guess there's also been a number of attempted heists foiled by adequate protection systems. As for dope, I'm sure there is tons of it, coke mostly, which is very chic. But the local patrons probably pick it up at the corner store with *The New York Times*; all very peaceful and above board. Am I getting warm?"

McIlwane's face relaxed into a smile. "What would you say if I told you you are dead wrong?"

Crawford hooted loudly. "Of course I'm wrong or you wouldn't be playing this idiotic game."

McIlwane chuckled but by the time he'd lit a cigarette he was an aging cop presenting a brief again. "Crime is down, right across the board in that division," he said, cutting a swath through the air with his hand.

Crawford looked interested. He everted his lower lip in thought.

"Ewart still in charge there?"

McIlwane nodded.

"Then I'd say Ewart deserves the Nobel," said Crawford.

McIlwane glowered. "So does he! He thinks the whole thing is due to his unit's efficiency. The powers that be tend to think it's the changing demography."

"And you don't think it's either."

"It's kind of fishy, Rum, kind of fishy." At this, McIlwane pulled the top wad of computer printout towards him. The printout represented a year or more of PRPs, police report periods, which were a month-by-month statistical analysis and breakdown of criminal activity in the city. McIlwane had a reputation for being imaginative at interpreting trends in the statistics. Supervisors at the staff or district levels, when examining the report, usually paid more attention to degrees of change from the previous month, keeping an eye out for fluctuations which were not in keeping with seasonal rates. Like any other industry, crime has its peaks, shoulder seasons and lows, especially juvenile crime, which was McIlwane's particular area of competence. By the look of his copious notes he had subjected the PRPs to an unusually intensive going-over. He sucked deeply on his cigarette, exhaled a cloud of smoke, and began his story.

"Your synopsis would have been just about right a year ago. Then suddenly there was a rash of crimes – break and entry and thefts for the most part – that were out of line with anything that had gone on in the area before. Ewart didn't talk much about promotion then, I'll tell you. His rate of arrests was dreadful and what's more the stolen goods weren't going through the usual channels. Merchandise simply wasn't showing up. That meant, for one thing, that the local thieves had found themselves a new breed of fence. What interests me is that the crime wave seemed to be the work of kids. There would be the trail of muddy sneaker prints – size six – across the rug and the hi-fi gone. But what was really disconcerting was how well the jobs were pulled off; the timing was good, the break-ins were slick, and the kids seemed to know what they were after, rather than just goofing around. Not only that, one or two of us had the damnedest impression that the whole thing was a conspiracy and far too well tailored for kids, despite the muddy footprints. They were having a good time, Rum; they were showing off."

"Pranks, you mean?"

"Pranks!" McIlwane repeated the word as if to suggest it was not the right one but there was no other word in his vocabulary.

"Listen," he said unnecessarily since Crawford was all ears, "Alan Ritenour, one of the school trustees in the ward, discovered that every lock in his house had been changed, in an afternoon – couldn't get in."

Crawford looked amused. McIlwane found another dope sheet. "And this: a man arrives home to find most of his stereo gone, only the pre amp left. He phones the police, talks with them, and an hour later gets a phone call asking him to come down and identify the equipment. He hurries off to fifty-one division and finds they have made no such call and by the time he gets home the pre amp is gone."

Crawford laughed in spite of himself. "Damned insolence," said McIlwane. He sorted through the dope sheets for one more example of the conspiracy of practical jokes. "Here's one," he said. "On Friday, February 21, all the garbage was stolen on Metcalfe Street between Carlton and Winchester before the truck came in the morning. That night it was all returned. Where the hell do you hide that much garbage?" The question was rhetorical. McIlwane continued. "There was, understandably, a hue and cry from the ratepayers' association. We had someone from crime prevention doing talks at the local school and Ewart demanded and got reinforcements to try to curb the tide. And it worked, too, or at least it seemed to. The stats dropped more in line and slowly but surely have been dropping ever since."

"And Ewart's been polishing his badge ever since?" asked Crawford, amused by what seemed to be a particularly anti-climactic story. McIlwane held up a hand like a traffic cop.

"Not so fast," he said. "Before I tell you more about that let me tell you why I'm looking into the matter at all. The commission

70

wants a report on the changing dynamics of juvenile crime, with special emphasis on gangs. Vince Gas from Youth Bureau headquarters is on the task force with me and there's a couple of others I don't think you know. We've been going over the records concerning crime rings to put together something.

"What particularly attracted me to the Cabbagetown problem of a year ago was that we never broke up any gang or arrested any ring leaders. When things got hot the gang just melted away, which suggests that the whole thing was spontaneous. Now I know kids and spontaneity. Anything can set them off, a movie, a new rock band – but spontaneity breeds recklessness and there was nothing reckless about this business. There was talent at work. What happened to all those spontaneous young *talented* punks? Things might cool down for a while but in this case things have been cooling down for a year. Did they all just spontaneously up and leave?"

It was obvious McIlwane didn't think so.

"What did happen?"

"Things cooled down when Ewart got in extra men," said McIlwane. "But if you look real closely at the PRPs, you'll see they didn't make all that many arrests. Not only that, things stayed hot for another month after the reinforcements came in and when a change did happen it was a sudden drop just as if somebody had yanked back the troops." The image was significant and McIlwane indicated by his expression he had chosen it wisely. He showed Crawford the figures representing the change between October and November of the previous year.

"Since then it's been a steady slide, everything has grown all nice and calm – almost. By almost I mean there has been four or five hefty heists in Cabbagetown in the past year, which you probably remember." Crawford remembered. "There was nothing childish about those jobs," continued McIlwane, "but you know something, Rum – and this is where I take the plunge – I think there *is* a connection."

The older man stopped and seemed to size up his audience. "Let me indulge in a little metaphor. Let's think of Cabbagetown as a nice-size pond where the water is always a little choppy, a lot like you remember it. Then all of a sudden let's say it gets really turbulent for a while, so much so that you end up pouring a lot of oil on the pond. Sure enough it calms down but suddenly you hear a very large splash and then another and another – only when your back is turned, mind you – when you turn around it's all calm as can be – "

"And you can't see anything below the surface because of the oil slick your troops laid down," added Crawford.

"What do you make of it?" McIlwane asked.

Crawford tugged on his moustache. "I don't know what I'd make of it but I think you're suggesting there are some very large fish in the pond and they're eating all the guppies."

McIlwane shrugged his shoulders not sure anymore whether his metaphor had served the intended purpose. He tried gamefully again. "There's no reason the big fish and the guppies can't share the same pond since they're not really after the same thing – "

"So the big fish are vegetarian?" volunteered Crawford.

"Oh, to hell with it!" said McIlwane, abandoning the metaphor altogether.

Crawford laughed. He understood where the whole thing had gone astray. There was no real or apparent reason why "the big fish" should care one way or another about the juvenile delinquents in the area as long as the kids stayed out of their way. What then was the answer to where all the guppies had gone?

As he thought he became engaged in a complex series of gestures which might have spoken volumes to a deaf person. It was as if he were checking all his features to make sure they were still in place; poking and pulling and scratching.

"Couldn't be some local vigilante group?" he said at last.

"Have you heard of one?" asked McIlwane.

The point was well taken. There were a lot of citizens' groups beginning to take action in the city but invariably they sought media exposure, feeling that good press coverage was the best deterrent to crime.

"Even if that's the answer I don't like it when people take the law into their own hands."

"Even if they do a better job than the police?" asked Crawford, deliberately provoking the supervisor.

"Especially when they do a better job than the police," he responded.

"You're power hungry, Colin," said Crawford. "What you really want to do is tie Ewart's britches in a knot." McIlwane harrumphed. Crawford considered the matter more seriously. "If I'm going to be the pawn in some top-drawer in-fighting maybe you had better explain what you *do* think."

McIlwane looked Crawford straight in the eye. "I don't know what I think, Rum. I just know I don't like it. I was in the artillery in World War Two. Now I'm not one of those cops like Wheeler who thinks police work is conducted on a never-ending battleground, but I do suffer some residue of combat duty. I get real edgy when the guns stop. Especially when they drop a few big bombs behind your lines. None of those big robberies has been solved to this day. That, however, is not my domain. I just want to know where the kids are."

Crawford smiled. "Maybe they all grew up?"

"That is precisely what I'm afraid of," said McIlwane. He looked at the pile of reports in front of him, and from the expression on his face he might have seen them for the first time for what they really were: columns of numbers in a jungle of rubric.

"Get me something tangible, Rum. Shuffle around and find out what's happening...that is, if you're interested."

10

On a dilapidated sheet of painted cork in the local laundromat Stink looked for messages from Gob. His own notice advising Gob of the tramp who had surprised him at the phone booth had been retrieved. The cork board was Stink's "post office." Each member of the gang had a "post office," usually a public bulletin board or sometimes simply a telephone pole littered with notices of lost cats, impending garage sales or offers of guitar lessons. To an outsider the messages left by Gob or his Scrogglings would not have made sense for they were in code. Stink had never once seen Gob enter the laundromat but the messages were left and collected nonetheless. There was no notice of a meeting.

Stink made his way to the local schoolyard where for days he had kept a vigil, watching for Teri. He had been careful not to be seen, but today she caught a glimpse of him and Stink determined that tomorrow he would approach her; talk to her if he dared.

He had the strongest desire to take her somewhere, to take her away, and he spent the rest of the day imagining where. Passing a travel agency with racks out on the sidewalk, a brochure caught his eye. Las Vegas. It burst into his imagination like a fire cracker. There were pictures and Stink could see Teri and himself in them. He could hear Teri whispering in his ear in some casino as a cashier tallied up his chips.

The next day at the schoolyard he watched for her. It shouldn't have surprised him to see her with a friend. It was another girl but to Stink it was one person too many. What's more Teri was laughing and holding the girl's arm. He turned on his heels. A roman candle burst into points of light over the Nevada desert and illuminated nothing. Las Vegas had vanished as quickly as it had appeared.

He didn't hear her call at first. He had been walking fast, almost running, and besides she had called him Stuart. When he turned she was running after him. She had a sweater around her shoulders and was wearing a dress. It was strange to see her pale skinny legs. The dress was black with a diagonal red stripe. When she at last caught up to him, all breathless, he noticed that the stripe cut across the nipple of her right breast in a way that alarmed him. "Who was she?" was all he could think to ask.

"I thought it was you," she said, and turned back, waving goodbye to her friend. "Kate Mercer." She waved again. "I told her you were my boyfriend. Hope you don't mind."

Hopelessly inept, Stink muttered: "Oh that's okay."

"Arlo told me your real name," she explained.

She started to walk with him. The exertion had made her cheeks and neck red. He could not take his eyes off the pulse in her neck.

"Kate is rich. She says her Dad is in media or something. Anyway, she likes to play like she's a punk and she gets off on me. Gob says I should encourage her...."

Stink heard only bits and pieces of what followed. Teri had sensed his shyness and so she chattered on. Las Vegas rose back out of the desert and Stink was there fumbling for his room key while Teri leaned drunkenly on his shoulder. In Stink's mind sex was something that only happened somewhere else; somewhere very far away.

"Arlo told me about some place called Suzette's. Will you take me there?" Stink heard that much.

A few minutes later they were sitting in a stall at Suzette's, a grubby little hole-in-the-wall on Gerrard Street. Suzette's seemed always to be open and if the coffee was burnt it was hot. Suzette was a 250-pound ex-stevedore from Macedonia. Nobody knew what his real name was; it sounded like Suzette. The fact that he spoke little English, was partially deaf, and spent most of his time in the back room listening to Macedonian folk dances on his record player, added enormously to the restaurant's charm. One could simply overlook the smell and highly volatile oil vats. Suzette entered the business end of his café long enough to pour two cups of coffee. Then he returned to the back room where he was soon singing lustily a song of oriental mode.

Teri prattled on. For his part Stink could have gladly listened to her all day for her voice drowned out a thousand other voices, even Suzette's, which bellowed from the back.

Gob had taken little time initiating Teri to the gang's modus operandi. He had a social worker's instinct for insinuating his Scrogglings into the community: washing windows, mowing lawns, sitting babies, all without stealing a thing but always with the ear open and the eye peeled. Teri's situation showed promise. Not only had she befriended a rich girl but there was talk of Kate's parents taking Teri in since Teri's own living arrangements were miserable. In this vein, Teri told Stink about herself, stopping now and then to sip pale coffee from a saucer poised on the tips of slender fingers.

Eventually, the conversation drifted to the Knot and Vernon Pilchard's arrest, which Teri had heard about from Arlo.

"What if he rats?" she asked in a conspiratorial whisper.

"He won't," said Stink, fidgeting uncomfortably.

"Why not?"

Stink reiterated that he wouldn't, making it seem as if he were reserving some secret knowledge. Teri sensed the implication but was by no means convinced.

Stink then told Teri of Captain Hakum. Hakum had claimed at least four lives, two since he had joined the Knot, ostensibly at Gob's command. There were others quite capable of carrying out such orders. Vernon, despite his brief sojourn in the ranks of the gang, would have heard all the grim stories. Whatever else he might have thought of the Knot, he would think twice before informing.

Teri did not seem reassured but, as in the moment when Gob had shone his torch full in her face, she did not blink. Stink watched her closely, as he fumbled through the assorted anecdotes of violence relating to members of the gang.

"Did Gob mention anything to you about the revolution?" he asked at last and it was strange to hear the word out in the open like that.

"What revolution?" she asked.

It was difficult to know where to start. "There is gonna be this revolution...some day." There, he had given the idea a time frame and, unclear as to how to continue, he looked down. He pushed a spoon, left-handed, through a slalom course of coffee splatters on the formica table.

Sensing his reticence, and glad to leave morbid topics behind, Teri joined in the guessing game. "And Gob is gonna make this revolution happen?"

He looked up quickly to see if she was poking fun at him, but she wasn't. "Everything is so complicated," he said, not able to look her in the eyes. "But one day there will be this revolution. It will be a time like when things will be a lot better and there will be more things – more money – for everyone, not just the rich – everyone."

Just then Suzette screeched horribly as though in pain. It was only the final dramatic note of his aria. Teri spilled coffee all down her front. She giggled and dabbed at her chest with a napkin. Stink couldn't help noticing that her nipples were no longer apparent. Women had so many mysteries.

"Arlo called you a Hood-pick – what's that?"

Stink smiled, thin lips drawn over his teeth. "It's like a skin flint – because I save my money. I've saved a lot," he said.

She nodded. "How long you known him?"

"Gob?"

"Arlo."

Stink told her about himself and Arlo in their voodoo days, and Teri laughed. She, in turn, told of how Arlo had come into her life when she had tried to steal his jacket at a rock concert. He had caught her and then offered the jacket, insisting she take it. In return she had to steal him another jacket of his choice from a store. She had done it. She could also pick pockets and win hearts. She was good with a sob story, she said, but hastened to add that she wasn't feeding Stink any line. She produced a silver pocket-watch she had figged on the weekend. Stink appraised it and handed it back, but she had meant him to have it.

"You don't mind if I call you Stuart, do you?" she asked.

Stink shook his head and tried at the same time to suppress a shiver that coursed down his spine, dissipating finally into a warm, liquid sensation in his groin.

11

Crunkscully had wandered right off his map. It had been a long day and a tiring one and had it not been for the school bell he would be home now, maybe drinking beer with the others. Instead, he watched children flying past him on bikes, shoving and teasing on the sidewalk or lolling about in the schoolyard. He searched their faces, and his imagination, defying genetic logic, found traces of himself in them all – blond, Negroid, Oriental – it didn't matter. There were his own eyes or Connie's dark hair. Once in a dream he had recorded on tape, Connie appeared to him chartreuse with red eyes and an ultramarine smudge down one side of her nose. There was no telling what Ross might look like.

Behind his back Crunkscully heard the creak of leather. The wind stirred and he heard a rattling noise. He had been aware of the invalid for some time but had hoped that by ignoring him he would go away. He hadn't. Crunkscully had seen him before many times. He had thought the man blind, but how could a blind man be following him? He sat in his wheelchair so close now that Crunkscully thought he could hear him breathe, even above the street noises.

Crunkscully didn't dare turn around. A memory began to explode in his head, disorienting him. It was applause, thunderous yet distant, like a rainstorm across a lake.

"Looking for someone?" the invalid finally asked. Crunkscully did not look around. He surveyed the now empty schoolyard. The noise was growing in his head. There was cheering and it was so clear to him that he instinctively snapped his mouth shut, as if he was the perpetrator, lest the beggar hear and assume the applause was meant for him.

"Is it a boy or a girl you are after?" asked the man.

Inside Crunkscully's head, hustings were shaking as footsteps clattered up to the podium. There was no privacy up here, everyone knew everything; everyone could see him.

Still patient, but with his voice raised belligerently, the invalid again addressed him. Crunkscully listened to the anonymous voice of public address announce him – Crunkscully – to the enthusiastic crowds assembled below. They went wild.

"Gob has many children. Perhaps Gob can find one for you."

"Scol-lard! Scol-lard!" cried the crowd in Crunkscully's head and dimly he realized that it wasn't him they wanted but Scol-lard. "Scollard," he said out loud.

"Scollard?" said the man.

The intrusion had a strange effect. Crunkscully spun around to face the voice. "No!" he said. And then to the other man's surprise he clapped his hands over his ears. His face was momentarily paralyzed with fear and he shut his eyes tightly to block out whatever vision it was, external or internal, that he found so painful. The memory, so shatteringly clear one moment, began to melt. It poured out of him like hot wax; the impression was lost. The storm passed. Opening his eyes and seeing the beggar there, he started to step backwards in faltering steps. He apologized, for what he wasn't sure. It was a habit he had picked up. He found his nose was dribbling and jabbed at it with his cuff. There was blood in the mucus.

Gob stared after him, flabbergasted. Lots of old rummies watched the children in the schoolyard, dreaming of some innocent time or love of one kind or another. But this one's performance was astonishing. He was certainly the man Stink had identified and he was quite obviously searching for something. If for no other reason than vulgar curiosity Gob decided to find out what; after all Cabbagetown was his Begler Bec. There was nothing to fear from this stranger, that much was clear. "Scollard." Was that his name or the name of his quarry?

✧

The confrontation with the invalid cut through Crunkscully's optimism of the past few days like a knife. It was as if his prospects were all painted on a bright curtain which once torn revealed a bleak terrain.

He stumbled home feeling curiously dejected, his legs like jelly and his head stuffed with gauze in the empty spot where the memory had been. Having wandered so far he was hard put to remember his way home, but his feet seemed to know the way. As tired as he was, he would have put off returning, had he foreseen what awaited him at home.

At 14 Elmsley Court the group was drinking Tokay, and had been since noon. Werner Boost had turned up with a case of the sweet, heavy wine and when Calmette said it tasted similar to the sacramental wine at his church Boost almost choked. Nobody asked any further questions.

Calmette turned down the television so that just the image remained. He was waiting for "Happy Days." "Where I go to church the pwiest is a lad just outa divinity school. Now he's just a boy, Di Fwanco's his name, but I call him fathah. I say, 'Good mawhning, Fathah Di Fwanco,' and he says, 'Good mawhning, my son.'" Calmette slapped his leg and fell backwards on the davenport, in stitches.

After a moment Tommy muttered fervently: "You know what I'd do? I'd kill the fucker!"

"No, no, no," said Calmette waving his hands about. "It's the way of things. Some men ah bawn to be fathahs and some men ah bawn to be sons."

"You mean some folks never grow up," said Chas ponderously. His deep and disturbing voice had a way of putting a lid on things usually, but not on Tommy.

"How can you sit there and take that?" Tommy demanded.

Calmette deliberated the question for a moment and then looked back at Tommy, perplexed. "Take what?"

"That Catholic horse turd, that's what!" Tommy's voice was raised in passion but before he could elaborate, Werner Boost interrupted him.

"Ach, you've got zee horses on zee brain," he said. He pointed at Tommy with one finger and behind his hand he muttered to the others in a stage whisper: "He's sore about zee Quinella at Greenwood." Then to Tommy: "Tell zem about you unt me at zee track." At this point Werner started to laugh a low belly laugh which created enough pressure across his midriff to pop a button on his wrinkled yellow shirt.

Frank, who had been replacing a fuse in the basement, arrived in the commonroom when the argument had progressed past the kindling point.

Werner, with much mischievous winking at the others, was drawing Tommy further and further into a pointless quarrel from which he was too stupid or too incensed to extricate himself. Scurrilously Werner persisted until finally he plucked the crow too close to the bone.

"Now zat you got no money," he said, "I guess you'll haf to see zoze friends of yours you tell us about, een zee Mafia. Yah?"

At the best of times Tommy Connacher was not one to provoke and for an instant there was a deathly hush. Tommy stood up very slowly. His face was as red as his hair. Suddenly, and with great dispatch, he raised the bottle of Tokay from which he had been drinking, intent on smashing Werner's skull. Instead of hitting Werner, however, he broke the light fixture suspended over his head.

It was almost dark outside and the fight was strangely back-lit by the patchy light emanating from the television. They were shadowboxing, with Tommy getting the worst of it for he had turned on Chas.

Frank stepped into the fray at precisely the wrong moment.

Tommy's wildly swinging fist connected with his face, shattering the left lens of his spectacles. With his eye tightly shut behind the empty rim, Frank looked more like Popeye than ever.

Tommy's fist was bloody. He was swearing but now there was a note of anguish in his voice. The others converged on him as he stumbled from the room backwards. He fumbled with the door knob and as they rushed him, Frank at the head, he flung the door open in their faces and dashed outside. In his feverish exit he tripped over the doorstep. He hurtled headlong across the porch and it was to this "welcome" that poor Crunkscully, weary and dejected, arrived home at last. He was flung back by the human projectile and he fell against the porch railing. Tommy scrambled to his feet. In his fall he had nicked his lip and blood trickled down his chin. He backed down the stairs. Chas came to Crunkscully's aid – he was dazed and, by now, hopelessly confused. The others crowded around him, staring at Tommy now standing halfway down the path. He glared at them but settled his gaze on Crunkscully who arbitrarily became in his crazy mind the villain of the piece.

"I'll get you," Tommy said. "I'll get you, you bastard!" And then he ran off.

Crunkscully went straight to bed.

❖

It was dark when Frank came up to see him. Crunkscully was sitting bolt upright in his bed. He had not had the wherewithal to undress.

Frank sat in silence for some time, his glasses tipped precariously on his nose. He spoke gently.

"I was thinking about something you said, Scully. Remember – something about a room with lots of controls and a window looking into another room?"

Crunkscully nodded vaguely.

Frank began to grin. "The way I see it, maybe you was an astronaut. Is that it?"

Crunkscully's brows knitted. There was nothing about astronauts on his tapes.

"You just crashed here in Neverland with the rest of us space cadets." Frank threw back his head and laughed. His Adam's apple shook in his great trunk of a throat. "I mean here we are, Scully, a bunch of space cadets in the middle of the city and a trillion miles from nowhere."

Crunkscully nodded solemnly. "I know about Tinker Bell," he said, poking Frank in the arm.

"Calmette show you that trick of his?" asked Frank.

Crunkscully eyed Frank suspiciously. "Why didn't they come and visit me anymore?"

"Who's that?" asked Frank.

"My friends. I had lots of friends, crowds of them. Too many to remember...they used to come."

Frank thought for a moment and then spoke mildly. "Well, friends can be pretty damn unfriendly sometimes. Can't be helped, I suppose."

"Connie came at first, but she never brought Ross with her."

"Connie your old lady?"

"She went away."

"You haven't seen your boy in a long time, have you?"

"I guess not."

"Like my kids," said Frank. He chuckled softly to himself and then rose to go.

"I *was* mayor, Frank," said Crunkscully. And he gave Frank such an agonizing look of inquiry it would have been foolish to ask him where or when, let alone how.

"Get some sleep, fellah," said Frank. "You'll feel better in the morning."

Frank shuffled to the door.

"I was," said Crunkscully.

But Frank had left.

12

Crawford, despite his earlier reluctance to participate in the project, now gave it a great deal of thought. There wasn't a case. There was no criminal running wild, there were no clues either, except on paper. What *was* going on?

There were two phenomena really: an evergrowing absence of juvenile delinquents and crimes related to juvenile delinquents; and the possibility of organized crime working in Cabbagetown. McIlwane had not said it, but three slick, large-scale heists in a six-block radius in four months signified as much. To Crawford the phenomena hung suspended one beside the other like items in a surreal painting, bearing no apparent relationship to one another yet poised in the same frame. McIlwane had supplied any number of images – big fish that jump when your back is turned; bombs that explode behind the lines of a still battlefield – but such images provided no clue as to what Crawford might be looking for, beyond a discrepancy from the norm, which is what McIlwane felt he had isolated. The investigation would, by necessity, be an oblique one. Although it was kids McIlwane was interested in, you can't send an agent into a pack of kids. No cop, Crawford least of all, looks fourteen. Only the best old-clothes man can pull off twenty.

Crawford's own particular genre was the mission crowd. It took little dissemblance on his part to fit in with them. He was compellingly drawn to derelicts. He enjoyed the speed at which tramps moved, even the sweet sherry they liked to drink. Though he was fastidious about his health, he never looked quite healthy; there was a sunkenness about the eyes. His physique, while limber, appeared to be on the verge of caving in. His thick, curly hair was streaked with grey. He attended to his own tonsorial duties, which gave the back of his head a ragged splendour no costume wig could approach. He was no chameleon, no master of disguises, but he did have the kind of face which faded into a crowd. He made a good "has been" and this area of the city still had its share of those.

Cabbagetown had pulled up its socks, and they were fashionable hose at that: woven with metallic yarn, bright hot pink, executive blue. Things, people, events, moved faster now but below the surface of things the left behinds, the ones with no socks, always seemed to have something to say about it.

Crawford liked to shuffle around. "Informed shuffling," he liked to call it. He had another talent which he had developed into something of an investigative technique. Distraction. He made room in his attention for the incidental and the extraneous. This made him quite a hit with winos.

The following morning Crawford took his next tentative step, as gingerly as a war vet on prostheses, but a step in the right direction. He found his way to 51 Division. It was ironic it should be there of all places that he should venture timidly out of his premature retirement, for, after all, it was at 51 he had started his career after returning from Hong Kong.

News of Crawford's enlistment preceded his arrival. He was greeted by those he knew but not without the odd smirk or raised eyebrow. Staff Supervisor Ewart was civil and accommodating but made it clear he thought McIlwane had a bee in his bonnet. He led Crawford to believe the office was at his disposal and Crawford thought he'd begin by just hanging around.

And so he did, for the better part of two days. He chatted with constables as they came on or off duty. He drank innumerable cups of coffee, and reacquainted himself with the drabness of a police division lunch room. He spent most of his days at the precinct unobtrusively picking up what he could of other people's conversations.

It was no wonder McIlwane's ideas were looked upon with lack of interest. There were five Youth Bureau workers in the division and they had their hands full, mostly with family-related problems coming from the Regent Park area. They were only too glad that things had cooled down in Cabbagetown. "The area is changing." Crawford heard it again and again. Lydia Creuse, the desk sergeant and an old acquaintance, felt that a lot of the displaced criminal element were heading out to the suburbs. Statistics did show that there was a significant rise in break-ins and incidental theft in the outlying areas of the city and this was certainly the most common juvenile crime after drunken driving.

While perusing the day book the recent arrest of one Vernon Pilchard came to his attention. Lydia told him it was a curious case because although Pilchard had been arrested any number of times before no one had ever "phoned ahead to book him a reservation." She had taken the anonymous call that had turned him in. He was out of jail now under the custody of his parole officer. He had been on probation before, after the last time he had been arrested. "Pilch," as he was referred to, was well known at 51 Division. He was what they called a "rounder"; he was always around. An interesting note was that before the recent arrest he had not dropped in for six months. This was the longest period he had been out of legal trouble since he was nine years old. He was now fifteen.

Lydia had booked him and Pilchard's behaviour after arrest had been far from normal, she explained, even for Pilchard. He had been erratic, boisterous, and had spoken in a strange jargon. He was scheduled for a psychiatric examination within the coming week. He was "good" at these examinations, so Lydia said, having "passed" several of them routinely. There had been an unsuccessful attempt by the D.A.'s office to keep him in custody. The judge had turned down the section eleven applied for which would have put his hearing before a criminal court judge instead of a juvenile court judge. The break-in was an indictable offence, but Pilch, for all his arrests, was still a minor. The maximum time he could be held without trial was twenty-four hours, and he had been released after this period pending trial. There had to be a court appearance within ten days and there was a feeling that Vernon might be sent back to reform school.

Crawford was looking for kids who weren't getting caught. However, Pilchard might be the exception that could prove the rule, the discrepancy from the norm, and Crawford had to begin somewhere. He wasn't going to attempt talking directly to Pilchard. For one thing, without authority of an official investigation he couldn't interview a parolee, but that wasn't the primary reason. Until Pilchard stood trial he was on the street, even if he was under strict curfew. To talk to him would have meant revealing his own identity, and Crawford did not want to do that.

He did, however, decide to see Pilchard's parole officer, Larry Hickson, and they met that afternoon over strong coffee and baklava in a Greek restaurant on the Danforth near his office. Hickson, around forty with yellow teeth and a chin with too many facets to ever be really clean shaven, was with the Central Toronto Youth Services and worked with severely disturbed anti-social adolescents. He had a work load of only five cases but they kept him busy. He looked it.

Crawford liked him. They had grown up in the same neighbourhood, but didn't waste time reminiscing. Hickson wasn't much surprised at McIlwane's theory. Nothing much surprised him any more.

"Tell me about Vernon Pilchard."

"He's a twenty-seven incher," said Hickson with a crooked grin, indicating the size in the air. "That's how much space his file occupies in my filing cabinet. He probably takes up roughly the same amount of space over at your Youth Bureau and in half a dozen agencies between here and Kitchener." Hickson cut his baklava in half; honey oozed out the sides. "He's a born recidivist; his life – if you can call it a life – revolves around crime and institutions and has done since he was nine. He's been arrested seventeen times but he has committed a lot more criminal acts; a hundred, maybe two hundred, at a guess. Pilch has been remanded for psychiatric observation after every conviction and they can't find anything wrong with him." Hickson grinned wearily. He licked honey from a large squat yellow finger. "My job," he said frankly, "is to keep him from killing someone."

With a second coffee ordered, Hickson continued. It seemed that Vernon Pilchard had been a loner and proud of it until six months earlier. "For a while he arrived for his sessions with me like a cat with a mouthful of feathers," he said. "I thought maybe he was in love." The statement was intended as irony. Hickson did not think Vernon Pilchard capable of love. "At one point he paraded some merchandise in front of me, made a big deal of showing me the bill of sale and all, said his uncle gave him the bread. I reminded him of the conditions of his probation and told him to watch his step. He didn't show me anything after that. I tried to find out what he was up to but he got particularly secretive. I probably should have got on his tail a bit more but I was glad enough to see him staying out of any real trouble." Hickson gave Crawford a quick and challenging glance.

Crawford sensed the challenge and chose to avoid it. "I heard he started talking funny?"

Hickson continued. "Yeah, he started talking funny. At first I figured it was just the latest hip-talk – we're always the last to know what's happening. Over the weeks it got more and more complicated, like a whole language. It was like Dickens or maybe more like something from a penny dreadful. You wanna hear some of it?"

Crawford's surprise must have shown. Hickson smiled as he produced a tape machine from his jacket pocket.

"The kids know I tape stuff. They can erase what they don't like."

He pushed a button and reversed the tape, stopping it after a moment. "He must have said this a hundred times – listen."

There was the cracked voice of a boy saying something he had memorized in order to show off. It was a set piece. "The Ruffian will nab the cuffin queer and let the harmanbeck trine with his kinchins 'round his colquarren."

Hickson stopped the machine. "What do you make of that?"

Crawford wasn't sure. Meanwhile the social worker replaced the recorder in his pocket.

"Gangs like to have buzz-words, secret codes, etcetera, but I wouldn't have thought Vernon would go for that kind of polka-dot malarkey. He's a loner. But let me tell you something. Anyone who can make Vernon Pilchard happy even for one month has really got something going."

Hickson gave Crawford the address of Pilchard's foster parents.

"How is he now, since his arrest?" asked Crawford.

"He's blue – in a real funk. By the revised terms of his parole he has to see me three times a day. He shows up on time and has stopped giving me any lip. That could be bad or good."

Crawford asked Hickson if he could find out more about Pilchard's generous uncle. Hickson agreed to try. "What do *you* think is happening?" he asked.

Crawford thought a moment and smiled. "Well you see there's this pond which is normally very rough...."

❖

Crawford dug out his "battle dress." He favoured the brown suit with the shiny knees and ass. He liked the aged and torn Beatles T-shirt, and a very long, muddy, tassled scarf of magenta wool for a touch of class. His black Wallabees completed the costume.

He took his place in the line-ups at the mission soup kitchen. He rummaged through clothes at the Sally Ann, and he hung out by the local liquor control board. He joined the sleepers and the pacers in the parkette the city had devised to disguise the awkward intersection at Parliament and Gerrard. It was all part of the territory and part of the rites of initiation. Shuffling, sitting, drinking, feeding the birds; it was a slow, unfulfilling process, satisfying only an endless curiosity in the variety of human response to failure. Crawford had forgotten one thing about drop-outs: for all the drudgery of their condition they finally were free of that most devastating of social fears; the fear of becoming a drop-out.

The eccentrics particularly fascinated Crawford and prominent among these major loonies was a man known as Gob. His wheelchair was outfitted with light metal frames, projecting like flying-machine wings behind him and to either side. Upon these frames were fixed cardboard signs, and on the signs, annotated in colourful array the crimes against him in what, to all appearances, was a life of unrivalled persecution. The culprits were not only individuals. God and ITT and assorted demons from other planets had ganged together, according to the signs, to drive poor Gob to the very edge of despair. If you could get close enough to read the small print (and one seldom dared) you would find that Duncan Hines had crippled him and Christ himself (in a moment of pique, no doubt), had blinded him. He was unapproachable, cursing anyone who came near him. Crawford felt sure his blindness was a sham but there was enough of that around. It was a harmless enough conceit and served to emphasize his delusion of grand persecution. Crawford found himself wondering if the wheelchair was another prop. Gob was a performer. Crawford listened to him rant on a street corner – there was no mention of gangs or kids. Cabbagetown supported more than its share of street theatre. He turned his attention elsewhere.

Anyone sitting idly at his window, observing the ebb and flow of human traffic through the streets of Cabbagetown, would not have singled out Crawford. It was not a question of stealth but of degree of eccentricity. He was not as noisy as Gob or the Ant Man, who screamed in terror while stamping on ants, half the time imaginary. He was not appealingly quixotic like the Chessman with the snow-white ponytail who played chess, solitaire, in the park, nor hideously misshapen like the poor creature Crawford called the Spider. In short, he was not ostentatious. He had already made a number of acquaintances, social conventions being what they were in the circles in which he travelled. When anyone asked him what he was up to, he said he was looking for something. If they asked why, which would have shown a surprising degree of perseverance, he said he was a cop. That always got a laugh.

After a few days he settled into a routine. It was sobering to reflect on how easy it became. Since his accident it had crossed Crawford's mind on bad days that were he to leave the force he would probably end up on Skid Row. He had no romantic illusion about a life free of responsibility but he couldn't think of any occupation for which he was better equipped. Outside of his house he didn't think of himself as belonging anywhere in particular. He tried not to think about it too much.

13

It was like a shipwreck. Crunkscully tossed in a turbulent wreckage of sleep before finally sinking into dreams. The surface was dangerous, the choppy waters strewn with the flotsam of memories; a whole cargo splintered and threatening to shatter his skull with each new wave, not one fragment of which was large enough to grab on to or hold his weight. Or perhaps he was just not strong enough to hang on. He was part of the jetsam of a sinking ship. On the surface of sleep, semi-conscious, Crunkscully was only another memory to himself.

Exhaustion dragged him under. As he descended, the darkness closed around him. He hoped that he would sink forever but some shift in his body equilibrium would not let him and he hung suspended in the dark somewhere between the turbulence on the surface and whatever awaited him below. Without knowing it he was being moved. Less violent currents pushed him at the speed of sleep into shallow reaches. The atmosphere around him grew less and less dark until, looking upwards, he could see a face hovering above the water. Now the weights which had dragged him into sleep fell away, and gently he rose again. As his head broke the surface he opened his eyes.

"Thought we'd lost you that time," said a voice.

Crunkscully pulled the sheets up to his chin.

Outside, rain pelted against the window.

"Been like that all night," said the voice, gesturing at the rain.

It was a familiar voice. "Thought we all might float away," it said and laughed softly. "I stuffed some fabric in those cracks around the window. One of these days I'll get around to caulking 'em up right. A guy needs fresh air, but not so much! Here, I brought you some soup."

The man was holding a mug of soup. Crunkscully's mouth felt like sandpaper. As quickly as he could he propped himself up in his bed, the springs strained with the shift in weight. He took the cup and then, feeling he should say something, he mumbled: "Thank you, Doctor."

The man who handed him the soup chuckled. "Better taste it before you thank me. I made it myself." He sat on the edge of the bed. "Got my glasses fixed. See?" He held them up for inspection. "There's this place down on Queen Street that can do it in ten minutes. Next thing you know they'll have drive-ins."

Crunkscully slurped the soup thankfully and gazed, wide-eyed, around the room. He looked at the dresser, at the notes on the glass, and at the neat pile of cassettes. He looked at the places on the wall where pictures had once hung. Last of all he peered over the rim of the mug at the cheery if puzzled face of the man sitting beside him. "Frank," he said, doubtful of the name.

"Thought we'd lost you, Scully."

Crunkscully sipped the comforting broth. There were letters in it all mixed up, spelling improbable words. He felt very tired.

"You was in a hospital, weren't you?" The question was rhetorical. "D'ju escape?"

Crunkscully nodded. "Walked out," he said dribbling soup down his chin.

Frank laughed. "Well at least you couldn't be too dangerous."

Crunkscully shook his head gravely.

"I spent some time in an institution myself. I wouldn't hurry nobody back to one."

"I can't find Connie," said Crunkscully. "That's her on the mirror, or at least it says it is, but I don't think so any more."

Frank examined the picture. "She married into the big time," he said, giving a low whistle. He rocked back and forth indecisively on his feet. He puffed up his cheeks like a chipmunk and made a popping sound when he exhaled. "You ain't seen your boy – Ross, is it? – at all, have you?"

Crunkscully shook his head sadly. "Maybe once – I don't know anymore."

Later, when the man had gone, Crunkscully climbed out of bed and examined the cassettes on the dresser top. Gingerly he placed the earplug in his ear. A comforting voice coughed politely and began. It was, of course, his own voice but he didn't know it.

"It seems his memory has a mind of its own. It seems reality is, day by day, becoming a thing of the past. This is very boring. He is going to die of boredom."

The voice whispered: "Mr. Fowle is very near the end. The doctor showed him a picture of a beautiful woman in a skimpy bathing suit and Mr. Fowle, after staring at it for several moments, said to the doctor: 'Well, it's not a tractor but it might be a house?'"

❖

If Crunkscully's disease was inexorable, it was at least as vague in its attention span as was Crunkscully himself.

Through his tapes, his disciples, Crunkscully refamiliarized himself with his previous idea to find Ross, although his efforts were reduced and lacking in enthusiasm. One day he took his map out in the rain and the red and green markings trickled across its surface in a muddy stream of indistinguishability. He would need a better map or a better idea.

Despite its far from prophylactic standards and the absence of anything even vaguely resembling a regimen, he laboured for a while under the misconception that number 14 Elmsley Court was some kind of hospital. If there was a pronounced lack of medical staff to sustain this notion there was a suitable assortment of patients. Monsieur Calmette came to visit often, and often wearing his dressing gown and fluffy slippers. Werner

Boost visited him and read him a chapter or two from his *Roman Invasion of Canada*. He kept the manuscript in a large cardboard carton. Even Olga wandered in to visit and was as uncomfortable as a hospital visitor often is; she scratched a lot and commented on the room and talked about the rain. "I was looking for that cat of yours," she said one day. Crunkscully had forgotten all about the cat. Olga seemed relieved to hear that.

The institutional illusion was completed by Frank Qualtrough, who looked nothing like a nurse, but attended him with nursely concern and constant good spirit. The price for his ministrations was a ready ear, for Frank liked nothing better than to chat. If Crunkscully's health should worsen, or if he grew violent, which seemed unlikely, then Frank would decide what to do with him. He liked Crunkscully. He had the funny feeling he had seen him somewhere before.

Crunkscully took to sucking on his thumb and he chewed clear through one of the wings of his glasses. Frank lent him an elastic device which athletes use to keep their glasses on. The tightness hurt the bridge of his nose but he saw better than he had for some time. With Frank's help, Crunkscully regained the ground lost in the trauma of his confrontation with the man in the wheelchair and with Tommy Connacher. It was Frank who explained to him that he was not in Vancouver. As his health improved he took to ambling around the neighbourhood again. He developed what Frank called a rambling mind and wandering feet.

On one of his jaunts he was sure he had seen Tommy Connacher. He had seen his face through a car's windscreen. It had been for a second only before the image of Tommy's face became lost in Crunkscully's own reflection. It had given Crunkscully the eerie impression of Tommy with his fiery red hair laughing inside his own face. It scared him.

Then, that night in the commonroom, Crunkscully heard more about Tommy.

"I seen him," Chas informed the others. "He's got one of them little hats and he's driving for someone over on Montcalm."

"Yah, but for who?" asked Werner suspiciously.

"Some Mafioso, eh, Werner?" asked Frank.

Werner only cocked an eyebrow mysteriously, and then went up to his room.

"Goddamned little firebrand." Chas would have loved to get his hands on Tommy.

Crunkscully was more disturbed by the man in the wheelchair. He had seen him frequently in his rounds. Calmette once told Crunkscully the beggar's name was Gob. But when Calmette went on talking about him, Crunkscully covered up his ears. Like a disease, the crazed creature with his cardboard wings and fluttering banners, with his oaths and mirror eyes, worked his way into the very core of Crunkscully's imagination until Crunkscully could not always escape him, even in his dreams. In his dreams, now, he would see the pram with its high bright wheels and when he looked inside he would see Gob laughing at him and the pram would have transformed into a wheelchair.

14

In mid-October the rains began to let up. The weather cleared and in its place an Indian Summer settled like fine yellow muslin across the tall red houses and the cobblestone gardens of Cabbagetown. Phoenix-like, the deserted streets sprang into life. On Sunday the wealthier parishioners, dressed in tweeds and designer jeans, were walking exotic dogs, and lining up at the corner store to chat and collect their *New York Times*. Many took the opportunity to fix storm windows and gutters, and soon ladders were up all over. The real estate agents were busy, and there was an open-house on every block. The streets were sluggish with a steady stream of "window shoppers" anxious to join, or just ogle, the upwardly mobile at home.

The sun also fell on the outposts of slumdom scattered throughout the neighbourhood. For the boarders at number 14, the warmer weather meant beer on the front porch. For a while at least the television was not on, having been replaced by a more entertaining parade of tourists on the street.

Crunkscully returned from the day's jaunt very tired. The walk had become protracted when he decided that it was Vancouver to which he had meant to go. He got as far as Riverdale Park before turning back but then he got lost in the network of alleyways which honeycomb the neighbourhood. It was a surprise to suddenly come upon the two familiar faces of Frank and the new lodger, Buck.

When Tommy Connacher had left Frank had placed a "Room for Rent" sign in the window. It was answered almost immediately by Buck, who had been living in a rooming house up the street destined to be torn down. Buck had cerebral palsy. He walked slowly, gyrating one arm as he did, and he talked with a bad stammer. Buck worked in a sheltered workshop in the basement of a local church, and held the honour of being the only resident at number 14 who was permanently employed. He tended to keep to his room or out back where he was constantly tinkering with his car, a mammoth, rusted, '68 Cadillac, which he parked in the alley behind Frank's Golden Hawk.

With great perseverance now, Buck was attempting to pour oil into the Caddy's crankcase. Frank was dreamily buffing the roof of his Studebaker, and, judging by the sheen, he had been at it for quite a while.

The two men noticed Crunkscully at about the same time and greeted him each in their way; Buck with the shaky tipping of an imaginary cap and Frank with a loud shout. "Scully! Get your butt over here and be prepared for the treat of your life. Where've you been? I went looking for you." He examined Crunkscully's dishevelled clothes like an anxious mother, but only for a moment. Something far more important was on his mind.

He climbed behind the wheel of his gleaming car and switched on the ignition. "Listen to this," he said with pride. After only a slight delay the engine roared into life. "That's a Thunderbolt 289-V8," he said above the noise. "Why the Lord Studebaker folded instead of Chrysler, I'll never know." Frank punctuated his statement by hitting the oval steering wheel with the palms of his hands and accidently sounded the horn. "Come on, get in!" he continued enthusiastically and, leaning across the passenger's seat, he opened the other door.

Obediently, and with a sense of awe, Buck climbed in the back of the car and Crunkscully got in the front.

Frank laughed. "The others would rather sit on the stoop guzzling beer, but you two are getting the rare privilege of a ride on the wings of the Hawk. Remember? I promised you this,

Scully." Frank engaged the clutch and then very carefully placed his hand over the black rod sticking up from the gear box.

"Th-th-there isn't any kn-kn-knob," said Buck, leaning forward over Frank's shoulder.

Frank frowned and looked briefly in the rear-view mirror. "That's right, Buckeroo. Why do you think somebody would do something like that?"

"F-fo-for money!" said Buck with conviction.

Frank only frowned and sighed a long, drawn-out sigh. Then he carefully put the car into first gear and pulled out onto the rutted, overgrown track which constituted Elmsley Lane.

❖

Down the alley Stink slid out of sight behind a tree. He had been watching the house for days for just such an opportunity. There was a back door and a fire escape attached to the two upper stories of number 14. If the others stayed safely on the porch there would be little chance of being caught. He didn't waste any time. As soon as the car turned the corner he approached the back entrance of the house.

❖

Crunkscully was far too tired for a ride "on the wings of the Hawk," and with one of his rare displays of temper, made this abundantly clear. He was dropped off with the promise of a rain-check. "Some other time," Frank called after him, unflappable as ever. Then he and Buck roared off.

Crunkscully walked the few blocks back to number 14, and, grunting at the others sitting on the porch, he went immediately to his room.

The boy spun around when Crunkscully entered. Crunkscully stumbled back against the door, closing it in his astonishment. Man and boy stared at each other without moving. Crunkscully smiled wanly. "Are you Ross?" he asked.

The dresser drawers had been ransacked; the closet stood open, and what few clothes Crunkscully had lay strewn about on the floor. The boy grabbed Crunkscully's old walking stick and, wielding it like a baseball bat, he stood his ground, ribs heaving under his black cotton T-shirt. "Who *are* you?" he snapped. Crunkscully looked at his collection of tapes in disarray on the dresser.

"Don't you know?" asked Crunkscully.

Stink was taken aback. He regarded the man quizzically.

Crunkscully winced as if from a blow. "Oh," he said. Then to the boy's surprise he walked around the perimeter of the room to a hard-backed chair on the opposite side of his bed from the boy and, sitting down, he proceeded to take his shoes off.

The boy lowered his make-shift weapon. He could leave without obstruction now but also without having completed his task. "Give me your wallet," he said. To his annoyance Crunkscully just laughed. He didn't even look up.

"You'll have to see Frank about money," he said, huffing and puffing as he struggled with his tired shoes.

"I gotta know who you are!" barked the boy.

Now Crunkscully looked at him, frowning uncertainly. "Crunkscully," he said. Then he smiled and shrugged his shoulders. "I don't know. I forget, and I haven't got a wallet." He turned his pockets inside out, one after the other.

Stink waved the walking stick menacingly. He was back-lit by the sun and his features were reduced to shadows. His hair stood out in spiky silhouette.

"I'm very tired," said the man. He slumped in his chair and with a note of irritation in his voice he added: "I thought you were Ross." He thought a moment longer and his face brightened. "Maybe you know him. He might be your age."

Stink was speechless. The man was calm, as if he knew something Stink didn't know and would never find out. He had no idea what to do next.

Luckily the man supplied the answer. He seemed to snap suddenly out of a reverie. "No," he said shaking his head. "You aren't Ross and you don't know him either. I'm not nuts, you're the one who is nuts. I didn't come storming in here demanding to know who I was. I didn't scare me. *You* did." After this tirade his voice dropped a little. He appeared thoughtful.

"We'll find out anyway," blurted Stink. "You can't get away." Crunkscully nodded his head. He had known that much all along.

"I'll tell you who I am. I'm somebody. And when I've forgotten who that somebody is I'll still be somebody."

Stink, after one more frustrated look at the man and his barren room, edged towards the door. The other showed no signs of following him. Stink walked out and shut the door. In the hallway he waited a moment, and tried to think what his next move should be. The man's voice called after him. "I took the precaution of remembering who I am. My memory is safely stored outside me, where my brain can't get at it."

Inside the room Crunkscully stood and raised his voice. "It's all on the tape. That's who I am." It was his finest moment. His pulse raced. He hurried to the door and opened it. The hallway was empty. Swiftly he made his way down the stairs, almost slipping in his stocking feet.

On the porch Chas was sitting as he had been on the railing, his back against the post. He was staring ruminatively at the label of the beer bottle he was nursing. Olga was walking around in a circle across the path and through the overgrown patch of grass that was the front lawn. Every now and then she would kick at a hapless divot. She was talking very quietly to herself and smiling. Werner was watching passersby from a lawn chair, stooping from time to time over a notebook to scribble furiously some observation he had made, and Calmette was carefully cutting out the Sunshine Girl from the Sunday *Sun* to add to the collection taped to his bedroom wall. He was the only one who looked up when Crunkscully walked out on the porch, asking: "Did a boy come by?"

"Youah son, Mistah Cwunkscully?"

"No, just some boy," said Crunkscully.

"A boy," said Olga, beaming from the lawn. She spoke as if Crunkscully had made his announcement to expectants in a maternity waiting room.

Werner Boost looked up from his writing. He wore a dusty pair of glasses on the end of his nose.

"A strange boy vas een our haus?" he asked.

"Them kids," said Chas. "Them wicked sons of bitches."

"I haf bin expectingk zem," said Werner darkly.

"Did they steal anything?" asked Calmette.

Crunkscully looked confused. "There was just one boy."

Werner grimaced. "Jus' von, he says. Ha!"

"What did they take?" asked Calmette excitedly.

"Nothing. Nothing," said Crunkscully, aggravated by them.

"No, of course not," said Werner with grim assurance. He was on his feet now leaning against the porch railing. He turned and looked squarely at Crunkscully. "Zey vill haf escaped by now. You needn't vorry. Eet ees me for whom zey are lookingk for."

"Those damn bastards," said Chas with passion.

Werner wasn't finished. Another idea had sprung to mind. "Zey are stakingk out zee place for Hallove'en!" The others gasped.

"Shit!" said Chas.

Crunkscully mumbled an apology for having disturbed everyone, and retreated into the house. His burst of energy had left him listless. When he entered his room again he knew immediately something was wrong; something was missing. The dresser top was empty. All twelve of his tapes were gone. So were his recorder and his notes. There was nothing left on the mirror but his own shocked reflection.

15

The Indian Summer could not last. The rains set in again as
October lengthened. It was more than a week till Hallowe'en
when Gob called the Knot together again. The clandestine
assembly met in its usual spot while in the trees of the park
above and along the road skirting the necropolis, and in the
wide, grassy gutters beside the Bayview Extension, child guards,
armed with walkie-talkies, played Bo Peep in the rain.

Stink was early but not the earliest to arrive. Gob was there
and, to Stink's shock, so was Teri. Gob said nothing but he looked
Stink over with an amused expression on his face. Teri had been
drying her hair with a small towel which she held out to Stink.
She smiled at him timidly. He took the towel in silence.

Gob continued eyeing him. The corner of his rough old mouth
twisted into a grin. "What mubble-fubble's brewing in that
tormented noodle?" he said, squinting until his eyes were slits.
Then he sighed and suddenly snapped his eyes shut. His head,
like a turtle's, sank into the multiple folds of garment around his
neck and he folded his hands in his lap. He seemed actually to
nap, and in the uncomfortable quiet Stink sat down, jabbing at
his wet hair in a desultory way. Teri picked at a thread hanging
from her jacket, twisting it around her finger until the end
turned white. The rain clattered like drum sticks on the copper
roof.

Others arrived, sniffling and coughing, with jackets pulled

over their heads. The shed filled like a backed-up sewer, pungent with the slow steam of damp clothing. Body heat turned the mud floor into a soup. The usual chatter was subdued, drowned to some extent by the din on the roof but Gob, still maintaining his pretence of sleep, could hear enough.

In a little while, the meeting began without Gob's usual opening monologue. He saw no reason to impress his minions with his superiority this night. Vernon Pilchard's arrest spoke for itself, though no one but Gob and Stink knew the details of the boy's capture.

Kiki gave the first report, on Simon Tisler Jr. She had made some progress. It seemed with all his wealth Simon was running out of entertainment and as a very willing piece of jail-bait she had proved the perfect divertissement. Kiki had been taken on a guided tour of the rooms above Simon's restaurant. The entire storey was a vault full of erotic art. The works were not on display but Simon had hung a few paintings and uncovered a sculpture or two which he thought might whet the appetite of his young and forbidden fruit.

Kiki was graphic in her description of what followed. It was a burlesque for the benefit of her fellow crew mates made more titillating by the T-shirt she wore, which bore an arrow pointing to her crotch, and the statement "The line starts here" emblazoned across her chest.

Gob was pleased but he wanted more information. He outlined to Kiki specifically what information he required about means of access and security systems. He outlined precisely what he knew the Grand Vizier would require. When Gob had first made his pact with the Grand Vizier his obeisance had been genuine, he was even sycophantic, for it had been a coup to even catch the attention of such a man let alone enter his employ. Gob had been fastidious in exhibiting to his Underlings the deference due this great power, but as time wore on he began to reveal something of his growing frustration. The Grand Vizier was, Gob had imagined, the road to the top; but the road had turned out to be a great deal longer than Gob had expected. By now the

Grand Vizier must be very close to recouping his investment in Gob's little army of spies, or so Gob suspected, and the Tisler collection would rake in a considerable amount on the Black Market.

What began to rankle Gob was the nature of his dependency. He felt confident that he and his crew of urchins could have pulled off any of the thefts the Grand Vizier had accomplished, but Gob, as good a fence as he was, could never have found a market for the stolen merchandise. The Grand Vizier, on the other hand, could. He had contacts and clients around the world, waiting for every conceivable commodity from rare prize dogs to hoards of Roman coins, or, for that matter, a sizeable collection of modern erotica.

Gob realized he was little more than a glorified messenger boy, no different in kind from his own band of Afterlings. What's more, the Grand Vizier didn't dignify Gob by meeting with him face to face, or not very often, at least. Instead they communicated through an obnoxious go-between who smoked foul French cigarettes and had the unlikely name of Llaldhar Arnoldin. Llaldhar never interfered with the running of the Knot but he was always around and watchful. His services had been loaned to Gob. Nominally he was in Gob's employ but his real role was obvious. He was a spy for his superior. Gob was aware, not for the first time, of the waste of it all. The Grand Vizier had real power.

Something had been brewing in Gob. Fed by gnawing resentment, the idea took shape until he could contain it no longer, and suddenly it burst from his lips, interrupting Kiki, who had resumed her report. "Enough!" he said.

Kiki sat down. The room grew still.

"Perhaps it is time for the Knot to come into its own. What do you say, my Scrogglings?" No one spoke. Gob continued. "What if I were to tell you that a most interesting piece of information has fallen into our hands, and that if we were to make the most of it, we could all become rich. *We* ourselves, that is; for what I have in mind will not require the services of the Grand Vizier."

This created a buzz, as Gob knew it must. He was talking out and out revolt.

"What if I were to tell you that in Cabbagetown there lives a man of such wealth he could probably buy a dozen Grand Viziers! You would be surprised, wouldn't you? 'Where?' you would say, for you think you know the neighbourhood well, and indeed you do. And I would point to a modest little row house on Wellesley and say 'There. There lives Bernard K. Muraskin; the billionaire Bernard K. Muraskin.' The fact is, he's seldom around. He lives all over the world, and alights here only on very special occasions. I am proposing to you that the Knot might supply him with just such an occasion." Gob looked quickly around the shed at the frank incomprehension on the faces of his crew.

"The details are not worked out; the information has only very recently come my way, thanks to the tireless work of our young Whip Jack."

Stink bowed his head under the gaze of his crew mates.

Gob continued. "Stink has even been so good as to supply us with a gentleman who will do most of the work for us. It is yet to be ascertained to what extent we can count on this gentleman's support, but he has already – how shall I say – cased out the situation quite adequately."

Suddenly a familiar muffled crackle could be heard within the crowded shed. From out of his many coats Gob withdrew a two-way radio. In the midst of static there was a youthful voice. It told of an intruder, approaching the shed through the park. Co-ordinates were given, advice asked for. The man was apparently a tramp, a wino by the looks of him, the voice said. Gob's instruction was quick in coming. "Detain him," he said. "We'll send the Captain to make the sign on him. A little lesson for wandering around drunk in the rain, and a little something to remember us by."

The co-ordinates were repeated for Captain Hakum, who

could hardly wait to be set loose. He wriggled like a greyhound waiting for the starting gate to open, and then he was off into the park. His footfall crunched briefly on the gravel path leading away from the shed, and then the sound was obliterated by the rain.

Gob seemed quite content. His mouth tasted sweet again. His rage had flown off into the night on Hakum's shoulders and Hakum's propensity to violence was equal to Gob's own imagination. It gave Gob pleasure, from time to time, to inspire his Afterlings to acts of cruelty. In his real madness Gob was far more the director than the actor. His orders would be carried out and, as in classical Greek drama, the tragedy would occur off stage.

He decided to speak no further of the grand plan involving Muraskin that night. He needed time to think. From the eager expressions on the faces of his crew, he had seen they were intrigued at the prospect, what little edge of it he had revealed.

❖

Werner Boost had been watching the park, on and off, for months. Tonight, he had felt a presence that he could neither see nor hear through the walls of rain. But he was not surprised by it, he expected it – he lived with it – in the sense that he knew the enemy was entrenched everywhere. Tonight he could perceive them close at hand, he could see them in his mind's eye for there is a paradox to seeing which Werner understood implicitly: one sees that which makes itself invisible.

He should, by rights, have been content with this observation, subtle as it was, but emboldened by drink he ventured across the park, growing more alert as he approached the eastern end, the farm, on the lip of the hill which rolled down into the valley. He was heading to the path which passed through the zoo, when he was suddenly and noiselessly confronted by several small cloaked bodies. He didn't need to turn to know he was cornered. He felt for a moment, as Gulliver might have, that such small creatures could not possibly overcome him, but they were as lithe as cats. His stocky legs and sheer mass made toppling him difficult, although he offered little resistance.

He was eventually felled onto the wet grass. In another moment small bodies swarmed over him until he was pinioned by bony knees. One of them tore off his scarf and shoved most of it in his mouth. It was cold and soggy and Werner gagged. Another boy arrived and it was for him the six or seven hooligans had been waiting. The newcomer was a tall teenager with almost white hair, and it took him only a second to straddle Werner's chest and sink his knees painfully into Werner's armpits. He flicked a stiletto switchblade in front of Werner's nose and made as if to remove the great red dong from its place. Instead the knife nicked the skin of his cheek. Werner was drunk and while adrenalin almost destroyed the anaesthetic effect of alcohol it did not quite. He choked on a scream that unleashed would have filled the rain-filled park but instead reported back like a stifled echo until his head was vibrating from within. He was able to realize through the pain that this mute Viking was carving some pattern on him, and the realization made him faint.

He was not unconscious for long but when he came to they were gone, like a dream. His face hurt too agonizingly for it to have been a dream but it had all been as fleeting. Finding himself free Werner clumsily found his feet and made it as fast as he could back across the park. He kept hearing his attacker pounding after him but it was only the rain. It swept up in gusts into his face; a mixed blessing because while it cooled his face it stung the ragged cut like a suture needle.

At Elmsley Court the television was on and with great relief Werner stumbled up the path towards that wan light. He even found it in himself to smile a bit, though his face would not risk the pain of communicating the expression. Now they would believe him, he thought. From tonight on, they would believe him.

❖

After the meeting, Stink walked with Teri in silence. The rain had stopped but the air was soaking wet. Hakum had not returned to the meeting having probably retired to his lair to lick his claws and teeth. The guards were gone, the park was quiet. Stink had no idea why Gob should send the Captain to carve up a rummy. Surely rummies were not the enemy of the revolution. Stink didn't like it. And why had Teri been at the meeting so early and alone with Gob?

At one point she almost spoke, but apart from that Teri seemed self-absorbed.

His own mind kept returning to the Coffee Shop's vivid description of the debauch at Simon's, but he suspected that wasn't what had claimed Teri's attention. It had been a strange and confusing evening. He had no idea who Bernard K. Muraskin was, nor could he believe that the old man who called himself Crunkscully could be contemplating a crime of any kind. He was a lame brain who could hardly remember his own name and yet it must have been him to whom Gob was referring. Not least of all, the prospect of pulling any kind of heist behind the Grand Vizier's back was not a comforting thought.

Before he knew it they were at Teri's doorstep. She turned and kissed him. It was an awkward gesture; she did not even remove her hands from her pockets. It was so unexpected that Stink stood for several astonished moments after she had gone. The kiss ignited him.

Later that night, tied in knots in his flannel sheets, he tentatively released some of the tension building in him over Teri. His sleep was not peaceful, all the same.

16

It was two nights before the Grand Vizier's men struck Tisler's but it was not until the early hours of the following morning that the alarm was raised. Three blocks away from Tisler's elegant watering hole, at Elmsley Court, Crunkscully's sleep buzzed and echoed with sirens, as cruisers swarmed to the scene of the crime.

Simon Tisler Jr.'s precious and extensive stash had been compromised. The impregnable storage vaults had been raped and the contents decimated – fifty canvases expertly chosen, had been carefully removed from stretchers, rolled up, and taken. It had been a meticulous and professional robbery which Tisler estimated would net somewhere in the neighbourhood of a half a million dollars on the Black Market.

Among the pressing crowd of sightseers and quidnuncs gathering outside Tisler's renowned eatery, and watching the police come and go with a curiosity matching that of the other onlookers, was R. Rum Crawford. He stood next to a pickpocket named Pickles, with whom he had been chumming around for the last couple of days.

After a while Crawford grew bored and shuffled off. Pickles caught up to him eventually, flourishing a wallet he had scored at the gathering. The two of them made their way to the Winchester Hotel to wait for the bar to open. It was only 11:00 A.M. but there was nothing much else to do. The wind was brisk, winter not far behind.

Pickles was growing tiresome. He was a willing enough raconteur, but he was leading Crawford nowhere. His latest topic of interest concerned immigrants, who were wrecking the economy. "They'll do any kinda work," he complained as if work were a disgusting habit. Crawford intended to lose him in the Winchester that day and pick up with someone new. The palaver was thick outside the hotel and he prepared himself for more of the same. The "same" consisted of verbal autobiography, readily spun out, and the politics of victimization.

Finally noon rolled around and the victims filed into the bar. Crawford and Pickles shared a table with two other acquaintances. A bag lady named Gladiola with a face as scuffed as a deflated soccer ball, and a man named Drum, whose conversation was limited to grunts at the Submarine sandwich he devoured with toothless rapacity. Crumbs and hot peppers gathered in his long, shaggy beard and oil greased his subereous cheeks.

After about an hour, Pickles left for the washroom, and was seen leaving the hotel shortly thereafter.

"So what do you hear about mysterious gangs in the neighbourhood?" Crawford asked bluntly. Gladiola eyed him with a pale grey eye and, with the confidence of a fortune teller, handed him a ticket from her purse. It bore the name of a dye cutter in Sarnia but she seemed to have made a mistake because she snapped it back and gave him a different card. This one, even more mysterious, warned him that his tires were soft. Drum burped fruitily. Staying would be a waste of time, and Crawford was about to leave when a large shadow fell across the table.

"You are a policeman, yah?"

Crawford craned his neck to see a huge nose on an enormous head topped by a lick of hair.

"Sure," said Crawford. "Why not?" He gestured to a seat which the stranger accepted.

Drum had finished his Submarine and stared into his greasy hands, transfixed. Gladiola removed herself to more convivial company.

The heavy German ordered a drink. His bespectacled eyes

were particularly small and straddled his nose like stirrups across the flank of a large red horse. The skin of his face was pale but for a pulsing tracery of blood vessels which mottled flabby cheeks. On the left at precisely the spot where the mandible hooks into the cranium the man bore the terrible welt of a wound which upon closer inspection looked remarkably like a letter. Crawford averted his eyes.

The other had been inspecting him with equal interest. "Zee name ees Verner Boost," he said. "You are admiringk my cicatrix, yah? You sink perhaps I am von of zoze Wienneze hot-shots who vair zair vounds as a mark of manhood." Crawford had not been thinking anything of the kind but since the wound was now the topic of conversation he had an excuse to peer at it. He raised his upper lip in distaste. Amidst the bruised flesh he recognized the letter "K."

"Vhat do you sink zey started to write?"

Crawford's eyes must have opened very wide for Boost laughed heartily. He wagged a finger at Crawford for no apparent reason and the latter couldn't help noticing the hand was incongruous to the body. It was finely shaped and sharply pointed. He probably had small feet, too, thought Crawford inconsequentially.

Boost's drink arrived, a double scotch, and with a twinkle in his eyes Boost indicated that Crawford would pay. Crawford did so in silver. Pleased with the transaction, Boost took a sip from his glass in a dainty fashion, pinky raised, and sat back in his chair with a sigh.

"You know zis expression, nark? Een my mozer's tongue zis vord means spy, but," he emphasized the conjunction with a warning finger, "eet also means decoy."

"Sure," said Crawford, somewhat dumbfounded.

"My mozer was a gypsy who stole my fahzer's heart from him. Nark ees zee gypsy's word for nose," he said, thumbing his own giant conk with obvious pride.

Crawford was looking at the "K" on the man's cheek. "Maybe they were going to write 'KKK,'" he suggested.

Werner shook his head. "No, no, no," he said. "Zey didn't vair no sheets and besides zey vere jus' children."

Crawford could not conceal his surprise.

"You are eenterested, yah?"

Crawford nodded, wiping beer from his chin, leaving foam in the bristly edges of his moustache.

Boost leaned very close and whispered in his ear with a hiss.

"Vhat took you so long?"

Crawford was nonplussed. He turned to face the stranger and for a moment their noses almost touched.

"Tell me about your wound," said Crawford.

"I'll do better zan zat," said Boost finishing his scotch in a swallow.

"I'll show you vhere eet happened."

So saying the man rose to his feet and marched through the tables. Crawford wasted no time in following, and as he passed Drum he clapped him joyously on the back, without disturbing the old man's Submarine-induced catalepsy.

In Riverdale Park the wind swooshed down on them in waves, scattering the leaves. The air smelled of woodsmoke and snow.

"I did not vander down here by accident," Werner assured Crawford. "Zey meet here."

"Who?"

"Zeez children of zee devil," Werner said.

Werner recounted his observations. He had known for months about the children meeting in the park. He had become suspicious of certain bulletins pinned to a telephone pole near his house, when he saw the same child retrieving them. He had begun to keep records of the frequency of their appearance. On several occasions he followed the child to the park, but until the night of his injury he had never actually ventured into the park. He led Crawford to the spot where he had been attacked and, gesticulating grandly with his fine, thin hands, he narrated the events of that night like a tour guide at Bunker Hill.

Crawford was enthralled but he – or McIlwane – would need material evidence that Werner Boost's carved cheek was anything more than a singular act of savagery. Crawford listened patiently nonetheless as Boost dug repeatedly into a grab bag of surmise and circumstantial evidence which he called his *Anschauung*. To Boost, it seemed, opinion was significant; opinion amounted to material evidence. Another investigator might have given up on Boost, so easily did the ridiculous become the sublime in the latter's imagination. But Crawford could do no better for the time being than to encourage the old German's friendship.

After a while Boost announced he had an engagement and the two men arranged to meet again the following day.

In the line of duty Crawford had been drinking too much and too early in the day. He went home with a headache coming on and tried to get some sleep. He forgot to put on the answering machine and an hour later Larry Hickson phoned. The social worker spoke too loudly and his voice was like a wedge in Crawford's head until finally the meaning of what he was saying came through. Vernon Pilchard had jumped from his foster parents' apartment balcony and had fallen twenty-three storeys. They had just phoned him.

Crawford asked if it was conclusively suicide. "Come and see for yourself," answered Hickson, not cynically but overexcitedly. "If you mean did he leave a note, no, he didn't. If you mean can I imagine Pilchard doing it, no, I can't."

"You said he was depressed," said Crawford.

"Depressed isn't dead."

Crawford considered this for a minute. The lack of a note seemed unusual. From his experience suicides liked to take someone with them; spread the guilt around or absolve someone from guilt, which amounted to the same thing. He said as much and Hickson laughed one convulsive laugh. He wasn't surprised. Pilchard couldn't write.

Without much delay Crawford contacted the police to follow up on Hickson's information. There was nothing definite. The foster parents had been out. There may or may not have been a visitor but there was no sign of a scuffle. A routine autopsy was scheduled and Crawford was to be informed of the results. His headache, forgotten in the excitement, now made its presence painfully known. Crawford crawled up to his bed ostensibly to go back to sleep. But he lay there thinking. He felt uneasy. He closed his eyes and a dead man stared at him. In his hand the dead man held a gun.

❖

Werner Boost did not show up the next day as he and Crawford had planned. Crawford looked for him in all the bars and on the street but saw nothing of him. He panicked slightly, feeling a potential lead slip through his fingers. He went down to the 51.

Vernon Pilchard's death proved not to have been a clear case of suicide and definitely not an accident. His fall, while doing nothing for his features, may not necessarily have killed him, but arsenic had, or had been about to when he had obliterated himself. Trace levels in his hair and nails indicated a gradual and prolonged ingestion of the poison, but the coroner also found evidence of circulatory collapse indicating a single massive dose. Police uncovered a substantial stash of cocaine and assorted other drugs in Pilchard's room and, upon analysis, the cocaine was found to be cut with arsenic.

So Vernon had been dying for some time, and then one night he died a lot more, speeding up – deliberately or otherwise – the inevitable. Bad drugs were plentiful in the street, and no doubt the police would regard Vernon's death as another case of street-drug impurity. But Crawford wasn't so sure. Cutting coke with arsenic wasn't quite the same as cutting it with icing sugar. And whether it was under the influence of McIlwane's obsession or Werner Boost's, Crawford began to believe the possibility of murder.

When a second day came and went with no sign of the German, Crawford began to worry; the man may have been obsessive, but Crawford could not dismiss him as unreliable. Consequently, Crawford found himself roaming the streets looking for a sign of Werner Boost, and was engaged in that activity when a rather curious event distracted him from his search. While there was nothing extraordinary about it, it seemed nonetheless significant. Informed shuffling has one feature which most other crime detection methodologies do not boast, although they depend on it. Luck. Informed shuffling stimulates the occurrence of luck. It doesn't make it happen but teaches you to recognize it when it does.

One of the eccentric regulars on the street was an enigmatic character Crawford had nicknamed the Mapman because he carried a large map around with him and seemed always to be lost. Today Crawford found the Mapman looking more neurotic than usual. He looked dreadfully lost. His face was an expressive one, a face which had more than once turned Crawford's head, though he couldn't say why.

Crawford was about to cross the street to offer his services when a black Peugeot with tinted windows pulled up smoothly to the curb in front of the Mapman and the rear door swung open directly before him. Crawford saw no one in the car so darkly tinted was the glass. He only saw an arm coaxing the shy, vague creature to enter, which he did with grave misgivings. The car then pulled quietly away from the curb and sped off towards Parliament Street.

Crawford had noticed something else. A boy, kitty-corner to himself, had also been observing the event, and he jumped from his hiding spot to gaze after the car. The boy was wiry and black-haired. He looked as if he was about to chase after the car but stopped, as if aware with animal-like sensitivity that he was being watched. He jerked his head around until his quick eyes met Crawford's and held there for a prolonged instant until he suddenly scampered off. His eyes, for the millisecond they had been in contact with Crawford's, had been as wary as an animal's.

The entire incident couldn't have taken more than a minute. Instinctively Crawford bracketed the event. Like the moment of an assassination caught on film it had been dramatic but had too many facets to be quickly comprehended. Crawford wanted to see it again in slow motion. Concentrating, he was able to. It had undoubtedly been a mundane occurrence, made dramatic by its isolation. There would certainly be a reasonable explanation, an explanation he decided to uncover. He had all the information he needed. He had memorized the licence plate. For the time being, Crawford abandoned his search for the enigmatic Werner Boost.

17

Crunkscully couldn't see where he was being taken but the experience was vivid nonetheless. He was blindfolded, which served to heighten his already sensitive powers of hearing. Primarily, though, he *felt* the trip. He felt himself lean into the door as the car negotiated a long arc of a turn and he felt his stomach rise as the car accelerated down into a valley. Later, he heard wheels rattling in deeply rutted tracks while he jiggled slightly in rich leather suspension. It was quiet – like the country – all wind and rustle and birds.

Crunkscully had caught a glimpse of the chauffeur in the rear-view mirror before the blindfold had been slipped in place. His hair was trimmed army short, which made his neck seem exceedingly pink – red stubble on excessively white skin. It was Tommy Connacher. He remembered Tommy Connacher well enough. There was a man beside Crunkscully who did not speak, but who chainsmoked strong-smelling cigarettes.

The car stopped at last in an abandoned wrecking yard in an avenue of rusted hulks. Thistles grew from every window and every manner of grass and weed clogged the wheels and bumpers of these metal skeletons. Tommy Connacher got out, stretched, and then urinated against a '53 De Soto sedan.

Outside it was cool. Even before the blindfold was withdrawn Crunkscully felt the splash of a snowflake against his cheek and involuntarily he shuddered. His eyes took a moment to adjust to daylight, dull though it was. The man with the flat face, who had sat beside him, pointed to his jacket pocket and Crunkscully found his spectacles there. Nervously he attempted to clean them on his tie, and fumbled, dropping them in the wet grass. The stranger picked them up. Then he lit a cigarette and, leaning against the car, he directed Crunkscully up the rise beyond the lot where, amongst the trees, stood a small, dilapidated barn. A flurry of swallows circled the building, dipping suddenly and disappearing under the eaves. As he approached, the chatter of unseen birds grew louder. The barn was a characterless building, its windows shuttered with weathered plywood. A path led through underbrush to a side entrance.

At the doorway Crunkscully turned, hoping for a reprieve, but the man with the flat face below gestured for him to enter. Crunkscully pulled open the door. It was dark inside, but a square of yellow light seemed to hang in the darkness. A room within a room; a window opening into another room. Crunkscully's arrival startled the birds and sent them into noisy paroxysms of flight. He blinked, and when he looked again the brooding cloud cover must have parted briefly because a sickly white light filtered down through holes in the sagging barn roof. Crunkscully's poor eyes perceived a glimmer like a stationary bolt of silver lightning, a silver sword in a weathered sheath. Crunkscully was looking at a large aluminum mobile home. It was an Airstream; long and curvaceous, almost entirely filling the barn.

A yellow carpet of light led up a wooden ramp to a low door in the trailer's convex side. From inside a whistling noise grew frenzied, and a surly voice beckoned him to enter. "Come in, come in, come in from out of the znuz."

At the front end of the trailer, with his back turned and bent over a hotplate, the strange host sat in a wheelchair. He was stirring something vigorously on one element while on the other, a kettle screamed. Without turning to greet his guest he poured the boiling water into a ceramic pot. He wore a tattered blanket over his rounded shoulders and the impression was one of a witch labouring over a magic brew. This did nothing to

120

alleviate Crunkscully's fear; it was not intended to.

The inside of the trailer was an extraordinary vision. The compact storage units and compartments which lined the walls had been stuffed with every conceivable oddity. Drawers, bins, and cupboards hung open as if they'd been recently ransacked. The entire trailer was a chaos of assorted objects. There was a bird cage hanging empty but for several bright feathers, and the floor was littered with overflowing cartons of cameras, televisions, adding machines, and all manner of small motor. There were the heads of parking meters and several automatic rifles lay in a heap. Behind them, there hung a brace of revolvers, like game on a line. There were books, too, and jewellery boxes, china and carpets, and rolls of canvas roped together like faggots. A fluorescent light shone hotly on a card table littered with telephones, one of which had been disassembled, exposing its innards. Beside it stood an open tool box appearing in the bright light like a malevolent doctor's kit. Stuffed in the backmost corner of the trailer was an unmade bed, looking for all the world as if it, too, had been stolen right from under some unsuspecting sleeping soul. On a ledge by the bed a guinea pig raced on its treadmill, frantic, not escaping.

Crunkscully saw everything and nothing. Mostly he saw menace. Pandemonium. The room assailed his weakened senses. He sank heavily into a chair. Behind him there was a gentle click as the trailer door shut. "Excuse me," Crunkscully apologized, not knowing quite why.

"Some tea!" exclaimed the man, swinging his chair around at last, and, with two glass mugs in one large hand, he wheeled himself to where Crunkscully sat. "This will diffuse the givenders," he said.

Crunkscully's hand shook as he accepted a mug. The hot liquid was alizarin and translucent.

"Madder's blood," said the man.

It was the beggar's voice as near as Crunkscully remembered but the face was all wrong, and the chair had no wings. He had little faith in his powers of recollection but he was disconcerted beyond words. The man said something about food but each word seemed more obscure than the last. A light flickered in Crunkscully's brain, in the control sector where sound and reason were sometimes linked.

The man wheeled back to the hotplate and spooned out a thick porridge onto a plate. When he returned, he lowered from the wall an ironing board, an improvised table, upon which he placed the steaming food in front of his guest. "A most nutritious gruel: bulgur and chickpeas, cooked in marmite and soy sauce and seasoned with bay and a pinch of dill." So saying, he pressed a spoon into Crunkscully's hand.

The latter, not knowing what else to do, tasted the concoction with the same trepidation as he had the tea. It was surprisingly good.

"I have so few guests," said the stranger sitting in the beggar's old wheelchair. Crunkscully looked away. "Admiring my scruffy little lair, are you?" The voice had changed. It was not surly anymore. "Believe me, I spend as little time here as possible, but it is conveniently out of the way. I hope your drive was not too unpleasant?" There was little sincerity in the question. Crunkscully didn't bother to respond.

The man in the wheelchair threw off the ratty blanket. Under a tweed sportscoat, he wore a green turtleneck flecked with gold. A smile played about the edges of his mouth and eyes. The slim, angular face was handsome, and boasted a crown of rich black waves of hair which were swept back off the forehead like a matinee idol's. His eyes were icy blue.

"I believe these are yours," he said, taking two piles of tapes from a shelf near at hand and placing them on the ironing board before his bewildered guest.

"You stole them," muttered Crunkscully. Then he began to scoop them up, hesitantly at first, and greedily when no opposition was offered.

"I really only borrowed them," said the man. "Fascinating, really, and edifying. A diary of encroaching madness. There are some things, however, I don't quite understand, which is why I wished to speak to you in person."

"You stole them," repeated Crunkscully with unaccustomed courage.

"No!" said the man with a voice like scissors cutting. "Gob did. Gob or one of his Scrogglings. Do you know what a Scroggling is, Mr. Crunkscully? A Scroggling is one of the worthless little apples left hanging from the tree when the crop is harvested. Gob gathers this worthless worm-eaten fruit. He has cart-loads of them. Gob is their salvation, their cargo ship – no, their *rocket*ship – out of this crumbling asshole of a world." The man said all this without apparent concern. He withdrew a newspaper clipping from his pocket and held it up. "This is Connie, your ex-wife, is it?"

The picture looked all wrong. An advertisement on the verso was distorting the picture so that Connie looked even less like Connie than she had before. "I don't know," Crunkscully said.

From another pocket of his sportscoat the man pulled a pair of photographs. Both were of a boy, one from middle distance, and one close-up, but with the graininess of features produced by a telephoto lens. The boy wore grey flannel trousers and a white shirt open at the throat. His tie and blazer were swung over his shoulder. He was not aware of the camera. It was a handsome face, a bright, careless face which laughed at some joke shared with several friends.

"Is that your boy?" asked the man.

Crunkscully wanted it to be. It was like a dream come true; Ross, a healthy happy young teenager. It was what he had hoped for and why shouldn't it be so? Yet while it was a dream come true he recognized it for what it was – a dream. Crunkscully bowed his head. "Is it him?" he asked.

The man frowned. He watched Crunkscully's face closely. When the latter made to hand him back the photos the man refused them and Crunkscully, not knowing what else to say, shoved them into his own pocket.

"Let's just say it *is* him, shall we?" said the man. In a fret of indecision, he drummed on his lower lip with two fingers, and reviewed his plans. "Do you remember the beggar, Gob?" The man sounded amused. "He is a memorable character. Frightening; usually only to children, but then...." He let the sentence finish itself in a gesture. "You will be hearing from our friend Gob in the next little while. You may still suit his purposes. And you will help, won't you, for Ross's sake?" It was a demand in the form of a question, as if the man delighted in creating and destroying choice at one and the same time.

"I've done some research, Mr. Crunkscully; a man has to be prepared when he is about to embark on a very big project. In my research I discovered you were a remarkable man. I hope you won't let us down."

✧

Crunkscully was blindfolded for the drive back, but this time he heard nothing; felt nothing. It was as if he had travelled somewhere and had never returned.

It was dark when he was let off at number 14. He went straight to his room and wearily undressed. Frank had caulked around the window and it did not wobble as much in its frame although the wind had picked up. He stared at his dresser, where he had replaced his cassettes and his tape recorder; the ark restored to its shrine.

He remembered little of what had happened except that it had the quality of a particularly virulent dream with few of the usual clues. At least he had his memory back, the taped one, for what it was worth. He looked at it now displayed in its cartridges. He took one and fed it to his tape recorder and fed the earplug to his ear. There was no music. Neither was there the comforting voice which spoke in the third person and always in the present tense. He pushed Fast Forward and then stopped the tape at various points, but there was nothing. Frantically he ejected the tape and replaced it with another with the same horrible result. His disciples would not speak to him, none, that is, but the one labelled "The Idea." In his relief at hearing anything at all it took a moment for it to dawn on him that it was nothing he had ever heard before. It was not his own voice but a parody of that voice which had once been his own. His memory had been perverted but not quite out of all recognition. There was still the essence of "The Idea" to find Ross; only now it all seemed a lot less pleasant a prospect than he had hoped it would be.

18

The black Peugeot which had gathered the Mapman into its shadowy bosom had vanished. Crawford had convinced McIlwane to follow up the incident and the licence had been traced. The car was owned by Winona Enterprises, a major contractor and residential developer, busy and highly visible in Cabbagetown. The owner, Dato Duranovitch, had a city address in the area, on pretty Montcalm Street.

McIlwane reached Crawford at home the following day having followed the bare lead a little further, with interesting results. Duranovitch had a big project under way in Cabbagetown, a condominium called the Royal Hawk Mews. It was being subsidized by a holding company called DurCan Investments, the "Can" of which turned out to be a man named Anselmo Cannelli. Police Intelligence had suspected Cannelli of Mafia connections for some time. The presence of an underworld figure in Cabbagetown in and of itself meant nothing, of course, but McIlwane liked the connection and arranged to have the car followed surreptitiously if and when it showed up. The conversation ended with Crawford suggesting they meet at headquarters for lunch. He was hungry for rational company.

It had not gone unnoticed by Crawford that one of McIlwane's theories, that of organized crime operating in the juvenile sector, was extremely close to Werner Boost's theory. McIlwane based his opinion on an imaginative interpretation of statistics. Boost based his on observation and an equally imaginative interpretation of those observations. It was not impossible that Boost was onto something and Crawford resumed his search for the German with enthusiasm. Boost found Crawford first. Crawford was resting his feet sitting on a park bench when the large man plunked down beside him, grinning from ear to ear.

He was safe and sound, and in good spirits. He said he'd been off following a lead, but the lead had to do with horses not crooks and he had apparently done quite well. To celebrate he had gone on a three-day bender, but he assured Crawford he had been thinking about the case, as he called it, all along. Crawford resisted the urge to tell Boost about the Mapman and the Peugeot, holding some residue of doubt about how far he could afford to take him into his confidence.

"How did you know I was a cop?" Crawford asked him at one point.

"I oberheard you tell somevon," he answered.

"But they didn't believe me," replied Crawford. "Why did you?"

Boost looked at him awry and said: "I belief eferysink I hear unt at zee same time I belief nosink!"

It went a long way towards explaining the man. He was irrational and in some ways naive; he was also unbiased. His research into the history of the Mafia was a fairytale but like any fairytale it was peppered with very real aspects; reality observed through a distorted glass, no less real for the distortion.

Seen through Boost's eyes Cabbagetown seemed as mysterious as hell. He told Crawford about the rooming house where he lived, about his housemates, particularly one former resident named Tommy Connacher, and how he had come to be thrown out and had vowed revenge. There were rumours that Tommy was driving for the Mafia and had been seen behind the wheel of a fancy black car.

"With tinted windows," said Crawford.

"Zat's zee von!" said Boost. "So you know Tommy already?"
Crawford didn't, but let Boost assume he did. Boost swelled with self-esteem.

Unfortunately the discovery that the two men might very well be on the same trail did not have the result Crawford might have expected. Instead of Werner spilling out all he knew on the spot he was suddenly impatient to go home, apparently to update the book he was writing. It was called *The Roman Invasion of Canada*, he told Crawford, but from his brief description it sounded more like a diary; a day-by-day account of Herr Werner Boost's topsy-turvy life. He promised to keep in touch as he waved Crawford goodbye.

It was as much as Crawford could hope for.

He returned to his rounds of the neighbourhood until it was time to meet McIlwane at headquarters.

The supervisor was in high spirits. Apparently, the singular episode involving the Peugeot and the old man had unwound a little further. It seemed a radio car had picked up the trail of the Peugeot, and a plainclothes car had been dispatched to follow it. It had done so until the car had turned into a large construction stockyard in the valley. There was no cover for the police car since the stockyard was the only address, commercial or otherwise, on that particularly empty stretch of the Bayview Extension. Therefore the cops had done all they could do without raising suspicions, which was to make passes of the yard. The vehicle had not been sighted again. The compound was in fact the property of Duranovitch's company, Winona Enterprises. It was extensive, with large warehouses, several Quonset huts, innumerable temporary facilities, and a platoon of heavy construction equipment for highway operations.

Under the pretence of following up a parking violation an officer, under McIlwane's orders, had discovered some rather strange facts. The car was usually employed in chauffeuring Duranovitch around, but he was away in Florida and had been since the first of September. He was not due back until Christmas. Otherwise the car was generally used by upper management people in Winona. Duranovitch's secretary had been unable to establish who was presently using the Peugeot, but apparently was not concerned since occasionally in the past "Dato" unofficially lent it out. When asked if the president could be reached she had made it seem highly unlikely. The officer had not pressed the point, having had no reason to do so. McIlwane had held back on any further enquiry, but there was an all-points bulletin out on the car.

It was late when Crawford left police headquarters. He didn't walk straight home, taking the opportunity to clear his head. The snow that had threatened days earlier had been a tease yet the air was expectant; cold and still.

Before he knew it, he had walked the day away. The moon shone down preternaturally bright. When he at last reached Cabbagetown, the street lights were on. He walked down Montcalm Street past Duranovitch's ostentatiously renovated townhouse. Crawford watched the darkened house for several minutes and, as he watched, the lights came on. But of course there would be no silhouette since no one had turned them on. They had come on in several rooms simultaneously, switched on by timers.

Further south, in the older, meaner stretch of Cabbagetown nearer the railroad tracks and home, Crawford stopped by a rundown inner-city schoolyard. Three black kids were playing basketball in the dark with the moon casting strange, thin shadows. For some reason Crawford felt his skin crawl.

19

Crawford was surprised to hear from McIlwane again the following morning. He wanted to see him pronto. This time not at headquarters but in the second-floor offices of the Youth Bureau on Davenport. The Youth Bureau offices were primarily a statistics-keeping unit and a central clearing house of information on youth-related crime.

Staff Sergeant Gas, who was serving on the task force with McIlwane, worked at the bureau. He joined Crawford and McIlwane in the conference room and produced several documents which had already been described to McIlwane over the phone but which came as a complete surprise to Crawford, who pored over the slim portfolio, while chewing vigorously on the end of his moustache. Each of seven items on 8½ x 11 bond was sandwiched in clear plastic. The messages were neatly and professionally typed and centred on the page. There were several copies of each message. Crawford read the first again slowly:

"I am the festering grimace which lies,
Like disease, in your flabby smile.
I'm the fowl breadth of your pecuniousness,
Bound on choking and cramping your style.
Watch out for Scrogglings who creep in the night
Watch out for Afterlings claiming their rights."

After allowing Crawford sufficient digestion of this anomaly, Colin McIlwane spoke. "All delivered in brown envelopes to addresses in Cabbagetown, invoice included. Check out the delivery invoice."

In the portfolio were several invoices. Crawford couldn't suppress a smile. The receipts, printed on a letter press, were legitimate in appearance but the delivery company's name was an impudent hoax: "B & E Messenger Service."

"That's for our benefit," said McIlwane sourly.

"The return address is fictitious," added Sergeant Gas. "The phone number turns out to be Dial-A-Prayer." Crawford permitted himself a chuckle. Gas continued. "We have had several sketchy descriptions of the delivery boys. They wore brown uniforms and caps and were, from all reports, courteous."

Crawford was impressed and speechless. He made a clicking noise with his tongue which irritated McIlwane. Gas continued. "People have a habit of relegating such threats to the trash can. Can't say as I blame them. We have no idea how many of them there might have been. The notes were delivered between 10:00 and noon on the same day. It was a co-ordinated campaign."

"Well organized," said Crawford.

"Damn gimmicky!" said McIlwane angrily.

Crawford nodded his head vaguely. He muttered the second message out loud:

"'Pitchkettled old fleak
At the loss of your pet?
Fretfull that doggy's seen the
Last of his vet?
Dig flesh-spades in pockets,
Salvations at hand;
Just wait for directions
And follow demands!'"

There was a footnote which read:

"'Don't keak to the coppers,
Don't delay and don't squiddle.
It would give me great pleasure
To make Max into viddles!'"

"Max?" he asked.

131

Gas said: "Each of the people who received that note has a dog; none of the dogs is called 'Max.'"

"Well, the delivery-boy routine is stylish," said Crawford at last, "even if the poetry isn't."

"But it's effective," said Gas. "It's meant to scare, and the recipients are scared. They want to know what the police plan on doing."

McIlwane got up and, shoving his big hands in his pockets, he walked over to the window. "It doesn't jive," he said. "The whole thing is skew wiff. One moment you can hear a pin drop in that quarter and now they are blowing trumpets. I don't know which bugs me more."

"It's like last year all over again," said Gas, not certain how much Crawford knew of the previous rash of crime and the pranks that had gone along with them. Gas was calling it terrorism.

Crawford read the third note. "And blackmail," he thought.

"A hoyden, a strumpet
a quean in her house
(while cuckholded hubby's
away at his work)
is joined at her table
and joined quite well
leaving hubby a dog's part
– a lick and a smell."

"Kinky," said Crawford after a moment. "Maybe we should bring the vice squad in on this."

The superintendent talked to the window. "It's ingenious, all right, but it's too...too – "

"Showy?" suggested Gas.

McIlwane ignored him. "What kind of a modus operandi is that? It's too – "

"Cute?" suggested Crawford.

"Why in hell would they want to start advertising their

presence all of a sudden, just when they're getting everything nicely quieted down?"

It was Gas's turn to answer. "Maybe they're about to open up shop?"

"It's too quirky," said McIlwane at last as if that was the elusive word he had been looking for all along.

Crawford was thinking along entirely different lines. "If I were you I'd be pouring champagne, Colin."

Colin McIlwane turned from the window with a stunned look on his face.

Crawford was smiling. "Isn't this just the kind of thing you needed to get a full-scale investigation? It shows uncommon resourcefulness, a co-ordinated campaign, and kids doing the leg work. Why aren't you down at fifty-one waving this in Ewart's face?"

"You trying to get out of this?" asked McIlwane, much to Crawford's surprise. Crawford wasn't sure. He shrugged his shoulders. "You're right, I suppose," McIlwane continued, "I could make a case out of it but I'd sure like to know more. This B & E horseshit makes me wonder. I feel like I just sat down to play chess against a redoubtable opponent and find he's put a whoopee cushion on my seat. You know what I mean?" The other two nodded but McIlwane hardly noticed. He was angry. "This business isn't slick, it's insolent." With that McIlwane retired into his own thoughts.

Gas was called to answer the phone in the outer office, leaving Crawford to consider his own position. The prank was significant. It didn't explain what was going on in Cabbagetown but it was tangible proof that something was going on, something Ewart hadn't stopped. "What am I supposed to do now?" he asked the supervisor finally.

McIlwane must have been considering the same question. He rubbed his face with his hand. "Keep at it for now, Rum. I am seeing Ewart later today. It'll be interesting to see how he interprets this. If an official investigation is going to be launched, and I'm pretty sure there will be, maybe you'll consider coming back to work full time, assuming I can clear it with Wheeler and those concerned. Why don't you think about it anyway."

Crawford indicated that he would do just that and was about to leave when McIlwane called after him.

"That crazy German, has he got any leads?"

Crawford smiled wryly. "Thousands of them," he said.

✥

Walking up Parliament Street towards the Winchester, Crawford found his mind drifting unmethodically; tacking here, tacking there, into the wind. He began to sink again back into the ambiguity of purpose he had felt when McIlwane first approached him about the job. He found himself considering some detail of house renovation as if his mind had accepted the inevitability of his return to retirement. He felt a kind of relief. Things could go as fast as they wanted, as long as he didn't have to keep up. Wheeler wouldn't lend him to McIlwane – real investigation or not – and there wasn't much reason he should. Crawford had not found anything spectacular to warrant special involvement, and yet he felt specially involved. He found himself growing grumpier and grumpier at the prospect of *not* working on the damn case. In this state he wandered into the Winchester Hotel.

All the regulars were in place. It was difficult to imagine they ever left. But as colourful as some of the regulars could be Crawford was struck on entering by the lack of colour in the bar. The clientele were all in shades of brown and grey. What was more, they all seemed as grumpy as he did. Across the room by the broken juke box sat Werner Boost, and beside him a roly-poly little man wearing fuzzy slippers, whose feet didn't reach the ground.

Crawford joined them and the little man smiled brightly, despite the fact that he looked particularly pale around the gills. "I'm Calmette," he announced. "And you ah Wehneh's police fwiend, ahn't you?" Crawford nodded.

"Why you just missed *owah* fwiend, Mistah Cwunkscully. He hasn't been well and has gone home," said Calmette.

Boost was sullen and cheered up only slightly when Crawford bought a round. He did, however, fish his little black notebook from his pocket and hand Crawford a list written in a spidery hand. "Leads," he said without further explanation.

Crawford read a list of enigmas Werner had thought to bring to his attention. The list depressed Crawford; it was nonsense and he wasn't in a mood for humouring Boost.

Calmette talked merrily about a variety of things, primarily of "As the World Turns," which had attracted him to the Winchester's bar to watch on the colour television.

Crawford found his mind drifting off, but it was snapped back to attention by an off-hand remark of Werner's.

"Zee gangk will meet again in two nights."

"You know?" asked Crawford.

Werner tapped his head. "I guess," he said. "Zee gangk zat did zis," he added as an afterthought, indicating his wounded cheek.

"Why do you say in two nights?"

"Eet ees – how shall I say? – appropriate," said Werner.

"I get it!" said Calmette. Crawford didn't. Calmette explained: "Hallowe'en."

Boost leaned back in his chair and stared Crawford in the eyes. "I haf a plan. I take you zair, okay? You vill see zeez creatures for yourself."

❖

Crawford was still considering Werner's rather ominous invitation when he arrived home to find a message on his answering machine to phone Barry Hickson, which he did.

Hickson had some information for Crawford. A friend at the Children's Aid had told him about a girl named Sally Paza who had been a graduate student in social work doing research into power dynamics with reference to juvenile gangs. According to Hickson's friend, Sally Paza had run into some trouble in Cabbagetown early in the year, although his friend had not elaborated. Crawford thanked Hickson. Hickson said: "Sure. And maybe you could do me a favour. Find the fucker that killed Vernon Pilchard."

Sally Paza was not in the phonebook. Crawford tried the universities and got a response at Wilfrid Laurier. He was put through to the Dean of Graduate Studies in the Social Work Department. Curiously, Sally had quit the program while in the final term of study for her M.S.W. She had not explained her change of heart. Crawford was given a home address and phone number in St. Catharines, and from her home he received her phone number at work. She was uncommunicative, but Crawford, sensing something behind her reticence, convinced her to see him in person. He phoned an old friend who lived in Grantham, near St. Catharines, and planned to meet him for dinner the next night.

The drive in the morning was a treat, especially liberating since he drove against the traffic. It gave the expedition the true flavour of escape. The sun came out and shone on Lake Ontario. Some intrepid or just crazy sailor bobbed among the white caps.

Crawford met Sally at her father's field office. She was a pretty girl with dull eyes, dissembling in dress and manner, more complicated than she looked, he guessed. Her father was a consulting engineer and she was between jobs. She had volunteered to help around the office. Presently she was testing concrete cylinders on a pressure machine, which she operated with calm efficiency. Crawford stood aside, holding in place a pitted sheet of 3/4-inch plywood as a shield, while she cranked up the p.s.i. He watched as the hairline fractures spread around the concrete cylinder until it finally shattered against the plywood. Sally recorded the breaking points.

He assumed she was taciturn by nature but she was positively close-mouthed to the subject on which Crawford addressed her. He explained a little about McIlwane's conjecture, and his own findings to date. She listened without response, except to indicate that such a gang did exist – "a super gang," she called it. At one point she apologized for wasting Crawford's time. Her studies in social work were over. The subject of gangs or juvenile activities of any kind no longer intrigued her, she said. Crawford pressed her, cautiously.

It was the chance mention of Werner Boost and his injury which finally brought about a response. She stared at Crawford for a moment and then, to his surprise, she took his arm and led him into a vacant office. Then she did a most bizarre thing. Placing her right foot on a chair, she hoisted up her skirt. In a ragged tattoo across her thigh were three words: "Eyebit by Devilshine." The "shine" was partially hidden by pubic hair. "That," she said, "is some of the work of the gang you're after." There was more to show but her spontaneous expression of frankness deserted her. Modesty kept her from showing him that on her right buttock they had left their signature, and Crawford learned what would have been added to the "K" on Werner's cheek. "Knot."

"Were you raped?"

She laughed at that, but the laughter caught in her throat. "Mr. Crawford, I'm not at all sure they were old enough to rape me, not the ones I met. I think there are others," she said.

❖

Crawford joined his friend Benny Cooperman for dinner and then drove home. The road wasn't such a treat in the dark and the escape from Toronto had been too short-lived. He arrived at Baseball Park Road after midnight and switched on his answering machine. McIlwane barked out the following message: "Duranovitch's Peugeot was sighted, chased at high speed, and lost in Cabbagetown. The two rookies responsible for their error in judgement are on shit duty at the stables – over and out!"

20

When the alarm went off it would be time for "Star Trek." Monsieur Calmette, sitting on the couch in the commonroom, watched the minute-hand shudder and jerk its way around the cheap face, listening in suspense to the noisy tick tock. His evening television viewing began with "Star Trek," and he hated to miss even so much as the theme music and "Space. The final frontier...."

At the other end of the davenport sat Crunkscully with a half-eaten plate of pork and beans on his lap. He was trying to make Tinker Bell dance on the edge of his knife; he seemed oblivious to anything else. He would often sit, just so, engaged in some small occupation, seemingly lost in thought but actually consumed by nothing more than the task at hand. He was not having much success at summoning up the fairy of light. There was little enough light left in the day. Frank was sitting at the table reading the newspaper with the aid of a magnifying glass. The room seemed very empty and still except for the clock ticking on the counter.

Crunkscully turned slowly and stared through the window. His gaze was quixotic – expectant one moment, apprehensive the next. He looked back at the stained knife. There were words and there were images and sometimes they coincided. For stretches of time his perception was taken up by an infantile oneness of vision. It was a kind of blindness; things went without name and therefore without identity.

Calmette's mouth hung open. He was breathing hard. His hands lay limply in his lap.

Finally the alarm rang, startling Crunkscully from his thoughts. Calmette smiled wanly and began to struggle off the davenport. "Made it," he said, as if concluding a race against the clock. But he spoke too fast. No sooner had his feet touched down than he fainted in a heap on the floor.

With more fretful consternation than actual bodily assistance Crunkscully helped Frank carry Calmette to his room. Crunkscully helped Frank drape a heavy blanket over the old man who was very white and shaking prodigiously. And then he sat on Calmette's bed while Frank went off in search of Aspirin.

Crunkscully looked with wonder at the walls lined with scantily clad Sunshine Girls, clipped from the newspaper and turning yellow on Monsieur Calmette's wall. After half an hour, Calmette fell into an uneasy sleep.

By the time Crunkscully and Frank returned to the common-room, Olga, Chas, and Buck had congregated there. There was a pronounced atmosphere of despair which was only heightened by the news of Monsieur Calmette's illness. It was October 31 – Hallowe'en – and an incipient anguish had settled on number 14.

Chas responded to the occasion by drinking himself into gloomy resignation. "This year they couldn't steal my radio," he scowled, "because I don't got no radio."

Olga adopted a warlike pose on the davenport. It was 6:30 but she was ready for the siege with a rolling pin in one hand and a bread knife in the other. Buck had come home from work earlier than usual and was preparing a T.V. dinner, which he said he intended to eat in his car. The previous Hallowe'en, scoundrels had scrawled obscenities all over his Cadillac and he had no intention of it happening again.

"Damn bastards," intoned Chas, ever empathetic.

Werner Boost arrived home half-drunk and with a brown bag, the contents of which would more than finish the job. His nose was like a beacon. He stood for a moment in the doorway, grinning, and then, to everyone's surprise, he yanked a package of chicken livers from his pants. "Dinner!" he announced loudly. The package was leaking down his leg and forming a puddle at his feet.

"Di-di-dis-gusting!" was the only response, laboriously provided by Buck. Wearing two coats and a blanket around his shoulders he passed Werner Boost and slammed the door behind him. The prospect of his lonely vigil had put him in a foul mood.

Werner Boost's festive spirit was tinged with cynicism. He made an elaborate game of opening and closing all the kitchen cabinets, saying over and over as he did so: "Vhere are zee candies? Vhat shall vee gif zee leetle treeksters? Me unt zee nark are goingk to do some treek or treatingk of our own," he confided with an air of self-importance. Then, as he cut up some onions and plopped them in a frying pan, he started to sing. Olga seemed to know the song and joined him in an eerie soprano.

"*Schadenfreude,*" Boost said. "Zat ees vhat eet ees. Zee maleecious enjoyment of ozers' misfortunes." His voice rose above the sizzling.

Dinner was served. Nobody ate much. Nobody talked.

After the meal, Frank, who had seemed preoccupied, left to attend to Calmette. Olga lay down on the davenport like a pharoah's mummy with her weapons crossed on her chest, and Chas soon went back to his room. Then, Werner Boost, whose earlier enthusiasm had deserted him, left, slamming the door behind him. It was 7:00 P.M.

Crunkscully sat for several moments in the quiet. After a while he began to twitch nervously. He got up and walked to the screen door and looked out to the dark street; there was something there, nothing he could see but a presence which oppressed the house and its inhabitants. He pushed the door open several times and let it swing shut with a bang before him. In this manner the nameless danger entered the house. Crunkscully sensed it. The house was under siege, it would be far safer in the street. He left without a word. The wind had dropped and there was a slight drizzle. He stood on the front pathway undecided as to what to do next.

On either side of number 14 parties were already under way. Rock 'n roll blared from number 16, and through uncurtained windows a red flashing light revealed silhouettes gyrating in vague rhythm. On the porch of number 12 stood a man in a complete Mickey Mouse outfit. He was shaking his massive round head. He had his hands on his hips and, beside him, kneeling on the porch, his wife, dressed as Cinderella, was trying to light a candle in a pumpkin. She had lost the matches in the pink chiffon ruffles of her voluminous gown and was swearing.

"Hi there," said Mickey to Crunkscully, waving an immaculate white-gloved hand with four sausage-like digits. Crunkscully waved and hurried away. Mickey tittered.

Elmsley Court was strangely quiet; the street was deserted. Crunkscully felt good to be out of the house. He listened to the sound of his footsteps, and stopped several times so that he could hear the sound start up again when he moved. It was comforting.

He emerged onto Sackville and here at last were troops of little people in costumes with chaperones and huge bags. His own footsteps merged with a hundred others: goblins, ghosts, and witches, and the various heroes of *Star Wars*. He tried to discern his distinctive shuffle from among the other sounds. The dark emphasized so many sounds: doorbells and screeches and squeals, the hiss of car tires on wet pavement. Indians and pirates darted by him. A gypsy, unaccountably equipped with a six-gun, held him up, but before he could respond a parent scolded the child and apologized to Crunkscully. It was fairyland.

When he could hear his footsteps and pick them out of all the rest, he tried to hear his breathing. He could see it – a pale cloud in front of him in the street light – but he wanted to hear it as well. Little else occupied his mind. He felt light-headed, and in this distracted state he wandered up and down the noisy streets until they were no longer noisy. He lost himself in the wet fairyland. Ill-cut, garish pumpkins with blazing eyes flickered and went out; the rain increased to a brief downpour. He felt oddly cozy alone in the streets, as if a man inside him had curled up in front of a fire to gaze out through his eyes at the rainy night.

Then suddenly the little man in his head was on his feet at the window clutching the sill, locking the windows and drawing the blinds quickly shut. Crunkscully blinked the rain out of his eyes in time to see the dark ghost just before it disappeared. It had glided across his path at an intersection not fifty yards ahead. Without recognizing the man, he knew him in that primitive sector of the brain which is not readily beguiled by mere appearance. Crunkscully took after him although not quite sure why. He felt simultaneously drawn to him and repelled. He caught up to him but dropped ten, twenty, thirty yards behind him.

Gob was draped with a huge, dark poncho which covered him and his wheelchair entirely. He was whistling, his thick lips puckered in the shadow of a rubber hood that was peaked like a wizard's hat. "Good," he said, when he realized who was following him. "A retinue." And he laughed loudly at the perverse irony of it.

Crunkscully recognized the laugh as the voice on the tape. He stopped stock still and let Gob glide further and further away, until at last he too stopped and swung around to face Crunkscully. Even in the light of a street lamp Gob's face was indistinguishable from shadow. His voice, however, was loud and clear above the rain.

"Are we anxious, then, my tired old moonbeam? Did you think Gob had forgotten you?"

Crunkscully ventured closer. "He said you'd come for me," he said quietly but the words were snatched away in a gust of rain.

Gob laughed and wheeled around and away.

After an agonizing hesitation Crunkscully followed. He would speak to him. He must.

Amelia Street jogs at Sumach, and presently ends at a beautiful little park, Wellesley Park, lined on one side by a row of houses. At the eastern extremity of the green, the sidewalk ends abruptly.

Some ten feet below, a sector of the enormous Toronto Necropolis rolls down a wooded hillside into the Rosedale Ravine.

At the end of the sidewalk Gob stopped. He rose suddenly from his wheelchair. It was an awesome display, for the dark poncho seemed to grow in Crunkscully's eyes like a volcano until its peak stood some six feet above the ground. Gob hooted, aware, as ever, of the impression he had made. He folded up the wheelchair and dropped it to the cemetery below, and then he turned to Crunkscully, waved once, and jumped after the wheelchair. He was there one moment like a small mountain and then he was gone.

Crunkscully was most disturbed. He hurried to the spot where the magic had taken place in time to see Gob below him fold out the wheelchair again and roll away up the cemetery road. He ran along the rampart, looking over the edge in complete despair. "I don't need you!" He cried loud enough for Gob to hear, for the latter could be heard laughing in grand style, derisively.

"I want to find him myself. Thank you for your concern. Leave me alone. You won't find him, I know...." The jumbled message clattered from his mouth. But Gob did not answer.

Scarcely knowing how he dared, Crunkscully jumped down into the cemetery. He felt a horrible pain in his legs; he fell sideways against an old tombstone and hugged it for support. He must let Gob know whatever he had planned was useless; only he, Crunkscully, could find Ross. It was all quite clear for a moment. Hoisting himself up he took off in pursuit. Up the slippery grass hill, under the dense umbrella of oak and willow rustling in the storm. At last he caught sight of Gob rolling along the crest of the serpentine roadway and Crunkscully began to run. He ran until his chest heaved and his lungs seemed to rattle his rib cage like prisoners in a cell. He pumped his knees, chest high, and between harsh breaths he cried out repeatedly: "You'll never find him. You'll never find him."

But what with the noise of the storm Gob remained oblivious to Crunkscully's cry. He whistled as he wheeled between the trees.

Crunkscully pushed on past the still memorials, catching glimpses of the squat ghost through the stones: the Celtic crosses and draped urns, the granite needles and classic pillars. At one point he tripped and fell headlong over a flat stone almost entirely lost in the grass. There was a whole family there, looking like a forgotten pathway. There was traffic noise now and only by straining could he hear Gob's whistling. Through the trees he could see the lights in the valley. The bluff dropped quickly down on all sides. Gob was visible only once more. Crunkscully paused to watch as the figure seemed to sink bit by bit, finally disappearing altogether in the underbrush.

Crunkscully almost fell down the embankment, slipping and regaining his balance only to slip again and slide on the seat of his pants. He knelt at last by the fence at what appeared to be the same spot where Gob had vanished. His sharp ears could hear someone on the other side of the fence, but there was no gate and the fence seemed otherwise intact.

The rustling continued. Crunkscully acknowledged physical but not moral defeat. "I don't need you!" he cried with all the energy he could muster. The vague noise stopped dead.

"But Gob needs you," said a hidden voice.

"No," replied Crunkscully to the bracken.

"You are part of his plans now," said the invisible adversary.

"You won't find Ross," said Crunkscully.

"Then we will *pretend* it is Ross, shall we?"

Crunkscully had no response to that. He leaned against the metal fence; it was cool on his brow. His breathing was very heavy now, louder even than the traffic in the valley. Louder than the rain, which was beginning now to let up. He remained still and concentrated on his breathing.

❖

It seemed much later that Crunkscully noticed the children. He had followed the fence, clinging to it like a life line that must lead him somewhere, preferably home. He shivered in the cold; his clothes stuck to him all over and he had lost a shoe in his precipitous descent into the ravine.

The children were above him in the trees. Long before he noticed them, however, they watched his movements to assess what danger he might represent. Then they lost interest and turned their watchful eyes elsewhere. It was as if the fence separated two lands and their guard duty did not concern itself with interlopers in the graveyard. Every hundred feet or so they were perched, half-concealed, in the crotches of trees, or straddling dark branches, as if mounted on patient black steeds that would move on command.

The fence climbed the southern boundary of the cemetery. He was climbing with it up a gradual incline, the way constantly obstructed by dense shrubbery, gorse to tear at his hands and evergreens laden with cold rain. As he walked he began to see more children. Never more than one at a time and always suddenly. They would appear out of the underbrush and make their way up the road until it curved out of his line of vision. They moved without a sound.

At the end of his endurance, Crunkscully rested in a patch of dry grass under a tree. The rain had cleared but there was a threatening stillness. In the long grass stood an old gravestone and leaning against it Crunkscully closed his eyes. He had just meant to rest but, exhausted, he fell into a fitful sleep.

21

Crawford had left in good time. He was to meet Boost at the Winchester at 8:00. In an alley near his home he passed a group of teenagers in a bottle-smashing debacle. He wondered if any of them might have etched "Eyebit by Devilshine" in a young woman's thigh. It did not make the prospect of the evening any more appealing. Before he reached his destination, the rain had ended.

In upper Cabbagetown the annual sweet quest was just about over, the downpour of earlier having brought with it an unwelcome curfew. The streets were empty and damp. The reflection of lights made the streets oddly diaphanous.

When he arrived at the hotel, the German was waiting for him. He wore a canvas jumpsuit affair with a hood fastened by strings under his chin. Inside he wore a day's worth of whiskey. The two men started to make their way to the park, a few blocks away, with hardly a word.

"Did you bringk a veapon?" asked Werner, finally. Crawford nodded. "So did I," said Werner approvingly.

Crawford didn't bother to explain that the 7.65 Walther in his pocket was unloaded. It weighed a ton. He hadn't so much as handled the service revolver for almost ten months.

Across from the park there is an ice-cream parlour, open but empty on this particularly wretched night. The two men went in and sat at a table, discussing strategy over their coffee. Boost explained his plan. He knew Tom the zoo keeper, who lived on the road bordering the Necropolis, and well within the gang's territory. The road was closed at night to traffic but there was a gate for pedestrians. Werner figured that if they made straight for Tom's house, the gang would not harm them. Crawford made it very clear he wanted no confrontation, and that under no circumstances would they venture further into the park. "No fireworks," he cautioned his absurdly dressed, red-faced colleague. Werner laid one slim hand on his chest as if to say: "Vhat, me?"

It was two hundred yards from the ice-cream parlour to the gates to the zoo keeper's road. The Necropolis loomed up to their left. They passed the chapel, the main entrance gate, and the guardhouse; all locked and dark. The walk down the zoo keeper's road was a nerve-racking experience. They walked conspicuously in the centre of the road. Rum, thin and sunken-chested; Werner, fatter than ever in his bizarre canvas bag – Laurel and Hardy in "another fine mess." Looking neither right nor left, they saw nothing unusual, but Crawford felt distinctly what Boost had described as the "wisibility of zat vhich has recently made eetself eenwisible." Crawford resisted the temptation to whistle. Nothing moved in the trees. Nothing approached them.

From behind scudding clouds a gibbous moon glimmered briefly and was again swallowed up by the night.

Tom's house was another two hundred yards from the gate, a walk of a few minutes. Only the porch light seemed to be on. The house was set back off the road, nestled in a tangle of plant life as dense as any English garden. It was a large angular house with a steep gabled roof silhouetted against the bleak sky. The house was reached by a narrow curving pathway encroached upon on either side by unruly bushes. It was fifteen feet from the road to the door but the road was lost to view when the two men stopped at last at the front door.

Werner knocked loudly. There was no reply.

"Where is he?" asked Crawford after a moment.

"How should I know?" said Werner. "Out, I guess."

"Out! But you – "

Werner chuckled. "I said vee vould wisit Tom. I never said he'd be home."

Crawford swore under his breath but his attention was diverted by a sound behind them on the road. He made his way noiselessly up to the path until he could see up the road. He heard the sound again. It was the crackle of a two-way radio. And then he saw the source. Thirty yards away a boy stood at the base of an oak tree dressed in an army poncho which he had momentarily hiked up in order to use the radio. He was now returning the radio to his belt. It was not a toy but a mitre set, precisely the kind the police used. Crawford wished he had one right now. Further up the road Crawford caught a glimpse of another child similarly dressed shinneying down a tree.

At Crawford's elbow a familiar voice whispered: "So now you see zee leetle buggers." Boost took Crawford's arm and led him back down the path towards the front door, but this time Werner made his way into the bordering bushes. Crawford followed. They made their way around the house until they reached the back. The land fell away steeply from where they stood and below them stretched the zoo and the park. There was an old shed perched there, leaning against the wall of the house, and the door opened with a creak of rusted hinges. Inside it stunk of wood rot. The tiny space was a jumble of old tools and refuse.

Werner made himself comfortable on a relatively sturdy box and drew a bottle from his coat. "Zis vill be our lookout."

There was one small window in the shed facing northwest. The window was hopelessly grimy and opaque with a fog of cobwebs which Crawford fought his way through and pried the window open. He looked out over the park. On a clear night it would have been a box seat, but the moon was hidden again behind the swollen clouds. Werner guzzled from his bottle contentedly, and muttered from time to time. Crawford paid no attention to him, waiting only for the moon to reappear. A half an hour passed and he began to wonder if the two children on the road were to be the sum total of the night's activity. Children with walkie-talkies was interesting but not exactly a "super gang."

He wanted more. Between the ragged edges of clouds the moon lit the park below and suddenly Crawford gasped, rousing Boost from his cups to join him at the window. The little shed was a crow's nest and Crawford had spotted the armada on the horizon. The moon would not stay still in the sky but in one bright moment Crawford had seen shadows peel themselves away from enshrouding shadows, slip from the shelter of bushes and trees, slide from buildings in the farm. Everywhere he looked there were small moving figures retreating as if on a universal command, heading west and north out of the park and into Cabbagetown. Werner was watching too now and any liquor-induced cockiness vanished.

"I haf vatched zis before zo not from such a wantage point. Vhen zey reach zee street you vill not see zem emerge togezer. Zey vill split up unt zen go zis vay unt zat as queek as cockroaches eento zee alleyvays. Vatch zat leetle bunch of zem – vatch!" He pointed to six shadowy figures approaching the open area of the upper park from the path which led from the reservoir.

As the two men watched from their crow's nest the six parted company and in another moment were gone. Then in the on-again off-again light Crawford counted twenty, thirty, forty more shadows.

"Enough to circle zee park," Werner said. Finally, when no more were seen, he added: "Eet must haf bin a short meetingk tonight. I vonder vhat else zey haf planned." It was only 8:50.

When Crawford felt quite sure the guards had dispersed he and his companion made their way back around the house to the path.

Before they reached the road they heard voices approaching, and stopped dead. Two girls, by the sound of it, filling the night air with idle chatter. It crossed Crawford's mind to warn the girls of the possible danger, but something made him disregard this good intention and they passed without seeing the two men on the path. Crawford peered after them as the two girls made their way down the hill. They were fifty yards away and clearly distinguishable in the now constant moonlight. Suddenly six boys tumbled out from the bushes on the side of the road and encircled the two girls, backing them up the slope on the far side of the road and against the cemetery fence. Crawford and Boost ducked back into the bushes and made their way as quietly as possible towards the scene.

Crawford had automatically reached for his gun but as his fingers gripped the handle, he felt an instantaneous nausea rise in him. A loud click behind him indicated that Werner Boost had cocked a pistol of some kind and when he turned he found inches from his own nose the nose of a .38. For one horrible instant he stared into Boost's dark little eyes, believing he had made the worst mistake of his life, that Boost had tricked him and was now going to blow his head off. The moment passed, dispelled by a nod from the German. "Vhat ees happenink?" he asked. They were in deep bush now, not more than twenty yards from where the boys had ambushed the girls.

One of the girls was yelling obscenities at the band of boys. The other girl screamed twice; she was shaking badly and clinging to her friend. Crawford told Boost to stay where he was, while he edged deeper still into the bushes to get a better view. Suddenly he noticed that he and Boost were not the only audience in attendance. Crawford froze as he recognized the Animal Boy, who stood not ten feet away from them back up the road. Crawford had the strange feeling that the boy was not this time merely an observer of the antics; he was waiting.

Below, the boys had closed ranks around the hapless girls. One of them reached out his hand to touch one of the girls and when she slapped it away he cuffed her hard across the face, causing the other girl to scream again. She stifled her scream by sinking her head deep into the shoulder of her more courageous friend.

Looking to his left, Crawford saw the lone observer move out of his cover, then stop, his fists clenched. Crawford could not let the ambush turn to rape, if he could stop it, but something convinced him to stay put.

Now, one of the group, a slim boy with long hair, suddenly

tackled the calmer of the two girls, and the next minute he howled and backed off, holding his hand, which it appeared the girl had bitten. The other boys laughed and suddenly two of them had the screamer by each arm and a third boy had the biter by her hair.

Crawford tensed for action. Beside him Werner breathed so heavily Crawford was sure the Animal Boy would hear them. Apparently he did not.

The frightened girl was now whimpering. The boy with the long hair held his arm out straight before him, and Crawford knew from the stance that the boy held a knife. This was enough to set Crawford in motion, but before he made a move the Animal Boy broke into a run and loped the remaining distance down the hill, yelling something indistinguishable, and again Crawford froze. The boy stopped ten paces short of the violent mêlée and the boy with the long hair turned to face him. The others stayed where they were. The leader held the knife straight-armed from the shoulder.

One of the girls screamed and tried to break away but she was thrown back brutally against the fence. In that instant of distraction the intruder attacked. He tackled the knife-bearer, low and expertly, rolling quickly to his right to avoid the slashing right arm of his opponent. Then he threw himself at the arm with the weapon, and the two boys rolled around, first on the pavement, then on the grass, the one trying to flee the other's grasp the other to free the knife. The knife fell and the boys dove for it. One of them stumbled to his feet and was able to kick it away before being wrestled down again. The others still did not move. The girls were silent, one had her head buried in her hands. Crawford's earlier reluctance to act was replaced by the certainty that he should not. He had witnessed many fights in schoolyards, on the street, in correctional institutions. He had broken up a number of squabbles. These boys were street wise, and if intimidated could fight ruthlessly, he suspected. There was a show going on.

Again the boys tumbled together and again the knife was

thrown free. Crawford gritted his teeth and automatically put a hand over Werner's gun barrel. Finally the Animal Boy rolled free. The long-haired boy dived at him and there was an awful cry. He tried to get to his feet but stumbled back onto his knees clutching his stomach. He was whining and coughing horribly and for an instant Crawford's blood ran cold. The long-haired boy looked at his hand and then crumpled in a heap on the ground.

"Ach du lieber..." whispered Boost in Crawford's ear.

There was a beat of silence and then two of the boys broke away from the scene and ran into the brush. One of the remaining boys made a move towards the victorious intruder, but the latter stood wielding the knife and his potential assailant quickly followed the others. The two remaining youths started to circle the victor, trying to get to their fallen comrade, but the Animal Boy started towards them and they ran off down the lane. He was holding the weapon in both hands like a pistol. He backed cautiously towards the girls, who were seemingly paralyzed with fear, and motioned with his head for them to follow him. As soon as they began to move, one of the girls started to moan and shake her head. Then she stopped dead in her tracks and finally had to be dragged from the spot by the other two.

They approached the spot where Crawford and Boost were hidden but were too engrossed in their escape to notice anything; running and hobbling, throwing furtive glances behind them. The Animal Boy held the knife in one hand now and scrambled up the steep grade, leaning on his fist; three-legged, like a chimp. They passed within a few yards of the men. Crawford craned his neck in order to look back over his shoulder. The three were now at the crest of the hill. There was an agonizing moment of waiting. Crawford didn't dare move in case any of the boys decided to make their way back to their fallen comrade.

Then there was a cautious low shout from down the hill. The shout was answered and then suddenly there was laughter. One of the boys cupped his hands and yelled, and from the bracken at the side of the road the three boys who had earlier fled emerged and joined the rest of their companions.

By the time they arrived, the long-haired boy was on his feet and talking excitedly. He howled as if in pain and relived his death throes for his audience. The others laughed. After several moments of banter the troupe made their way back up the hill. In another moment they too had gone. It was quiet again.

Crawford waited, but this time there was no curtain call. Boost was dumbfounded and still breathing heavily. Crawford closed his eyes for just a moment. His decision not to interfere had been a mixture of instinct and fear. He had been proved right but it had been a calculated risk. The whole fight had been a sham – for whose benefit, he couldn't guess. He slipped from his hiding spot, leaving Boost behind, and made his way carefully up the lane. The strange dream was not over.

To his right a voice cried out, shocking him in its immediacy and with its profoundly woeful chant.

"He didn't kill him.... He knows that.... How could he kill him...he's lost, that's all, lost. Terribly, terribly lost.... Poor Ross...."

"*Gott im himmel!* Poor Crunkscully!" said Boost, now at Crawford's side.

Crawford saw a man on the other side of the graveyard fence. He was propped against a gravestone. As they approached him the poor man's eyes grew enormous. He tried to speak but instead gagged, small bubbles appearing between his lips. As Crawford leaned down, the tormented man shrunk down into a heap. Then his expression changed and he leaned towards Crawford until his lips almost touched the chain-link fence. "He isn't dead, is he?"

Crawford shook his head. "No. It was only a game."

The man looked only vaguely relieved.

Crawford stared at Boost. "You know him?"

Boost nodded. "I live viz him."

Crawford had the uncontrollable urge to laugh. The Mapman and Boost lived together – of course! For a brief moment he wasn't sure that the whole thing hadn't been a terrible farce,

153

masterminded by McIlwane, and cast with a suitably outrageous bunch of lunatics, to test his sanity. Had he passed or had he failed? He had no idea.

"Let's get you out of here," Crawford said to Crunkscully.

"How do vee do zat?" asked Boost looking at the stout fence.

"How should I know?" said Crawford.

❖

At the very bottom of the hill where the pavement stopped and the lane petered out with nowhere left to go, Gob stood with his wheelchair folded and carried under his arm. He had seen the whole show, including the surprising sequel. Arlo had overacted his part and the audience had included some uninvited strangers but he had to admit it had been entertaining. There would be little time for such wrinkles in the weeks to come. Hallowe'en pranks aside, his grand plan now claimed the greater part of his attention. All along he had known the opportunity would have to come his way eventually. But in what a strange guise; in a man prematurely old, harmlessly searching for a lost son and in the process leading Gob to his fortune. What a show that would be!

❖

Crunkscully was adrift; further from shore than he ever remembered being, deeper than he had ever dreamt. There were no words out here at all. Speech was wrecked and this time the flotsam was in minute fragment, there was nothing to grab onto and no ideas clear enough to give language any form. He forced wind through his larynx more from habit than from inspiration but the resulting sounds were undifferentiated grunts and groans. The mouth and tongue had forgotten the steps to their articulate dance.

By the time Crawford had found a phone and contacted the authorities of the Necropolis, and they had sent someone to unlock the gate to the cemetery, Crunkscully had recovered from his fit of jabbering and Crawford privately concluded he was merely very drunk.

The three of them walked back to number 14 Elmsley Court, Werner hiccupping, Crunkscully mumbling to himself, and Crawford in a state of exhausted confusion. He felt almost bewitched by the rapid sequence of events. Nothing seemed quite real except the weight of Crunkscully on his shoulder.

People were already leaving the posh party at number 12. A pumpkin climbed into his BMW and fumbled for his keys; a rabbit and a banana passed, giggling, and climbed into a Saab. At number 16 the rock music pulsed loudly, and the sound of breaking glass and overturning furniture denoted an escalation in the festivities.

Number 14 stood darkly silent between, winking with one frosty eye: the eerie light from the television. Frank had been watching the news when he heard the heavy footsteps on the porch. With no more than a few words of exclamation he set about helping Crawford and Boost with their ungainly load. They sat Crunkscully on the davenport and stood breathing heavily over him while he gaped around the room, his eyes finally alighting on the television, where they stayed. On the bleary screen a raincoated newsman reported before a raging fire. Firemen lowered a child from an inferno.

"Where'd he get to?" asked Frank of Boost.

"Zee cemetery."

Crawford rolled his head trying to loosen a kink in his neck.

"I wonder what he was up to there? Kinda looks like a truck hit him," said Frank.

"He's not injured," said Crawford.

"Yeah, but he's right out there, ain't he?"

Crawford looked at Crunkscully's vacuous gaze. "Who is he?"

"He's Scully," said Frank. "And I'm Frank Qualtrough, super, nursemaid, and confidant." He pulled a chair from the table and indicated to Crawford to do the same.

155

"Scully," muttered Crawford.

"That's what I call him," Frank continued. "He calls himself Crunkscully. It's Swedish. Funny, though; he reminds me of someone; I don't know who."

"He reminds me of someone," said Crawford. Frank seemed pleased.

Boost was at the refrigerator rummaging for food and beer. He handed one to Crawford. Then he turned suddenly and asked after Monsieur Calmette.

"Whoosh!" said Frank, as if he had forgotten about his other invalid. "Things are never dull in Neverland," he said to Crawford.

Crawford nodded in commiseration. So that's where he was, Neverland. It explained everything.

"The news," said Crunkscully dreamily.

"We always watch the news around here," said Frank proudly.

At that instant a hijacker was shot and he fell on the tarmac. Then again in slow motion. Crawford's mind was beginning to reel.

"Who are you?" asked Frank.

"Rum Crawford."

"Oh, you're Werner's nark?" said Frank, looking him over matter of factly. "You sure look like a cop, come to think of it."

Crawford winced.

"Crunkscully didn't do nothing wrong, did he?" asked Frank.

Crunkscully. Crawford said the name to himself like a connoisseur trying to discover the ingredients in a complex flavour. As he watched his Mapman, a gentle dim-witted creature, he wondered again what his connection could possibly be to a sleek, black Peugeot. He drew on his beer.

"Were you looking for him?" Frank persisted, but Crawford was lost in thought. "He's sure got his troubles. He's outa hospital, skidaddled, or so he says. He's scared and he can't find his kid who he's looking for."

"Ross," said Crunkscully with great clarity. Then he drew

from his pocket the two photographs the man had given him and the newspaper clipping.

"I never seen these," said Frank, indicating the photographs, "but this here is his old lady, 'cept she remarried into the *hoi polloi.*"

Crawford took Crunkscully's offering, then passed the photographs to Werner, who was breathing over his shoulder. More than the *hoi polloi*, thought Crawford, reading some of the clipping. Muraskin was definitely more than *hoi polloi.*

"Sisyphus," said Crunkscully pointing at the yellowed newspaper clipping. No one knew what he meant. After a moment he returned his attention to the television.

"He ain't got two memories to rub together," said Frank discreetly, or so he thought.

"Ross is his son?" asked Crawford, trying to keep on track.

"That's what he told us before," said Frank. Then he noticed Crunkscully was shaking, and so he busied himself with wrapping him in an old army blanket. "I'd better get some soup into him," he said and made his way to the cupboard above the counter.

Crawford stared at Crunkscully. He squatted and looked into his face. Crunkscully reached out and took his beer from him and took a healthy guzzle. His eyes were very tired and lustreless. Beyond having seen him on the streets, the old man looked familiar, but Crawford couldn't put his finger on why.

Then Boost decided to retire for the evening. "I haf a lot of singks to consider about zee case," he said, self-importantly. At the foot of the stairs, he stopped. "Mista Crawford, tell Frank zair about zee kids. Tell him it's true vhat I haf bin sayingk all alongk. You do zat for me, yah?" And then he went up.

"Is it true?" asked Frank as soon as Werner was out of earshot.

"What's he told you?" responded Crawford.

"Lots!" said Frank. He was at the range pouring into a pot a can of Campbell's with a yellow sticker proclaiming it to be "The Manhandler." He reconsidered his reply. "Stuff about a gang – kids, children of the Mafia, that kinda thing. Is it true?"

Crawford felt he had lost all track of what was true. Everything that had happened seemed no more than a cluster of bright, elusive, and random baubles without a thread to hold them together. The strangest thing of all was that it was happening *to* him. He didn't feel anything like a cop on the trail of something. It was more like something was on his trail, distracting him at every turn so that he could not get a sense of what he was after.

Frank was waiting for an answer. He was staring at Crawford with a pot of soup in one hand and a waiting cup in the other.

"Is it true?" Frank asked again.

A smile escaped the corner of Crawford's mouth and got lost in the bristles of his moustache. His eyes lit up crazily. "Who knows," he said.

22

It had gone just as Gob had said it would except for one small thing; Arlo had carried the contrivance too far. He wasn't supposed to die.

"To fight the crib," Gob had said. A sham. To Gob it made perfect sense, and Stink's role was obvious, undeniable, for Teri's rich friend Kate recognized Stink as Teri's boyfriend. As such he would rescue the two girls from certain rape. For her part Teri need only think of some excuse to get Kate to the intended scene of the exercise, which was easy since Kate followed her like a lamb. Teri's real work came later, back at Kate's home. Teri was well liked by the Mercers; Gob was pleased.

Reuben Mercer collected things: letters, documents, etchings, etcetera. Teri hadn't understood why anybody would collect letters but Mr. Mercer had been delighted to explain. In his enthusiasm for the subject he had shown her his most valuable possessions and given her some idea of the enormous value of them in dollars and cents. That much Teri understood. Reuben was a trusting soul but not a fool; the most precious pieces in his collection were stored in a safe and all the pieces, whether framed or in portfolio, were locked in his library under electronic protection. To lift one solitary article would require a professional well informed with the comings and goings of the household. The idea had been to get Teri into the house on a more permanent basis; the rest would follow. Teri had made sure the Mercers knew that her mother was an alcoholic, and a sick woman. She beat Teri and didn't seem to care whether she lived or died. Gob had counted on the generosity and soft-heartedness of the Mercers. He reasoned that they would eventually take Teri in, especially with Kate's urging. To cement Kate's and Teri's relationship Gob had contrived the "rape." "A particularly nubile wooden horse," Gob had explained to Teri, before the last meeting, though she hadn't understood. He was delighted with himself at the ruse. Teri and Kate would be thrown together, sisters in an unthinkable drama – inseparable in adversity. After he had beaten off the thugs, all Stink had to do was get the girls home and incidentally become a hero in the process.

On the way home, Kate was hysterical and in her excited ramblings it was clear she was more frightened by the tragic consequence of the fight than by the sexual assault she had come so close to suffering.

"He got up," Stink lied to her, for he had not seen Arlo move. "Honest I saw him; it's okay." He caught Teri's glance and saw a reflection of his own fear, magnified in her eyes. It was *not* okay. It was possible, even likely, that the Mercers would not call the police over an assault or possible rape attempt, but a murder, even in self-defence, was another matter. If Arlo was dead, Stink was in big trouble and if he wasn't there would be some explaining to do.

He made to leave them as the trio crossed the Mercers' front lawn, but before he could extricate himself from Kate's hold the door opened in response to her loud whimpering and suddenly it was too late to do anything. If he ran away he would hardly seem the hero. Stink swallowed hard; his throat was parched, his tongue felt like sandpaper.

Reuben Mercer reacted much as Stink had feared he might. "Killed? The boy was *killed?*" Distraught, he rushed to the phone while Siobhan Mercer tried to comfort the girls, both of whom were crying uncontrollably now.

Stink shouted urgently: "No, not killed. I saw him get up. Honest." He fought back a growing nausea.

"But...those groans," Kate managed between sobs, and then she fell back into her mother's arm.

"He was faking it," Stink improvised. He watched out of the corner of his eye and saw the blood rush to Teri's cheeks. He felt his neck grow hot.

"What do you mean?" asked Reuben. "Do you mean to say it was some kind of game?"

"No, not a game," Stink said quickly. "He just faked being stabbed so that I'd get scared and stop beating on him."

It was a desperate explanation but it had the effect of delaying Reuben's phone call. Reuben sat down heavily in a chair, deep in thought. After a moment he spoke. "You're quite sure you saw him get up?"

"If you call the cops there won't be nothing there." Stink tried to sound confident.

"Honey." There was a special pleading in Siobhan's voice. Without words her expression said what Gob had told them she would say. "Please, no authorities, it's distressing enough."

Reuben did not seem entirely convinced as to the wisdom of this and Stink made one last attempt. He was thinking fast. "I'll go back and check, if you want. I mean, if I stabbed a guy we should get an ambulance or something. I don't want to get in no trouble."

This at last shook Reuben's resolve to phone the police. "No, son, you've done enough for one night. I can go myself."

This brought a shrill cry of protest from Kate, who flung her arms around her father. Siobhan spoke softly. "If he's certain he saw the boy recover...." She left the sentence unfinished, and to Stink's relief Reuben Mercer nodded reluctantly, patting his daughter's head. He was ashen.

Siobhan gathered up "her girls" and, with an attempt at cheeriness, whisked them upstairs to a bath and a change of clothes.

Minutes later, she called down the stairs to her husband and he left the living room. When he returned, he had a blanket, which he wrapped around Stink's wet, bony shoulders. "I don't know about you, Stuart, but I could do with a stiff drink." He didn't wait for a reply, but went straight to a cupboard and poured scotch into two crystal glasses.

Stink was shaking and he pulled the blanket closely to him. It had gone smoothly, after all, but his nerves were shattered. The drink was delivered. The room was quiet then for a moment, except for the clinking of ice. It was a room unaccustomed to loud noises. There was a Persian rug with a nap like velvet and tall plants everywhere in Chinese vases.

Stink sipped readily at his drink now and Reuben smiled broadly. "I didn't even ask if you drank scotch," he said, amused at the idea. He lit a cigarette, and offered one to Stink, who refused.

Stink's tongue was all pins and needles from the drink. I should go, he thought, but the room, blond and warm, held him there.

"That was a brave thing you did, Stuart. I can't tell you how dreadful it would have been had anything happened to Kate, or Teri, for that matter. She's almost part of the family."

Oh God, thought Stink, scarcely able to believe his ears. He suddenly felt transparent. Reuben Mercer must have been blind not to notice. But he shook the thought from his head and tried to concentrate on what the man was saying to him. His senses were lulled. The scotch, the blanket, the warm room, helped to loosen the knots in his stomach; even the pain in his bruised legs lessened to a dull throbbing, but he still felt uneasy. Unhappy.

Siobhan returned after a while and mixed herself a drink. "My girls send their love and have gone to bed," she announced. She sat beside her husband on a soft, pale-coloured couch and, smiling at Stink, she explained that Kate had begged her to let Teri stay the night. She had agreed on the condition that Teri phone her mother first. "That woman," she said and imbued it with the scorn of a much more derogatory epithet.

"Bleeding hearts," Gob had called them, after hearing one of Teri's reports. "Let us see what happens, my Scrogglings, when we prick a bleeding heart."

When he had finished his drink, Reuben was determined to

162

go and check the scene of the crime and, too tired to argue, Stink offered to accompany him. If Arlo really was dead, Stink could always take off, disappear. Or could he, for what then would happen to Teri? Everything seemed so complicated. Outside the air was colder than it had been earlier, and the wind had stopped.

"There'll be snow soon," said Reuben. "Snow that'll stay."

The lane by the cemetery was empty.

Part Two

"...when memory takes over and corrects
fact...makes it tolerable..."
Edward Albee

23

Crawford didn't sleep well. In his subconscious mind, the night crawled with grotesque, many-legged children who scurried from the light of the moon. Children not in the flagrantly ugly masks of Hallowe'en but in the much more disturbing masks of obscurity. Camouflage. Battle dress. Other children joined this army in his dream, images from television of twelve-year-old Nicaraguan guerrillas. Doe-eyed innocents with submachine-guns. The armies vanished and were replaced by two single opponents who circled one another, thrust and parried, thrust and parried, in tiresome repetition. The fight didn't end; it was neither escaped nor won and underscoring it was yet another duel which Crawford had been avoiding. Suddenly he could avoid it no longer. He fell headlong through his dream into a nightmare.

He was back in a warehouse across town. There was a resounding gunshot and he felt a burning sensation in his leg; his legs crumpled beneath him. He tried to struggle up and out of the nightmare but instead he fell still deeper. His dream-self reached for the power switch as he fell, bringing the lights down with him. It was quiet, the echoey quiet of being in the belly of a huge dark place. There was no further shot. He waited in agony. The madman was over him somewhere in the rafters, then suddenly something heavy fell, landing not fifteen feet from where Crawford lay wounded. There was no scream or groan to indicate that what had fallen was human, only the expulsion of breath upon impact. Crawford tossed in his sleep trying to rid himself of the nightmare but oblivious to him his dream-self took a flashlight from his coat and shone it across the warehouse floor. There was the fallen angel watching him. Crawford was transfixed; he wanted to flick off the flashlight but he couldn't. The fallen angel looked clear through him but there was no light in his eyes. The man was dead. He held a gun in his hand, which was aimed at Crawford, but the man was dead. His neck was broken, Crawford could see that, but it was as if some cruel instinct in the madman still tried to trick his finger into pulling the trigger. Crawford held his own gun in his other hand but he too was frozen into inactivity. He could not fire and he lay waiting, joined to a dead man across the beam of his flashlight. He was still waiting when reinforcements arrived. He had no idea how long that was.

He woke up.

He lay breathing heavily in his bed, safe in his own home. He listened but there was no sound but the muffled city. He was still waiting for that shot, the one that would finish him off. The doctors had removed a bullet from his leg but this other, this simulacrum, was still lodged firmly in his imagination.

It might be some time before he could risk sleep again that night and so Crawford went downstairs. He poured himself a drink and looked from his kitchen at the ramshackle backyard with its lumber and torn out plumbing parts, wet and glistening in the moonlight. The wind which had come up with the end of the storm had blown itself out. Standing on the cool tile floor sipping bourbon, Crawford tried to make sense out of his life.

He knew one thing; he could no longer play at being a cop. He could no longer accept the ambiguous role McIlwane had created for him – the nut case on the not case. That was over.

He refreshed his drink, thinking briefly how pleasant an expression that was. He made his way through the dark kitchen, feeling ahead with his toes, pushing aside various tools that had spilled from a tool box. In the living room he sunk into a corner of his mother's settee under the skylight window, at the very bottom of a lunar shaft. In the luminescent dark he noticed only the solidity of things and the pervasive smell of the room. It was a good, comforting smell: sawdust – the opposite of decay.

His thoughts drifted back to the park, to the Animal Boy, to the mysteriously vague Mr. Crunkscully. He had seen the face before – before he had ever seen the Mapman. But where?

The bourbon began to work its magic, turning Crawford's nerves into lacework. He curled up on the settee and under a tattered quilt of velvet remnants he slept.

It had begun to snow.

❖

McIlwane phoned at 7:00. Crawford, only barely awake, was surprisingly lucid in describing the previous evening's sequence of absurdities. McIlwane grunted from time to time and Crawford found himself listening for the tell-tale sign of disbelief.

His narrative finished, Crawford surprised himself and McIlwane. "I want this case," he said. "That's what you were hoping I would say all along, isn't it?"

McIlwane was evasive. He resorted to officialese to describe the process by which Crawford's position might be normalized.

"I don't think you understand," said Crawford more impatiently than he meant to. "I either take on this case or I quit." It didn't sound right; it sounded like a threat. Crawford listened to his senior's measured breath over the line.

He wanted to explain, to cry out: "There's a dead man with his gun pointed at my head. He can't shoot me and I can't shoot him and I can't shake him off." But he said nothing.

"Do you want to know why I phoned?" Colin asked. Crawford sighed.

"I suppose so," he answered.

"I phoned to say I spent most of yesterday in meetings with Ewart and the steering committee of the commission who set up my task force. I got an agreement in principle out of them to start an investigation, based on the B & E Messenger Service business. No modus operandi for the investigation was discussed, and no funding, but I think between Vince Gas and myself, we convinced them that you should head whatever team they see fit to grant us. I phoned to see if you were interested but, quite frankly, I'm just a little perturbed to find you *so* interested. You sound like you've been eating speed-injected candy apples, or something." McIlwane didn't wait for a retort but got down to business. "What you witnessed last night might convince the commission to broaden the base of the investigation and give us a bit more support. There's a helluva lot of loose ends. Our big problem will be convincing Wheeler to transfer you laterally to my safekeeping. The commission will need a full written report of what you've got so far, and since they'll need time to consider the report, it behooves you to get it done as soon as possible."

Crawford's brief moment of enthusiasm had flagged. He saluted the phone, held at arm's length, but said nothing. McIlwane continued. "To be frank with you, Rum, you sound edgy, and writing up a report will dampen your spirits to a level that the commissioners can deal with. You know what I'm saying?"

Crawford was good at reports. He had an advantage over other detectives; he was literate. But that didn't mean he liked writing them. He was smarting a little from the schoolboy business. He guessed it was his narration of the evening's events, which had not been tailored for official ears. He agreed to write the report but first he wanted to take an investigative team down into the lower park at Riverdale as soon as possible. It was from that direction the gang had come and the shed on the reservoir island seemed a likely meeting spot. McIlwane agreed to help him out by pulling some strings.

❖

Crawford realized that the snow had probably obliterated any signs of the previous night's activities, but the trip was not categorically a failure. Within the hour, he and his experts had scoured the lower park and checked out the shed. There were fine hairs clinging to the bars on the windows suggesting blankets had been draped over them as improvised curtains. The mud floor of the shed had been scraped, implying that whoever had been in the shed had wanted to disguise their presence. What couldn't be determined, of course, was how many people might have been present there, or their ages. All that was left behind was a piece of cigarette paper, one wad of gum, and a marijuana roach.

There was one interesting find which Crawford made and kept to himself. It was a small black notebook with writing in crabbed German. He recognized it immediately as Werner Boost's book of mysterious leads. Crawford had discovered it on the path, covered with a dusting of snow. Boost must have been there some time in the night after Crawford had left him at Elmsley Court. He was surprised at the man's bravery or else his sheer stupidity. He was also concerned that Boost may not have dropped the book simply out of carelessness. He hoped the old man had not got himself beaten up again.

Crawford left the unit at the shed and drove his own car over to 14 Elmsley Court. The door was answered by a vision in strangeness, who introduced herself as the Countess Olga. She was wearing a tiara but there was nothing else regal about her. Crawford felt awkward in her presence for she made no attempt to hide her attraction to him. He asked for Werner Boost.

"No, he isn't at home," she said, and then, pleased with the statement, she repeated the statement for everyone who wasn't home, including Frank and Crunkscully.

Crawford thought better of leaving the notebook in Olga's safekeeping, but did ask if Werner was all right. Hearing he was well he asked after Crunkscully.

Olga immediately became suspicious. "I didn't steal his cat!" she spat at him, and closed the door without another word.

Crawford didn't wait around. He went home and immediately started work on the report McIlwane had recommended. It took him a while to find his typewriter and, not to his surprise, it was clogged with sawdust. But it didn't slow him down. He felt about ten months of inertia slipping away.

24

Reuben Mercer had been right about the snow. It had stayed – all through the weekend. Stink stared from his bedroom window, on Monday morning, across the drift-covered courtyard of the apartment complex. Some idiot neighbour had left her washing out; it was frozen in slabs and swung on the line like so many shop signs. The early-morning light was diffuse and cold, and Stink shivered. His head throbbed badly. He had developed a cold which sat as compressed as a snowball between his ears, pressing against the back of his eyes. There was a pressure in his stomach burning like dry ice; the remnants of an imaginary knife which had entered him and then had its handle snapped off leaving the hurt and no means to wrench it out.

He had not stabbed Arlo on Hallowe'en. He had run into him the following day on Yonge Street, very much alive, and shiny with shades in place, smiling with only his upper lip while he took sidelong stock of himself in pinball arcade glass. Arlo alluded to Gob's grand plan as if he knew something Stink didn't and he toasted its success from a silver mickey flask.

Stink had almost wanted to kill him then for real. Instead he blubbered about how nervous he was for Teri in the home of the bleeding hearts. Arlo only laughed. He wasn't cut out for commiseration.

Later the same day Stink had managed to see Teri alone for a few minutes. She had told him the Mercers wanted her to stay.

She had been elated and sad. She had kissed him. That was all, and it was too much and not nearly enough.

Thinking about that now Stink realized something monstrous had happened to him. He was in love. It was not really an unusual phenomenon for a thirteen-year-old boy, but it was monstrous that it should have happened to him. He pounded his knuckle into the thin layer of frost along the inside of the window ledge until the ice cracked. Crossing the room, he listened at the door for his aunt. Hearing nothing, he guessed she was out, and he began to dig urgently through the junk in the bottom of his closet for a plastic rifle, a childhood toy. Disassembling the butt he removed the envelope which contained his savings, and when he had smoothed the blankets on his bed he laid the bills out face down like cards in a game of solitaire. Periodically over the year he had taken his accumulated cash to the bank and had exchanged it for crisp, new, hundred-dollar bills. Before him on the bed lay twenty-one pictures of a perfect fishing village. He kneeled at his bed with the money spread out before him and suddenly he felt weak all over. He wanted to be far away in a travel brochure or on the back of a bill. His father used to talk about going away, but he had never done it. Mostly he had sat drinking or paced the room. Stink could remember his father feeding him Cheezies, which he ate until his lips bled, and he remembered the day his father had punched the pet cat's teeth in with his bare fist.

Yesterday, Sunday, there had been a message in his post office in the laundromat. Then he had learned what Arlo had obviously known the day before; the grand plan was to go into effect today. The message didn't explain Stink's part in the proceedings, only that he was to be at Suzette's Café that night.

Stink rolled up the bills and shoved them back into the toy rifle. Outside, Monday hung on the line bleak and forbidding. Stink spent most of the day feeling very sorry for himself.

Late in the afternoon he phoned Teri at the Mercers', but someone who called herself the cleaning lady answered the call and she spoke little English. He phoned again at six and Kate answered. It was strange to talk to her at all but far stranger to hear the unguarded affection in her voice towards him. Teri was not at home and had apparently gone to see her mother, presumably to talk about leaving her.

Stink thought Kate sounded suspicious and, before he could stop himself, he blurted: "If she said she was going to see her mother, then that's where she was going."

"I know that!" said Kate. "I only wish she hadn't gone." Stink grunted in response. "She's my best friend," Kate said, as if to explain herself.

Stink heard Siobhan Mercer's voice in the background, and then Kate spoke. "My mother just reminded me to thank you for Friday night. I'm sorry we didn't see you before you had to go. Anyway...I mean, well...thanks."

Stink wasn't sure what to say. He hung on the line, caught up in the comforting background noise – kitchen sounds, a radio playing, Siobhan Mercer calling the cat.

Sensing she'd embarrassed Stink, Kate tried to draw him out of his silence. "Teri tells me you used to be in a gang where they called you Stink. Is that right?"

"I guess so."

Kate laughed brightly. "It's neat. I mean it's a pretty decent name, isn't it? Can I call you that?"

Stink felt strangely trapped. "I guess so."

He could hear Kate's mother talking to her, and then there was the muffled sound of a hand over the mouthpiece.

It cleared. "My mother says you should come here to dinner some time," Kate said. "How about tonight?"

For one moment Stink could smell and taste it and then the vision melted. He had to fight to answer. "I gotta eat with my aunt. She plays bingo tonight."

His excuse made no sense, it was the first thing that had come to his mind, but Kate responded cheerfully enough, if a little crestfallen. "Okay, some other time."

"Yeah," he answered. "I have to go now."

"Okay, Stink," she said.

He waited until she had hung up and then threw the receiver down into its cradle so hard that the telephone fell to the floor. After a moment it wailed its protest. He listened until the wailing stopped.

25

The day had grown cold, the night colder still. Curled up on the ground inside the college walls watching a darkened floor of second-storey windows, Arlo thought of the others waiting in the sleazy warmth of Suzette's. It was cold comfort to know that he, Arlo, was the key to the night's operation; that he would reap the greater reward. Earnie, Stink, and Benno would do nothing until they received his phone call.

By 10:00 he was becoming too numb to care. Even his flask of cheap whiskey had run out. Then, at long last, came the signal: three flashes from a flashlight. It hadn't been his idea but David Muraskin's. It was something his new acquaintance had read in an adventure comic and Arlo, the sycophant, had congratulated the boy on his ingenuity.

It had not been difficult to charm David from his protective environment and had taken less time than Arlo had expected. David was hungry for adventure. Once Gob had discovered his school it was only a matter of determining through observation who might be more successful at wooing the boy, Arlo or Kiki. Then, having established his favourite haunts on the occasions he left the school grounds, it was left to Arlo to single David out from his pack of schoolmates. The week prior to Hallowe'en Arlo had met David three times before suggesting the nocturnal adventure. It was to begin with a daring escape from the dormitory, which, like the signal, had been David's idea.

From the darkened washroom window fell a rope of sheets David had managed to gather. In ten minutes he was down and Arlo was at his side immediately.

Someone on the dormitory walkway passed within twenty feet of them, and although there was no real danger of their discovery, Arlo pulled a knife from his jacket. When he replaced it again David noticed it fit into a belt across Arlo's chest; there were three slim companions to the one he had drawn. David began to experience very real misgivings. The college is surrounded by a stone wall and the gates are locked at night. But the wall on the north side of the soccer pitch was overgrown with ivy. They were out in twenty minutes.

The silver Airstream trailer was parked eight blocks away where Gob had said it would be. Normally it would have appeared hopelessly out of place in the prestigious neighbourhood bordering Upper Canada College, but it was parked at an intersection which was partially dug up and cordoned off by the city for repairs. The Airstream sat within the palings hitched to a pickup, and with the sign of a well-known construction company on its silver flank, it looked convincingly appropriate.

Now that the feat of escape was accomplished, the adventure was over for David. "I was thinking. If we could just get to a subway station I could get a transfer," said David hopefully.

Arlo looked blankly at him.

"With the date and time on it," David explained. "Then the guys would have to believe me. I mean, that I got out and everything."

Arlo laughed but it was not the bright and brittle laugh David had heard before. He was a different creature at night. David was frightened of him and unsure what to do. He said as much but Arlo wasn't listening.

When they drew alongside the Airstream, Arlo turned to the whining preppy at his side. "You want a real adventure?" he asked. For a moment David almost thought he did. Arlo's eyes were wide with excitement.

"What kind of adventure?" David stammered.

"We'll break into this trailer," he said hitting the door of the Airstream.

David was relieved. It didn't seem particularly dangerous and they were only a quarter of a mile from school. Once they had done it, he could return. He would have proved himself and Arlo would still like him. "Is it easy?" he asked.

"Oh, sure," said Arlo turning his attention to the door handle. Arlo put on a good show of picking the lock. The door clicked open. Arlo looked to see that they weren't observed. The streets were deserted. "Come on," he whispered.

David took one last look around. Then they clambered up into the trailer, and the door clicked shut behind them.

Shortly after the trailer drove off it disgorged Arlo, and he watched the silver Airstream drift silently by and out onto St. Clair. He had been given a roll of bills, the likes of which he had never pocketed before. And there would be more, Gob had promised. He was heading for a phone booth from which he would call Suzette's.

❖

Stink had never been much for conversation. Benno Kashiki was stoned on quaaludes he had taken from the inside band of his yellow fedora. Gob's right-hand-man Earnie was the only one who had said much of anything. "Da whole ting is got really big money," he had repeated several times.

The time passed and tension grew. Suzette was entertaining in his back room and a few noisy visitors helped themselves to pieces of a very yellow lemon meringue pie, which sat in the display case behind the counter. The pie nauseated Stink. The waiting nauseated him.

"What's he want with Crunkscully?" Stink asked Earnie.

Earnie only laughed. "Gob like ta have his fon."

Stink's mind drifted to Teri. He imagined her in the Mercers' blond living room and he was jealous, of her and the Mercers – even of the room.

It was nearly 11:00 when the pay phone by the door rang. Earnie answered it and smiled back at his comrades. "It's on," he said at last, hanging up the receiver. "Let's go."

✧

"...His mind is like an arid place but like a desert capable of blooming mysteriously. His son is a bright flower in that desert and ripe for the picking....

"He has a strange new relationship with his memory, it controls him. His memory has solipsed his mind. He will do whatever his memory tells him to do...."

On and on the Judas tape continued. Why Crunkscully listened at all was difficult to say. The taped voice mocked him. It was as if his memory bore him a grudge for how badly it was treated and had turned on him to express its dissatisfaction. He had allowed the tape to speak to him out loud rather than in secret through his earplug. There was no reason to keep what Judas said a secret. He punched the Off button, stopping the mutant memory, and slipped into bed in his pants and undershirt. He fell into an uneasy sleep. His dreams took him to a warm September day and to a Siamese cat which sidled up to him and rubbed against his legs. It seemed such a hopeful sign. He was dreaming of that cat when a noise woke him.

"Sisyphus?" said Crunkscully in a hoarse whisper. He thought he heard her jumping against the wall trying to scale her imaginary shelves, trying to escape. At first there was only the light from the curtainless window, the sparkling light of a street lamp reflected in the fallen snow. He heard her jump again. "Sisyphus?" If only he had a string. He could tie it around her neck and she would lead him back to Ross. She would help him find his baby and he would be real this time, not just a sharp sliver in his imagination. He would be there crying in his pram, not gone with the lost boys.

Crunkscully suddenly saw the door open, just a crack. He raised himself in his bed. The door opened a bit further.

He hadn't his glasses on. Three watery shadows appeared to enter the room. He closed his eyes, hoping sleep would take him back for he had no energy to fight shadows. Small strong hands dragged him from his bed without a word, and he offered no resistance. He had known he would have to go sooner or later.

26

What with his report to the commission and ad hoc meetings with McIlwane, Ewart, and the inimitable Horse Sergeant, it was Tuesday morning before Crawford returned to Elmsley Court. He was really only dropping by to return Boost's notebook and was not in the least prepared for what he found.

Crunkscully was gone. Crawford tried to piece together what had happened from what Frank told him as they walked up to Crunkscully's room.

It seems that at 11:00 the previous night Frank had looked in on Calmette and found his condition had worsened so he bundled him up and drove him to the hospital. What with the registration at that time of night, he didn't get home until about 1:00, which was when he decided to peek in on his other invalid, as he usually did before going to bed. When he saw Crunkscully's tangled sheets, Frank guessed that he hadn't been able to sleep and had gone out walking, but when he hadn't returned in the morning, he didn't know what to think. He didn't phone the police. Phoning the police did not come naturally to him.

Frank didn't find it particularly strange that no one in the house had heard Crunkscully's departure. "Hell, this place supports every kind of nocturnal rambling."

There was no sign of a struggle in his room, but if Crunkscully had left on his own he had done so without his clothes or anything else. In the pocket of a rumpled shirt, Crawford found the yellowed newspaper clipping with the photo of a Cabbage-town couple, the Muraskins, and the two photographs of a boy in school uniform. On close inspection now, the pictures looked as if they had been taken surreptitiously with a telephoto lens. That was alarming.

At that moment Werner Boost entered Crunkscully's room. Absentmindedly Crawford handed him the black notebook which Werner reclaimed with the slightest of conspiratorial grins, as if he had expected Crawford would have found it.

"You vant to know vhat I found?" he asked. At that precise moment Crawford didn't really care one way or the other but Werner barrelled on. "Zee tracks of a vheelchair." Crawford looked momentarily perplexed and Werner winked at him. Crawford held his gaze steadily for a moment as he sized up the statement but his mind was preoccupied with Crunkscully's disappearance.

"You said there was an ex-housemate who drives a black limo with tinted windows?" he asked. Werner nodded. "I saw Crunk-scully picked up by a Peugeot – maybe the same one, I don't know – about two weeks ago. Any idea where he might have been heading?" Frank stared blankly. Werner nodded his head vigorously but said nothing. Crawford couldn't help believing something was very wrong. He told Frank and Werner about Duranovitch. He told them anything he could think of in the hope of getting information back in return. "I've got to know what's going on," he said. Frank scratched his stubbly head as if such a demand was beyond his powers. Crawford sat on the edge of Crunkscully's bed. "Tell me about Crunkscully," he asked and Frank's face brightened immediately.

"Scully's a space cadet," said Frank, tapping his head with a finger. "He told me he used to be the mayor."

Crawford looked at Frank. Maybe he saw it there in Frank's eyes, maybe they both realized it at the same time. The penny dropped. The face which had turned Crawford's head on the street suddenly had a name. The man had been looking for someone named Ross.

"Ross Scollard," said Crawford quietly. "He *was* mayor."

"Jesus H. Christ," Frank exclaimed.

Werner looked momentarily puzzled, but then he too unravelled the mystery. "He vas not mayor for long, yah?"

"Not long at all," said Crawford.

Werner's eyes grew very large for a moment and he slapped his little black book on the palm of his hand. "He has bin shankhaied!" he shouted.

"Scully?" cried Frank in disbelief. Then he turned to Crawford. "What do we do?"

Crawford looked at the clipping. "Find the Muraskins," he said.

Werner had other ideas which he wasn't prepared to discuss.

❖

Finding the Muraskins was easier said than done. Their address was *very* unlisted. It turned out they lived two blocks from Elmsley Court on Wellesley Street. By comparing the tattered clipping with the house it was obvious to Crawford that the woodwork had been painted white since the photo had been clipped from the newspaper the previous spring. He entered the garden through a wrought-iron gate, climbed three steps to the oak door, and pulled back the ring shot through the polished snout of a brass bull's-head knocker.

A housekeeper answered with a certain amount of surprise and a suspicious frown. "Are you from the school? No, of course you're not." She seemed annoyed with herself at having made such a foolish mistake. Without waiting for Crawford to enlighten her, she called out.

A very large man with a surprisingly small chin – apparently named Rory – came to the door. Rory, even in shirt sleeves, carried with him the pugnacious quality of the trained bodyguard. Nonetheless, he was immaculately groomed, over-cologned, and took obvious pride in appearing dangerous. Crawford fantasized that he would have rather been a policeman, but couldn't make the grade. This opinion was unwittingly confirmed by Rory's disdainful reaction when Crawford introduced himself as a police sergeant.

"The Muraskins will be arriving on the 9:45 from Jamaica tonight, Air Canada flight 631," Rory answered smugly to Crawford's first question. He replied guardedly to the second question. "What do you mean, is their son with them?"

Crawford had the distinct impression there was something he should know. Something to do with what the housekeeper had said. He ventured out on a limb by producing the photos which he had found in Crunkscully's shirt. "Do these mean anything to you?"

Rory raised a hairy eyebrow as he studied the photographs. "David is missing from his classes. The Muraskins were notified and have seen fit to return. What exactly is your business here?"

Crawford didn't answer. Under the circumstances he was not going to question these people regarding the disappearance of a strange tormented man in whose shirt pocket he'd found David Muraskin's photograph. He said simply that he would be back the following day, and left.

❖

From a C.P.I.C. terminal at police headquarters Crawford learned that Ross Scollard had been listed with missing persons since August. He had been a patient at the Dalton Geriatric Centre in Cooksville, northwest of Toronto, but had apparently escaped. Crawford had an idea where he could find more on the man. He had contacts in the media. There were journalists he had tipped who owed him favours; it was a symbiotic relationship every good detective entered into. He even liked some of them.

The one he had arranged to meet for late lunch that day was one of those, and he was the perfect man to talk to in this case. Jeff Brothers was now with Southam News Services. When Scollard had run for mayor, Brothers had been a political columnist for *Time* Canada. Like many of his breed, he had a prodigious memory and an avid curiosity. Given a morning's notice he was able to dig up information on the "Scollard Scandal."

"Sure it was a scandal," Brothers argued. "The public was outraged that a disease, of which they had never heard, could claim a newly appointed hero. Alzheimer's disease. It's a sad kind of disease, pathetic – scandalous."

In a way he was right, thought Crawford, but the journalistic turn of phrase made him cringe.

"Of course they can't be certain it's Alzheimer's until he's dead and they can cut him up," Brothers added.

Crawford wasn't sure what he wanted from Brothers. He was curious for one thing, in a morbid kind of way. What happens to a hero, a martyr, who doesn't really die, or at least not right away? One way or another Scollard was involved with the case and talking to Brothers would be faster than doing the background reading himself and more entertaining than police files.

He sipped on a Guinness while Brothers nursed a Marguerita. "You're a regular archaeologist," said Crawford, watching Brothers produce a briefcase-load of Xeroxed articles.

He handed them to Crawford. "The benefits of working for a news service. There is a lot of stuff. The story captured the public's imagination." Brothers smiled malevolently, with hooded eyes. "Actually, you aroused my curiosity, one of those 'what ever happened to' pieces."

Crawford told him he had found Scollard. He didn't say he'd lost him again.

"I'll get a story out of this, Crawford, one way or another."

Brothers then began the story between mouthfuls of spinach salad. There were pictures and although only six years had elapsed since the election, Crawford found it strange to compare Scollard's picture to the wan and disoriented creature he had known as the Mapman. The younger face was strong, well-boned but fleshed out and softened by a substantial frame of hair. It looked to Crawford as if that face had been dropped somewhere in a desert and left to the wear of sandstorms. The hair, the dark, strong stuff in the photos, had been bleached to a ghost of its former self.

"I was there," said Brothers, showing him a picture of Scollard's headquarters on the night of the election. "What a hoot!" he said. "That picture must have been taken just after we watched Travis's concession speech on television. It wasn't a graceful speech at all. Scollard's supporters went wild with a kind of mad, vindictive triumph. The whole campaign was quite a scrap."

Crawford took the photo from Brothers. He searched among the waving hands and balloons and streamers for the candidate. "Is that his wife?" he asked, pointing to a blur of printer's ink beside Scollard on the podium.

"Could be," said the reporter, squinting to see more closely. "I think she was there. Don't look so surprised, Rum. There were a lot of bets on whether she would show up, victory or not. She kept a low profile during the whole race. *That* caused a lot of speculation. Of course, later, people understood why. The campaign must have been hell for her, knowing what she knew. His wife didn't want him to run, but at the time no one knew he was ill."

Crawford looked again at the picture, trying to see Scollard's wife to compare it to the face in the clipping of Connie Muraskin, but the more he stared the more abstract and meaningless the tiny image became. "Is there any picture of her?" asked Crawford suddenly, curious to see her face.

"How does she fit into your investigation?" asked Brothers.

"Apparently she remarried," said Crawford, picking his words carefully. Brothers was flicking through the portfolio.

"Uh-huh," he said. "And?"

"Someone named Muraskin." Crawford had meant to sound off-hand but Brothers looked up with astonishment.

"Who Muraskin?"

"Bernard K."

Brothers' eyes threatened to fall out of his head but he couldn't conceal his scepticism. "No offence, but if she did, she certainly moved up in the world. From mayor to Croesus; it's another Jackie O. story. I don't follow the society pages much, but I think that one would have been a hot item."

Crawford was sceptical himself but he tried to get back to the subject at hand.

"From what you say she must have known about the disease before the campaign. Surely it couldn't have just struck from out of the blue." Crawford spoke over an article called "Old Before Time."

"It wasn't sudden," said Brothers, sitting back in his chair contemplatively. "She had her doubts, but the indications were either ignored or misinterpreted. Memory is the first thing to go and Scollard was no exception but it was put down to the pressures of the campaign."

"But a politician without a memory?"

Brothers laughed. "Anyway," he shrugged his shoulders. "He compensated. All those years of reading the news might have helped."

"That's what he did!" said Crawford. "The CBC Radio six o'clock news."

"An invisible presence in a lot of peoples' lives," added Brothers. "I don't know. What I can glean from rereading doctors' reports in the paper, Scollard must have worked a helluva lot harder, which, by the way, didn't help his condition one bit. Alzheimer's disease is strongly affected by stress of any kind, especially any kind of trauma." Crawford remembered the fallen man in the bushes. He saw again the terrified face.

Brothers continued. "Do you remember all the speculation about him having suffered a breakdown during the campaign? It was kept pretty hush-hush but, oh, the rumours – drinking problems, marital problems, every kind of emotional instability. It turned out later that they started doing intensive neurological examinations about then, but it's a slow process; you only find Alzheimer's disease by eliminating a whole batch of other brain-damage-causing dementia."

There was another story. "Scollard Pulls Through in the

Crunch." There had been an all-candidates meeting just after the period when rumours had been flying concerning Scollard's health. Apparently he had shown up brilliantly and created a sensation.

"This is the big one," said Brothers suddenly, waving a notice in his hand. The *Sun* managed in its inimitable way to scoop the official press conference: "Mayor Elect Resigns." It was in red and juxtaposed to it was a picture of a mammoth-breasted female swimming in the clear waters off Bermuda.

"That, in a nutshell, is the newspaper business," muttered Crawford beneath his breath.

"Now, now, no need to be contemptuous," Brothers smiled broadly, but not altogether sincerely. "I'll never forget the following Saturday's issue. Every editor on the magazine had a story to file; the ramifications of a mayor-elect resigning was half the story, the other half was Alzheimer's disease. It was like an assassination. Beforehand you have never heard of the assassin and then within the week you know more than you ever wanted to know."

"And then it all faded away. The papers replaced it with some other scandal, some war, some other terror," said Crawford. It wasn't meant to sound as cynical as it did. He was getting progressively grumpier. He could understand now the fear in Crunkscully's eyes. It was fear of the unknown.

There was another article called "The Real Victims," dealing with the problems encountered by the family of the Alzheimer victim. It posed a number of startling questions: "What to do with your husband when he needs to use the washroom in a public place and can't remember how? How do you convince your mother that she just ate her dinner five minutes earlier, when you know that food is one of her greatest joys but she is growing dangerously overweight and getting less and less exercise? How do you convince your wife not to hide all her belongings because of a morbid persecution complex? How do you introduce your husband to his brother?" There had been a fund-raising campaign by the Alzheimer Society. It had been very successful. The pathos must have pushed the pen across quite a number of cheques.

"To catch you up," said Brothers at last, unaffected by Crawford's deflated spirits, "he finally had to be put away. Here's the story, it's a *Time* Canada," he added. "Remember them?" He made the quote marks in the air as he spoke. "From my own personal collection – worth a fortune."

The article was under the banner of "Medicine." Crawford checked the date. It was three years after Scollard's election and resignation. So he had been in hospital for three years when he had escaped in August. The article was called "Postscript, The Man Who Would Be Mayor." "The hurrahs of three years ago are little more than an echo for Ross Scollard, one-time radio announcer and briefly elected mayor of Toronto," Crawford read. His eyes skimmed over the pages. "...It is not the loss of memory one comes to expect of so-called 'benign senescence.' It is accompanied by a wide variety of possible behavioural and psychiatric symptoms and a wide range of physical ailments. This complicated by the fact that the patient is often woefully aware of his deteriorating mental state and, not being able to help himself, experiences a strong death wish. Against the possible mental anguish, obsessional anxiety, schizophrenia, depression, severe, sometimes psychotic, anger and aggression or just plain confusion, medicine has few defences...."

Crawford's mind wandered back to the Mapman, the sad creature in the graveyard on Hallowe'en. He tried to match him up to the man in *Time*.

"Scollard, by all accounts, is far from a typical patient," the article said. "He is one of those rare humans with a winning attitude. As one nurse put it: 'Stubbornness is a symptom of the disease and Scollard is as stubborn as a mule – he won't give in.'

"Can Scollard remember the 'Last Hurrah'? Apparently not with any clarity although there are times when he remembers a surprising amount. It is one of the most insidious tricks of the disease, that every now and then the patient will seem to be back to normal. Drug doses are cut back, even cancelled, and the patient might even go home for a weekend but it is only a malicious jest, the recovery is never a lasting one.

"We are left with the paradox that while we, the public, might only vaguely recall Scollard's phenomenal rise to fame, we remember the incident better than he himself. It is a sobering thought."

Crawford tugged on his moustache and looked thoughtfully at Brothers for a moment. "Got time for a brandy?" he asked quietly.

Brothers did.

"Scollard pulls through in the crunch." He hoped.

Brothers put the copious notes back in his briefcase. "She – I mean Connie Scollard – looked after him for three years. So it must have been in the last three years she married Muraskin. She could probably have gotten an annulment but she didn't seem the type."

"What about a son," asked Crawford.

Brothers thought for a moment and shook his head but he looked at Crawford inquisitively.

"Maybe he was previously married," suggested Crawford, regretting having told Brothers so much.

"Maybe," said Brothers. He tapped his brandy snifter with a silver toothpick. He was working on an angle and Crawford could hear the typewriter clicking already.

Crawford dedicated the rest of the day to getting his job back. McIlwane had gone to bat for him and all Crawford could do was wait. Obeisance to the jealous god of bureaucracy was conducted on hard benches outside offices. There were more ad hoc meetings and forms; he had almost forgotten about forms. It was a question of readjusting to the slowness-in-triplicate pace; getting shot was the least of his concerns. On that matter, however, the medical officer who had released him from his duty ten months ago now had to see him again and release him from the purgatory of an ambiguous retirement.

A phone call to Rory at the Muraskins' residence supplied Crawford with the name of David's school and he phoned the authorities there. Although Crawford refused for the time being to explain what had led him to phoning, his call startled the headmaster. The school had considered the disappearance of the previous night as a schoolboy prank. Bedsheets tied together and anchored to the bathroom radiator indicated an escape not an abduction. For his part, Crawford could not picture Scollard as a kidnapper, but his and David's disappearance on the same night was too much of a coincidence. Meanwhile, in the back of his head, he tried to braid together the strands of the case which had led him to Scollard in the first place. He couldn't dismiss from his mind the possibility that they were all somehow interwoven: Vernon Pilchard, Sally Paza, Werner Boost, Crunkscully, and David Muraskin. They had one thing in common; they were all victims.

❖

By the following day David's disappearance could no longer be looked on as a prank nor could it be kept from the media.

The press seemed to like the secrecy at first since it gave speculation free rein, and speculation made good copy. Muraskin's prodigious wealth, previously known only to the more diligent readers of the *Financial Post,* was now front-page news. The kidnappers could ask the world. But was it a case of money? Perhaps it was political. After all, Muraskin dealt in all kinds of commodities and numbered many shaky governments among his clients. Or maybe it was an enormous white-collar crime, whereby Muraskin, or his alter ego the Hermes Corporation, would be called upon to back down from some huge takeover bid. The *Sun* dug up sources which even suggested Muraskin owned a country somewhere in the Indies. Would he swap a country for his son and heir?

The police were not unaffected by Muraskin's importance either, nor were they indifferent to the international press coverage the case would receive. Crawford was recovered officially to the force, debriefed before a team of experts and then, taking into account his jump on the case, was immediately made official head of the investigative team to handle it. The M.O. rubberstamped his return to activity.

The team included an official spokesman, since Crawford wanted to maintain his anonymity to the public. There were to be four detectives and various back-up personnel as needed. Sergeant Beryl English was to trace the whereabouts of the Peugeot, specifically on October 20, the date of Crunkscully's suspected first abduction, and on the past Monday. An intensive search for the car was also to be mounted especially in Cabbagetown where it had given the police the slip. Sergeant Derrick Reuter was to supervise a search of the Winona Enterprises stockyard in the valley. Sergeant Bob Skene was to follow up any leads directly related to David Muraskin's leave-taking and generally to handle the kidnapping as if none of the other leads existed. Skene personally liked this idea. Unlike the others, he was amenable to the suggestion that the Cabbagetown clues Crawford had gathered in his shuffling were nothing but coincidence and unrelated to the case at hand. Crawford was keeping Cabbagetown for himself. Meanwhile Riverdale Park was to go under day and night undercover surveillance and descriptions of Ross Scollard and the Animal Boy were to be circulated to all patrol units. Crawford assisted the police artists to produce a good Identikit portrait of the latter and even had the artists retouch a photograph of Scollard to reduce him to his present characteristics. Crawford somehow doubted they would be seen on the street.

His first meeting with the investigative team was only just over at 2:30 when the police were notified that the worst of their fears was justified. The Muraskins had received a ransom request. It had arrived at their door in the form of a tape cassette, delivered by a boy from the B & E Messenger Service. Crawford figured it was time to visit the Muraskins.

Rory answered the door, dressed in a black suit. As he swept the door open, a Siamese cat snaked through his feet, and launched itself out the doorway into the alert hands of Investigative Sergeant R. Rum Crawford. Rory swore and reached out for the aspiring runaway, now yowling mightily at her captor.

With inspired quickness Crawford hugged the cat to his chest. "Mrs. Muraskin," he said bluntly. The thug glared.

At that moment, Connie Muraskin arrived, and Crawford handed her the cat.

"Why must you do that?" she scolded the beast. "Last time we were here she ran off for a week. We were sure we'd lost her." Mrs. Muraskin invited Crawford to step in, and dismissed Rory with a nod. She was elegantly attired in a dark-green suit and a light-green silk blouse, the sheen of which shifted with the rhythm of her breath. Her face was expensively made up but pale for having been in Jamaica. She appeared older than the newspaper image of the previous spring, owing mostly to a deep furrow check-marked between her eyes.

"Come this way, Detective Crawford," she said, and since investigative sergeants love being called detectives, Crawford thought this was a promising beginning.

She led him into a sitting room beyond which, through a double door, Crawford caught sight of Bernard K., talking on the phone and pacing.

"Rory says you were by yesterday. I appreciate the quickness of your response. Does that mean you suspected a crime all along?" She said this with brusque efficiency, without the slightest quiver in her well-modulated voice.

She was, no doubt, distressed, but Crawford imagined that expressions of motherly concern would be saved for intimates. He came straight to the point. "When I came by yesterday, I was looking for someone else. In fact, I was investigating another case. Do the names Ross Scollard or Crunkscully mean anything to you?"

She didn't have to think; knowing peoples' names was an important part of her life and these meant nothing to her.

"Is David your son – yours and Mr. Muraskin's natural son?"

She answered yes, but her immaculately arched eyebrows flattened and her hand reached involuntarily to a cameo brooch on her lapel which she fingered nervously. It was not the line of question she had expected. It was her turn to cross-examine.

"Do I understand you to say that the man for whom you are searching might have something to do with David's disappearance?" It was a neat turn of phrase.

"I don't know. That's what I want to find out."

"Might he have kidnapped David?" Connie Muraskin persisted.

"It seems very unlikely but there is reason to believe he was interested in your son, that is, he may have been under the mistaken impression that your son was his own son."

Connie Muraskin's tact was failing her rapidly. "That's monstrous!" she said. "Is the man mad?"

Crawford quickly shook his head. "He isn't insane but he is sick...ill."

Muraskin had finished his phone call and his wife called him into the room. Succinctly and accurately she repeated her conversation with Crawford.

Muraskin responded vigorously. "If you are not looking for my son, may I ask who is?"

"A team of detectives is following up several promising leads," Crawford said in his most optimistic voice. "I am presently interested in the ransom tape and the method by which it was delivered."

Muraskin sized up Crawford and then called Rory, who entered the room hastily, as if he had been waiting for his cue. "Tell this man about the messenger boy," Muraskin said.

Rory was delighted. He described the boy well although he named nothing striking about his features. "He was in a smart brown uniform with a peaked cap. If you don't mind my saying, I don't believe he has anything to do with it."

"No?" asked Crawford, trying to hide his amusement at the man's sense of self-importance.

Rory shook his head. "The boy was most courteous. He saluted me when I signed for the package. Not enough of that kind of deference around anymore," he added.

"Thanks," said Crawford.

Even without knowing the past exploits of the B & E Messenger Service, Connie Muraskin sensed the irony in the boy's treatment of Rory. She dismissed him.

Then Muraskin brought a portable tape recorder from his study and switched it on.

Crawford found himself watching Mrs. Muraskin as she listened. Her pale complexion was not perceptively paler but her expression turned to ice.

"He is my son, Connie. I am his father," spoke the tape. "Of course you should be able to see him and that can be arranged. I don't want this to be hard for you, believe me. You can see him again for one and a half million dollars, but it must be delivered by Friday, November 14. I will let you know where and how in the next few days. If the deadline is not met, you will never see our son again. Not alive."

The three of them listened expectantly for something, anything, following that, but there was nothing.

"Is that this Scollard fellow you're after?" asked Muraskin.

"I think that may be his voice," corrected Crawford. "I would like to take this tape with me."

"I suggest you redouble your efforts to find him," Muraskin said in an even tone, and he left the room for his study, closing the doors behind him.

Connie Muraskin looked at Crawford questioningly. "I thought you said this man wasn't mad?"

It would have been foolish to try to explain to the woman that unless he was very much mistaken, the man whose voice she heard was at that moment being held captive himself.

"Do you wonder what my husband is thinking at this precise instant?" she asked and left the room.

Rory showed Crawford out.

❖

When Crawford eventually got home he was voracious. He stuffed himself with spicy Italian sausage and gobs of red cabbage and washed it all down with homemade beer.

Things were happening very fast. In a matter of hours he had gone from unofficial shuffler to head of an investigative team with nine days to find a kidnapped boy. From semi-retirement he had been thrown headlong back into the thick of things. Already he could feel the pressure mounting. The inordinant amount of food he had just eaten didn't help matters. Indeed the spicy sausages made him dream in technicolour; dreams he would rather not have dreamed.

27

Before leaving Baseball Park Road the following morning, Crawford listened to his telephone answering machine, which, in his exhaustion of the night before, he had left on. Jeff Brothers had phoned twice but had left no message beyond his name and Crawford didn't take the time to return the calls. In his first run-in with the press after his injury, they had been sympathetic but bothersome. He had been a wounded hero at the time; he wasn't sure what they wanted to cast him as now and could wait to find out.

He walked to upper Cabbagetown under a sun hazed to lemon fizz. The snow was melting and the streets were wet. He passed by Duranovitch's house on Montcalm, and turned up the alley six units down. It ran only as deep as the properties, about one hundred and fifty feet, he guessed. The sound of construction met him before he could see anything as he made his way down the muddy Caterpillar-rutted road. The Royal Hawk Mews, a Winona Enterprises project, stretched across the back end of the alleys, and was swarming with workers who looked like sailors on the skeletal scaffolding, suspended above a sea of mud. The back alley ran north and south, servicing the tenants on Montcalm who still had garages. Most of the tenants, however, had sacrificed that convenience for postage-stamp back gardens which were, in most cases, surrounded by tall cedar fences to conceal whatever modest pleasure could be conducted in such a space.

Duranovitch's meagre lot was surrounded by just such a fence, with a gate completely blocking visibility into the first-floor windows. The fenestration on the second floor included two floor-length translucent glass windows and a third smaller transparent one. An elaborate attic deck had been built but was also fenced. The northward leg of the alley ended at Duranovitch's house. Beyond his lot the properties were another twenty feet longer and butted up against the larger cinder-block wall of an auto body shop, the back entrance of which was on the alley reached by a short steep drive. "Our Town Auto Body/Repair," Crawford read on a faded sign but, peering through a very small window in the back door, he saw nothing by way of commerce in the gloomy interior. The large space was poorly lit by ancient and filthy skylights. The interior seemed empty, not only of cars but of benches and equipment. The shop was on a valuable piece of property. Duranovitch might well own it with plans to extend the mews up the entire length of Tepworth Lane to Winchester. It occurred to Crawford it would be interesting to know the extent of Duranovitch's holdings. As the owner of the Peugeot which had scooped up Scollard two weeks ago, he was the closest they had to a suspect.

Crawford made his way back down the lane and across the vacant lot to Montcalm Alley and turned his attention to the Royal Hawk Mews. Everywhere there was hammering and the pneumatic pulse of heavier equipment, and behind it all was the constant wheeze of a pump, which was ostensibly keeping the mews afloat.

He saw another sign, this one freshly painted. It was a large billboard announcing the mews to be a "Tradition in Fine Living." The fact that the elite estate was only now under construction, and that the tradition was therefore as old as the paint on the sign, was an irony not lost on Crawford. There were fourteen units surrounding a shallow courtyard soon to be the luxury grounds envisioned by the artist who had painted their portrait on the sign. The courtyard was presently a grey-brown smudge with isolated ridges of snow like crystallized white caps on the dirty sea of mud. All the windows of the luxury flats faced into the courtyard or at least would do, for presently the mews was blind, the apertures covered with plywood.

Crawford had only been watching the construction for a minute when he suddenly sensed that he was being observed. He didn't turn right away but he suppressed a shudder which coursed through him, making him cold all over. When it had passed, he turned, affecting an air of nonchalance, and confronted Werner Boost. The German stood in the vacant lot near the body shop. His old raincoat was flapping buttonlessly and although he smiled, his glasses had caught the sun and were opaque for a moment. Crawford could not easily erase the feeling of fear that had shot through him.

"Goot morningk, Mista Crawford!" called Boost.

Crawford joined him. "What are you up to, Werner?"

"Vee, zee Neverlanders, are on zee lookout for Mista Crunk-scully's abductors. Vee make regular checkups – a patrol – around here since you mentioned zis man, D'ranowitch."

"And how did you find out where he lived?" asked Crawford. Boost looked shocked. "From zee phonebook, of course."

Crawford's eyes must have wandered to the ever-present little notebook in Werner's hand for the German smiled and held it up. "You vant to know vhat I write?" he asked.

Crawford indicated that he did. Boost sidled nearer as though they might be overheard, despite the fact they were standing in a vacant lot.

"I am vonderingk where is Gob, all of a sudden." Crawford must have looked questioningly at him, because Boost sighed and shook his head. "For a cop you haf a lousy memory. Een zee park, remember? Zair vere vheelchair tracks! I saw zem viz my own eyes."

Crawford remembered him saying as much but had not connected the tracks with the cripple named Gob. "You think he's in on it?" he asked, humouring the German.

"I never said zat," Werner snapped. "I jus' vas vonderingk vhere he'd got to lately. He hasn't bin around since zee last few days. Funny, eferyvon disappearingk like zat, all at zee same time."

Crawford wasn't quite sure what to think and said nothing.

Boost invited him back to Elmsley Court and Crawford thought he might just have time for a coffee break. The rooming house was only three blocks away but first he wanted to ask Duranovitch's neighbours if they had seen anyone come or go from the house.

Werner waited for him on the street.

One neighbour stared anxiously back and forth between Crawford at her door and Boost, hands in pocket, on the street, and Crawford realized that the two of them looked a bit like gypsy con artists working as a team. For this reason Crawford drew his badge out of his coat and said: "We're working undercover." The woman looked only partially convinced.

Overhearing this, Werner was pleased to be included in the minor conceit and said grandly to Crawford: "If I had not become a crook as a youngk man I vould haf become a cop."

Another neighbour, the woman who shared the northern wall of Duranovitch's house, thought she might have heard a sound like a scream but had concluded it was just the raccoons. "They scream when they mate," she explained.

The results of Crawford's search were slim, and by the time he'd turned from the last house, Boost had wandered off and was nowhere in sight. Checking his watch, he decided against dropping in at Elmsley Court.

❖

Crawford had scheduled a working lunch for 1:00 at headquarters and arrived to find the small investigative team eating from boxes and bags. Before he joined them he made out the necessary applications for a search warrant of Duranovitch's house. Screaming raccoons or not, he wouldn't be content until he knew that the house was empty. He also set in motion a search proceedings on Duranovitch's holdings.

Beryl English made her report first. She had spent most of the morning with Duranovitch's personal secretary, whose name was Swaantje Bremane. The whereabouts of the Peugeot were still not known and, interestingly, Winona Enterprises had made no attempt to notify the police that the car was missing. Miss Bremane had made it clear that there was nothing extraordinary about this situation other than the inordinate interest of the police. She was not aware of the real reasons for the enquiry but gathered that a detective had not been sent out because of an overdue parking violation. "Dato" – as Miss Bremane called him – was "loose with the keys" to the company car, and the office staff had abnegated responsibility for it since a similar disappearance some time before. Dato had been the last to use the car before he left for Florida in September. He had left no directive as to who could use the car. Miss Bremane could not say who had taken Duranovitch to the airport.

Sergeant English had taken a list of employees from the secretary, intimate friends and family who had borrowed the car in the past. Through interviews at the office and on the phone, she felt she had narrowed this down to a short list of six, including Duranovitch's brother who called himself Gabriel Duran. Duran had been around earlier in October and had, on occasion, borrowed the car for extended periods of time. As an aside, Sergeant English mentioned that there seemed to be no love lost between Swaantje Bremane and Gabriel Duran. She couldn't, however, say the same about Bremane and her absent boss. "Which isn't to say she's some curvaceous, dim tart," said English acerbically, eyeing an associate who had leered in response to her observation. "Miss Bremane is extremely competent; almost too competent," she said without qualifying.

Sergeant Reuter reported next. The Winona Enterprise's stockyard in the Don Valley was an enormous property sprawling over ten acres along the northwest side of the Bayview Extension. Reuter and two constables had gone there at 8:00 that morning and had only just had time to complete their search before he had to return for the meeting. He enumerated the buildings: two large enclosed warehouses, three smaller ones, and five Quonset huts, temporary facilities for site headquarters, including both portable buildings and a fleet of six trailers. The Peugeot was not there and the stockyard foreman could not recall when he had last seen the car. At any rate, because of the tinted glass windows he couldn't always tell who was driving the vehicle unless they dropped by his hut and, needless to say, Duranovitch didn't bother identifying himself to the foreman on every visit he made, although visitors were supposed to check in with him. Crawford was reminded that so far it was the car, not the driver, that was under suspicion.

Reuter continued. There was only one entrance to the stockyard although there was another gate in the very back corner of the property. Beyond the fence lay a dried river bed, overgrown with weeds, and an earthen ramp led down into it from the back gate. Another ramp climbed up the far shore. Although steeply graded the ramps had apparently been built wide enough for the passage of heavy construction equipment. Many years of rain and ice, however, had etched deeply into the dirt surface of each and they showed no sign of recent vehicular use, a fact corroborated by the yard foreman. This back gate was held shut by a rusty length of chain and a stout lock.

Apparently Duranovitch had bought the property beyond his stockyard and some years earlier had planned to develop it. The gate had been put up at that time and some rudimentary ground work done on the far side of the river bed before the project had been cancelled. The land climbed steeply beyond the river. It was rough with wounds of graders and strewn with boulders. Had the elusive Peugeot gone through the gate it could not have travelled far.

Detective Skene reported last. He had interviewed half a dozen friends of David Muraskin, including the boys in the photographs, and there were indications that David had for a few days before he disappeared been seeing some boy whom none of the others seemed to know. Someone not from the school. The boy was slim and handsome and wore his hair long. One of David's friends had described the stranger as "pretty," and had said that David had kept the new chum to himself, which was apparently not like the normally gregarious David.

There was a lot of work to be done. While the tape received by the Muraskins yielded no clues to the lab specialists, the delivery linked the B & E Messenger Service with the case and also, less conclusively, to the group of kids Crawford and McIlwane had been trying to identify.

At this point McIlwane suggested having a forensic psychologist listen to the ransom tape. Doctor Peter Wenzel was contacted and later that afternoon, having heard the tape, he presented his views. He did not find the voice notably aggressive or threatening, considering the nature of its request. He was surprised by the calmness of the voice and after listening several more times to the tape suggested that the man could possibly be in some kind of hypnotic state.

Whether Scollard was victim or perpetrator was very much in the air. Although on the surface of things he certainly seemed a likely suspect, no one who had met the vague creature could have believed as much. But whether Scollard was captor or captive, the man had to be found.

❈

The hominess of Rum Crawford's house might well have eluded a more fastidious housekeeper, but for all its incompleteness of form and for the disarray of furnishings, it was still home. The tranquillity he so looked forward to upon his return that night was unexpectedly shattered, however, in the simple act of sitting down to read the evening paper. It is always a little disquieting to find your name on the front page.

There were two headlines, both exclusive and proud of it, judging by the size of type. The lesser of the two caught Crawford's eye first, not least of all for the photograph of himself. It was old – a shot taken by a former girlfriend, which had been dug up from heaven knows where. The police were not about to release an update, so he would not easily be recognized. The smaller headline gave him a twinge at first and then made him writhe in distaste. "Crack Detective Called Out of Retirement to Solve Kidnapping." Clearly Jeff Brothers' handiwork, and, thanks to him, Crawford's cover was now blown.

Then he read the headline above it. "Ex-Mayor Implicated in Muraskin Kidnapping?" While the headline was worthy of a tabloid, the copy was more cautious. "There are reasons to believe that Ross Scollard, former broadcaster and mayor of Toronto for the shortest term on record, may be implicated in the kidnapping of billionaire Bernard K. Muraskin's only son. Scollard, who was forced to resign as mayor only weeks after his election due to the organic brain syndrome, Alzheimer's disease, escaped from hospital late in August and was recently discovered living in a rooming house in Cabbagetown only a block or two from Muraskin's Toronto residence. He had assumed an alias and was apparently looking for his son, according to undisclosed sources. He believed the Muraskin boy to be his own son and the disappearance of both Scollard and Muraskin have police convinced there is a link up."

Undisclosed sources! Crawford found he was shaking as he read. Brothers must have based all of it on what Crawford had told him over lunch. Crawford swore very loudly, and continued swearing as he read further, curious to see how far Brothers could take the scant information he had at his disposal. He had done a bit of research of his own. After recounting briefly the nature of Scollard's illness, with emphasis on various aspects of the deterioration caused by the disease, and especially to the wide variety of behavioural changes that might occur, he intimated, without ever saying it, that Scollard was a psychotic. Brothers had succeeded in contacting Connie Scollard in Vancouver and had found out there was no son. He had also contacted the hospital and found out from them that he, Crawford, had called in connection with Scollard's disappearance.

The other article exhumed the case from which Crawford had spent nearly a year recovering. He only scanned the page, not wanting to relive it in detail. He threw down the paper.

Undisclosed sources! He'd give Brothers a piece of his undisclosed mind.

Brothers' voice was suave. "Rum, hi. I tried to reach you but you didn't answer my calls. Rumours were flying and I couldn't let it slip away."

"Well, it's hogwash!" said Crawford.

"Then let's straighten it out," said Brothers. "My pencil is poised."

Crawford had given Brothers enough of a scoop and was not about to give him more. "You've blown the whole thing wide open," he said.

"You were covering up the Scollard business?" Brothers asked. "Sorry, old man." Brothers didn't sound sorry. "Don't hesitate to phone with corrections," he added.

Crawford hung up. It had occurred to him mid-conversation that perhaps it was just as well the papers played up the Scollard angle. He had a feeling that was exactly what the real kidnappers wanted.

28

Stink's cold had turned into flu. He had spent the week in bed, and might not have seen the newspaper at all if he hadn't visited Teri. She had phoned him Sunday morning; Kate had put her up to it. The girls sounded giddy and Kate was going to make pancakes. As much as he wanted to see Teri, Stink declined at first but, hearing that Reuben and Siobhan were out for the day, he changed his mind.

There was a moment just after he had arrived when he was left alone in the kitchen. The cat he had heard Mrs. Mercer talking to was a fat, happy orange thing, which rubbed against his leg. The kitchen was spacious with a shiny wood floor and yellow pots hanging on the wall. Behind the glass cupboard doors, white dishes glistened. There was an old-fashioned heater in the corner which sent out waves of welcome heat.

He felt a sensation he had experienced before on break-ins. Taking a seat, or maybe licking the chocolate rim of a bowl. Stealing into someone's domestic life for just an instant and feeling it settle down like a warm sweater falling in slow motion around his bony shoulders. But this time, he had been invited. For the smallest period of time, he felt something like safety.

When he saw the newspaper on a kitchen chair, the picture of Scollard meant little to him. He could not at first link the face to that of Crunkscully, nor could he connect such events with his own life.

Then Teri returned to the kitchen, saying Kate was still upstairs. She smiled. The corners of her large mouth elevated, producing a V-shape, but her eyelids raised sadly. Her hair was shorter, making her face larger, not so hemmed in.

"I'm scared," she said.

"Well, leave," whispered Stink.

Teri looked first confused and then hurt.

"What'd they do to you?" Stink asked.

Teri looked up, more confused still. Then suddenly it dawned on her Stink had misinterpreted what she had said. "It's not the *Mercers* I'm ascared of, it's *this!*" With her finger she poked the newspaper, lying on the chair beside her. "I never met anyone like the Mercers," Teri went on, and before Stink could ask what she meant Kate returned.

Kate had heard nothing of what had been said but the expressions she encountered suggested some dreadful exchange. She suggested they start making pancakes, and delegated responsibilities.

Spirits were recovered somewhat, and then unexpectedly the Mercers arrived home. Stink felt a surge of panic. The thief in him sensed a trap and perhaps it was a trap because Siobhan Mercer smiled when she saw him and gave him a hug. He turned scarlet and Kate scolded her mother who only laughed, teasing them for their adolescent sense of propriety.

Feeling more and more an intruder in this domestic scene, Stink grew uncomfortable. Shortly he made some excuse and left. He had so wanted to talk to Teri and ask her what she had meant earlier but since there was no chance they would be alone he couldn't bear to stay.

As he rounded the corner onto Spruce Street he realized that the car behind him had that special anonymity peculiar to the police. Not for nothing was Stink known as Sly Boots. His senses were highly tuned and if he wasn't smart, he could at least think on his feet. Since the day he had watched Crunkscully get picked up by the Peugeot, and had noticed that he himself had been observed, he had wondered if someone was shadowing him. He was mad at himself because he shouldn't have been seen at all on that occasion since he was only to wait until Crunkscully left his house and then phone a number he had been given to relate the direction in which the old man was heading. It was out of curiosity he had followed to see what would happen to the man. He was paying for that mistake now.

He started to run just a little and the car accelerated. Then he knew for sure he was being followed and he dashed down someone's path towards the back garden. He heard brakes and the car door slam, and he heard footsteps in pursuit. At the end of the path there was a door into a garage, which he could see was open. He dashed through the garage and darted down the alley beyond. He lost his footing once but was up and off in a second. Cabbagetown is honeycombed with alleyways and secret passages and Stink knew them better than he knew his own mind but the plainclothes cops stayed with him and it was some time before he gave them the slip.

The rest of that day was terrible for Stink. He stayed in his room because his aunt was home and had some old ladies over. He dug out the pocket-watch Teri had given him in Suzette's. He stared at its face and counted the seconds. So much was happening so fast. He tried to think of something else, but the only thing worth thinking about was Teri and what she had said about being scared. His head was buzzing with a thousand conflicting thoughts, and when the walls threatened to close in on him, he went out into the street, expecting at any moment to be surrounded and taken away.

He passed Suzette's, open even though it was Sunday, and when he caught sight of Arlo sitting alone inside, he entered. Suzette was pounding meat in the back room, singing in rhythm with the thwacks of his cleaver.

This used to be a comforting place but now the sounds of the cleaver bothered Stink. He imagined the front door suddenly blocked by cops and himself trying to make his way out the back past three hundred pounds of solid Macedonian meat. He wouldn't sit. He would try to get Arlo to leave.

Arlo was pouring something into his coffee from a flask. He toasted Stink's arrival. "Welcome to the big time." He had his hair tied back in a tight pony tail. "Sit down. Take it easy," he said, dismissing Stink's anxious protestation. Then, as if anticipating Stink's thoughts: "Gob's got it under control, so cool it, man."

It would always be like this, thought Stink. Arlo and his kind would always know what was happening and Stink and his kind would always rely on their kindness. It suddenly was a tiresome prospect.

"I don't like this. I hate this."

Arlo, with affected camaraderie, said: "Don't we all." But the words meant nothing. He slipped into the lie like a crocodile into a swamp.

"Teri wants out," said Stink to test Arlo's reaction.

Arlo only shook his head. "No, she doesn't," he said, with so much certainty that Stink doubted his own impression and his own memory.

"She doesn't want out, Stink. Vernon Pilchard wanted out."

29

On Monday the Scollard connection to the sensational kidnapping was broadcast in an extraordinary exclusive to CBC Radio. A tape cassette had been sent to the newsroom just in time to be aired on the 6:00 news. It would be repeated every hour.

"He wants to go home," the tape said. "He misses school and is frightened. They have promised him he will be united with his parents and this pleases him and pleases his father. So his father will do everything he is asked. It is very important he does." The voice was timid at first, and then when the speaker cleared his throat it was more expressive. For a moment it was rich and controlled and then it wavered in pitch and fell to a murmur. From the same news desk Scollard had read the 6:00 news for four years before his mayoralty campaign had made it necessary to resign. Now, six years later, Scollard, or a ghost of him in his glory days, was again making news. The irony was demonic.

The police had decided to let the press believe they considered Scollard the chief suspect without actually coming out and saying it. This recording would go a long way to convincing the public, and with any luck the kidnappers, that the police were after Scollard. Brothers' story would now be generally supposed to be true and enterprising reporters would soon be combing Cabbagetown to find out exactly where Scollard had lived and with whom. Crawford hadn't told Jeff by what name Scollard was known but it was still possible someone might discover the

Elmsley Court rooming house. Crawford decided to drive over and warn the Neverlanders what to expect. He also wanted their confirmation that the voice belonged to the man they knew as Crunkscully. He would stress how important it was that they not let on the police had any doubts about Scollard being directly involved in the kidnapping. He arrived just in time for the 7:00 broadcast.

The Neverlanders gathered around the radio. "That's him all right," said Olga, beaming proudly as soon as the tape came on. Seemingly she had not grasped the significance of the recorded statement. Buck shook his hand jerkily. Chas pounded one huge fist into another and a frown cracked his face like a fissure. Werner Boost bowed his head and wrote a note in his book.

Frank switched off the radio vehemently and then pulled the plug. "It's him and it ain't him!" he said, making clear what Crawford understood, what all of them understood, with the exception of Olga.

"Somevon makes him do zis, yah?" intoned Werner.

Crawford made his pitch. "If you want to help Crunkscully, do not talk to reporters. Do not let on you've heard this tape and do not tell anyone what you think. As far as you know Crunkscully just disappeared one day as people in a rooming house sometimes do. Do you understand?"

"Oh, we'll lie real good," said Olga, seeing a golden opportunity.

"P-p-poor Scu-Scully," said Buck.

Frank walked Crawford to the door with a big arm on his shoulder. "You keep in touch, Rum Crawford," he demanded. "That Muraskin kid ain't the only one who's been took."

"I wish you could find him," shouted Olga sadly after them. "I wish I could find him."

Frank grinned a little hopelessly at Olga as he opened the door. In a voice meant for Crawford's ears only he said: "If wishes was horses then pigs would have wings." But his spirits picked up immediately. "Keep in touch," he demanded again. He said it with a sense of camaraderie, and more, with a sense of dignity.

Crawford was out the door when Werner caught up to him. "You saw me vatchingk zee area around zee haus of zis guy D'ranowitch? Vell, two days after you vas zair, I saw somesingk eenterestingk. Zair vas a trailer – a silwer von shaped like a bullet. Eet vas wery dirty unt had a sign on zee side like zis." He showed Crawford a pictogram in his notebook of a stylized tree over a wavy blue line that Crawford recognized as the emblem for Winona Enterprises.

Crawford explained that Winona was building the Royal Hawk Mews and it was probably a portable office.

Werner shook his head in vigorous denial. "Zey haf an office eenside zee buildingk eetself – I know zis unt eet vas Saturday, no von vas vorkingk zen. Unt vhat's more, eet vas gone Sunday morningk!"

Crawford looked at Boost for a moment, and Boost's eyes met his squarely. Crawford thanked him for the tip.

30

There were at least two people who had tuned in at 6:00 that Monday evening, knowing in advance the tape would be aired. The two sat in an expansive, darkly upholstered library.

One of the two men, older and larger than the other, sat behind a vast oak desk in a chair which dwarfed even his prolific frame. The other sat in a brocade-covered Louis Quattorze chair, without arms and with a back which did not inspire confidence. The man sat on the edge of the chair. Despite advanced age, the older man's face was not wrinkled except around the eyes. The forehead was high, what hair there was on his head was pale and straw-coloured, brushed down flat over the dome, and curled slightly around the lapel of a silk smoking jacket.

When the newscast was over the man behind the desk gestured with a soft, liver-spotted hand to the man on the edge of his seat that the radio should be turned off. "Very flashy, Gabriel," he said and sighed as if in resignation. His intense eyes belied the weariness in his voice. "You are a man of many parts. I might go so far as to say you show an occasional spark of brilliance. I knew that the moment I met you eighteen months ago. At that time I was also informed that you were prone to showing off. It should not come as news to you that this...disturbs me."

Gabriel Duran thought of something to say but bit his tongue. The other man continued. "We were setting up a long-term operation together. Your role was to establish a network that would provide our organization with information we could turn to profitable use. I might add that you were seeing some profits yourself. You *were* doing an exceptional job." He paused and watched the other's face for a sign. He apparently saw what he wished, for he allowed himself a slim smile. "Yes, I thought you would notice, but the use of the past tense does not necessarily indicate your usefulness to be at an end. If I were seriously considering a termination of our agreement it would not be revealed in a slip of the tongue. You might, however, take it as a warning." He coughed very slightly into one of his pale hands and then continued slowly, with great care, as if he were wording a contract. "I am a careful man, also a patient one. You are impatient and have this propensity towards vulgar display – braggadocio. A certain amount of it is effective, I dare say, in cajoling those young scamps into joining your enterprise, but it does not amuse me."

The door opened and a servant entered with a glass of milk and two pills on a silver tray. The old man took the pills and sipped like a bird from the cut-glass tumbler. The servant departed without a word, shutting the door silently.

The old man's face wrinkled and his thick tongue tried to clean away a distasteful residue on his teeth. "I don't like these hand-slapping sessions any more than you do," he said. "I do not like to babysit any of the operations under my auspices, but I cannot abide such flagrant sensationalism. This is not the stage, Gabriel. You have taken upon yourself a monumental task completely outside of our agreement, I might add."

Duran burst. "But I told you immediately!"

"Immediately *after* the deed was done," the man corrected.

"It couldn't wait. Once we'd found the boy – "

"Yes, yes I know all that," interrupted the old man. He waved away any further explanation. "You have brought this venture to my attention for two reasons, I suppose. One, you will need my help in the end, to do your 'banking,' and two, you wish to impress me. Fine. You shall be left to carry out your plan. You and your crew shall be left in peace and Arnoldin shall be left in your employ. Obviously, I will be monitoring your progress." He leaned forward and put both hands on the desk. "Suspend all this other nonsense. This is not a suggestion, it is a command. If you are going to enter the big time, act like you are. These petty harassments and jokes should stop – this B & E business especially. It is sheer spectacle and will only serve to undo your attempts to frame Scollard. The police are not fools. I do not like playing ring around the rosey with the police. Lately I have spoken to Miss Swaantje Bremane, your brother's secretary, and she informs me they are looking for his car. Why are they looking for his car?"

Gabriel Duran did not answer, nor was he meant to. It was another warning. The old man coughed again but this time the cough was more virulent and he took a silk handkerchief from his pocket. Having finished, he spoke again. "Let us be frank, Gabriel. You are an experiment. There are many talented individuals in my employ but none quite as uproarious as you and your gang of children. I am in the business of taking risks, but only so far. Be patient. If you insist on playing the fool, you will not last. It is that simple. I have not gotten rich playing the fool. Your brother has not gotten rich playing the fool. It is your turn, do not squander it."

The old man made no formal sign or statement of dismissal but the other perceived it was time to go, and he bowed ever so slightly and left. He would have liked to have bowed deeply – genuflected – with a broad sweep of arm and swoosh of plumed hat. "Thank you most merciful Grand Vizier," he would have liked to have said, "thank you." The man would not have appreciated the joke.

He thought of the man's stern face. It had been Duran's finest conceit to make that face Gob's face; it was a brilliant copy. Behind the Grand Vizier's borrowed features Gob ruled over his unruly Scrogglings. Behind that face Gob felt himself to be not merely inside the Grand Vizier's pocket, but inside his head. It was a place he longed to be.

31

It had all started innocently enough. Crawford was supposed to shuffle around, get his feet back; but instead, he felt his feet were being pulled from under him. His mood had become increasingly labile as the kidnapping investigation progressed. There were moments when he could see nothing but the negative aspects, the losing side, and then he would experience a sudden shift and everything would seem to be all right.

On the bleak side, the case was bogging down. Duranovitch could not or would not be reached. He was now in the Caribbean on his yacht and short of calling out the marines, there was no way of talking to him, which was all Crawford wanted to do. Alerted by the punctilious Swaantje Bremane, Duranovitch's legal counsel had successfully blocked Crawford's attempt to secure a search warrant for the house on Montcalm and the same counsel was making it difficult to establish Duranovitch's holdings. Investigation, however, had found another reference to the ubiquitous contractor in a most interesting place. The central police information data bank showed that Duranovitch had been indicted for espionage by the RCMP in 1964. It was an unexpected twist.

Under the auspices of Duranovitch & Son, Winona's parent company, started by Dato's father, Dato had secured an army contract to build experimental hangars for a Canadian Forces base on the DEW line. Suspicions had arisen because of Dato's known affiliation with certain underworld figures. But nothing more was brought forward to implicate Duranovitch and the charges were dropped.

Another negative aspect to the case was the fact that the park and the stockyards had been under day and night surveillance one week now since the previous Tuesday without a sign of any clandestine activity. The Animal Boy had been spotted a couple of days ago, had been chased, and had gotten away. The black Peugeot had vanished and Gob had vanished, too, according to Werner Boost. Crawford still couldn't see what connection a blind beggar could have to this business but Werner seemed utterly convinced there was a link.

None of Duranovitch's relatives or close friends most likely to have access to the Peugeot was really under suspicion although Sergeant Reuter was following up a lead on that account. He, too, had met Miss Bremane at Winona Enterprises and she had been more pleasant to him than to Sergeant English. Reuter was able to augment a point made earlier by English; not only did Bremane dislike Duran but apparently Dato disliked him, too. He had helped his brother out of innumerable jams, much to Swaantje Bremane's amazement. Time and time again Dato had gone beyond the bounds of familial duty. Sergeant Reuter wasn't able to determine from Bremane why. If Duran had access to his brother's pocketbook and car, he probably had access to his house, and Crawford wanted into that house, warrant or not.

There was one possibility suggested by Detective Skene by means of a leading question: "What if a patrol car was passing down Montcalm one night and suddenly the coppers happened to hear another scream coming from Duranovitch's house? Wouldn't it be their duty to get in one way or another?"

McIlwane, who sat on the team in an advisory capacity, didn't like the implications of the idea. One or two others nodded tacitly, one way or the other. It was an uncomfortable moment. Skene chuckled to himself. "It could always turn out to be another raccoon," he suggested. So for the time being the investigation came down to a search for the elusive Gabriel Duran.

Crawford felt sure Skene would make his break-in on Duranovitch's house, warrant or not.

There was another side to the case which worried Crawford. A man like Bernard Muraskin would have enemies; lots of them in high and low places. The kidnapping could easily be tied in with something very big – something along the lines the media had originally speculated – political or international intrigue. The RCMP were following up that angle. At his worst moment, Crawford got the ominous feeling he was leading an entire investigation on a false trail.

It was Tuesday, November 11. Something had to happen soon. There had been another meeting which had broken off for lunch and Crawford and Beryl English went to a not-very-quick lunch stand.

"You sound like my mother saying her rosary," said English, sitting across the formica from Crawford.

"I'm not praying," said Crawford, who had been mumbling. "Except that our lunch will arrive."

"I am," said English. "In fact on Sunday I lit a candle, one of the two-fifty models that'll burn for days."

"Till Friday?" asked Crawford pointedly.

English didn't think so.

⌖

Tuesday, November 11 brought one new development in the case. The Muraskins received a letter, by special delivery, informing them of a phone call that would be made to them at 4:00 that afternoon. David was to speak first and assure them of his identity by answering some simple family questions asked by Connie Muraskin. Then Bernard Muraskin was to say one of the following sentences: "Yes, I will pay the price of 1.5 million dollars in cash by Friday" or "No, I will not pay the price of 1.5 million dollars in cash by Friday." There were to be no alternatives whatsoever and if the answer was no the boy would be shot.

Crawford was at the house along with electronics personnel in order to tape the call. It soon was apparent that any attempt to locate the callers was being blocked electronically from the source.

As promised, David spoke first. Bravely and with little emotion he recited the following message: "I am fine. Please tell Daddy to pay for my release. This man Scollard will kill me if he doesn't." Connie, following the demands in the letter, asked him his grandmother Muraskin's nickname. For one moment he laughed as he answered "Pecksniff," and then he burst into tears and was forcibly dragged from the phone. Mrs. Muraskin also cried but with grim determination covered the receiver so as not to give her son's captors the pleasure of hearing her. Bernard Muraskin repeated the phrase, "Yes, I will pay the price of 1.5 million dollars in cash on Friday," with the control of a man talking to his investment advisor but he, too, was visibly shaken.

The voice of Scollard followed. "Directions will come shortly. Follow them. Do not try anything funny."

Later, listening to the recording of this phone call, the difference between the two speakers was quite clear. David had spoken directly into the phone; the voice they presumed to be Scollard's had been recorded. At 4:00 P.M., Tuesday, November 11, David Muraskin was still alive. Scollard might easily be dead.

Connie Muraskin recovered somewhat from her emotional outburst, cheered by her husband with the fact that David was still alive. She turned to Crawford. "The other man – his voice – it doesn't sound like the voice of a monster."

"It – he isn't," said Crawford. "Unless we're very much mistaken, he has been kidnapped, too. Like I said, he's ill, not sick." It wasn't a clear distinction but this time Connie Muraskin seemed to understand.

After departing reassurances, Crawford slipped through the police guard and the paparazzi milling at the Muraskins' front gate, and made his way over to Elmsley Court.

"Vhat about zee trailer?" said Boost, greeting him at the door.

"One of my men is checking into it," said Crawford. Reuter

had told him that Winona owned six Airstream trailers used as portables and Crawford had him check whether one of them might have been at the Royal Hawk Mews site on Saturday.

Crawford was invited for supper and accepted the invitation. Frank told him it was to be a special event and Crawford, deciding to contribute, left and returned in a while with wine and beer and a box of French pastries for dessert.

When he returned, Frank was wearing British army dress. "You're not the only sergeant," he said, saluting and proudly showing off his chevrons. He had served as a saper in the Second World War and wore his uniform every Armistice Day.

Werner, arriving in the commonroom, suggested with a wink that he would put on his uniform too. He chuckled when Frank glared at him. There were some things Frank did not find amusing and the Second World War was one of them.

Crawford launched in to helping with the dinner, and apart from the keen attention Olga rivetted to his every move, he soon felt at home in the strange house.

Listening to the Neverlanders, Crawford found himself thinking what a field day Doctor Wenzel would have with the group. From his own undergrad psychology courses he could itemize their problems: marked loosening of association, prone in their dialogue to becoming bogged down in a morass of trivia impeding the communication of a central idea, prone to outrageous circumstantiality, moods – labile, prone to flights of ideas and delusions of reference.

But such statements did not explain *who* they were or why Crawford liked them. They were survivors, that was part of it, and they were original. But there was more to it than that; something that Crawford had noticed before under cover on Skid Row. Despite the hardships of their day-to-day existence, they lived a simpler, less stressful life. There were few demands, conversation was easy. He had met a number of doctors and businessmen on the skids and although they lived with their regrets, they had no desire to return to the rat race. In a way they were the lucky ones; when the spring broke they didn't die of ulcers or a heart attack and they didn't go mad either. They found somewhere and some way to live with a broken spring rattling around inside.

In the case of the Neverlanders, fate had brought them kindly to 14 Elmsley Court and Frank Qualtrough. He served them now a recipe he picked up in France as befitted the occasion. He called it his "Top-o'-the-Stove Rat-a-Tat-Tooie" and it was good, if piquant.

The Neverlanders were interested in the case and to hear them talk there had been only one kidnapping – Crunk-scully's – for he was one of their own. They were doing their part towards recovering him. Taking their cue from Werner they had taken to roaming the streets and faithfully reporting any suspicious findings to Crawford. An Irish wolfhound with three legs had seemed particularly suspicious to Olga and she had followed it home. She had even memorized the address. Buck drove the streets late at night in his monstrous Caddy, sometimes he said with the lights out for extra secrecy, and with eyes p-p-peeled. Chas described Tommy to Crawford in vivid detail. He had decided to search for him, because he was quite certain Tommy was implicated. His ulterior motive was scarcely concealed. "The Elmsley Court Irregulars," said Frank, the proud ex-sergeant.

The evening wore on and Crawford got pleasantly drunk. He had his mitre set in case anyone wanted to reach him; beyond that, there was nothing he could do that night. Several times his thoughts went to Detective Skene who was probably pulling off his clandestine raid at that very minute, only a few blocks away.

His mind drifted in and out of the conversation but nobody seemed to mind since they were all doing the same thing. Drifting. Frank told war stories; the time he had thrown a hand grenade into a shed where a German sniper was hiding and the shed had been full of Camembert cheese. Chas played the harmonica and Olga talked about how difficult it was to be Adolf Hitler and how she would rather have been Hedy Lamarr.

Werner followed Crawford out to the porch when it was time to leave. It was a frosty night but Werner didn't seem to notice.

He stood in his shirt sleeves lightly clapping his fine fingers together in thought. "Haf you heard of zee *Vehmgericht?*" he said after a minute. Crawford hadn't. "Eet vas a tribunal set up een medieval times een Vestphalia. Een irregular and wery secret tribunals zey meted out justice on zoze who zey considered society's offenders. Zis Gob ees such a sing, yah?"

Crawford looked askance at him. Boost was like a bulldog when he got hold of an idea. "You really think Gob is involved in this?"

"Vhere ees he?" asked Boost. Crawford shook his head. "Zee tracks een zee park – zee *vheelchair* tracks. Eet all makes sense!"

Crawford raised and lowered his shoulders. "What about this *Vehmgericht* business?"

Werner continued. "Society has not bin so goot on me too, so vhat do I, Verner Boost, do? I rob a leetle. So who cares? I redress zee balance. But zis Gob, he screams at people on zee street unt he ees full of hate. So maybe zat ees all von big act but eet ees not an act at zee same time, if you see vhat I mean. I steal, yah, but I do not hate. But Gob hates. Mark my word eet ees *Vehmgericht*. Zee whole sing ees a wendetta."

Crawford nodded. "Against who?" he asked.

"All of us!" cried Boost.

Crawford thanked him and left.

32

Stink had been creeping around like a golem absorbed in his own shadow. Something was up, according to Arlo, and yet there had been no announcement of a meeting and the delay left him feeling abandoned. Finally, Tuesday, in the laundromat, on the chipped notice board beside the handwritten advertisements for movers and babysitters, Stink had at last found a coded message. There would be a meeting at 8:00 that night, somewhere new. The Royal Hawk Mews, number 6.

Stink had no desire this time to arrive early for the meeting. At 7:55, he found his way through the deeply rutted site by the illumination of a single light standard which wavered in the wind, making the construction-rough ground ambiguous with shadows. Number 6 was surrounded by a metal exoskeleton of scaffolding which chinked and squeaked in the wind. As the windows were boarded up with plywood sheets, Stink was momentarily confused. Then he saw the way to enter was through the basement, and he slithered down into an aluminum window-well and dropped through onto the floor. A tooth of aluminum filing caught his finger and he knelt on the cold concrete sucking at the tear until the warmth of saliva mingled with the blood and the stinging subsided. Upstairs he heard a familiar din.

The scene, however, was not familiar. The eyes which met his were recognizable yet strangely cast. The room seemed to reel like an hallucination. He saw in every face panic released in short, stifled high-pitched laughs. Stomach butterflies were choked with cigarette smoke. The chatter was different as well, subdued and yet electric. It was not only the enormity of the project that created this frisson but not having the security of the park cushioning them on all sides. Vulnerability sparked the excitement.

Gob was in rare form, parked in his wheelchair on a raised area overlooking a pit that was to be a sunken living room. In the pit the Knot sat on boxes of tiles and sawhorses. Some more adventurous souls sat on the unfinished staircase and still others sat, legs dangling, on the balcony which overlooked the living room on three sides. Gob could not have been happier. He was on stage. Number 6 was a theatre complete with pit and Gods. There was a man with him. No man other than Gob had ever attended a meeting of the Knot. Gob introduced him as Llaldhar Arnoldin. He was paunchy, middle aged, with curly hair, no cheek bones and a mouth like a fish. He leaned against a wall directly behind Gob with his hands on his hips so that his jacket hung open, revealing a revolver in a shoulder holster. Everyone but Stink was so distracted by the atmosphere of tension, and this stranger in their midst, that they didn't notice that Teri was not there. If Gob had noticed, he didn't say as much. Stink stole into a shadowy corner and perched himself on a drum of pitch. For him, the room was full of Teri's absence.

"You are not on the outskirts of Cabbagetown now but at its very heart," said Gob. And so the meeting began.

By shifting only slightly, Stink managed to curl his whole body into the shadows. He felt a strange sensation come over him; he had never been in Gob's presence and so far away from him at the same time. Stink had never seen a play but in his dark corner he imagined that's what it would be like. Gob's gaze seemed fixed on some point just above his audience's head.

He was talking about suspending all wreaks and wrinkles to please the Grand Vizier. He warned those with B & E Messenger Service uniforms to return them. Behind him, Llaldhar Arnoldin stifled a yawn and then started picking at his ear with a finishing nail. Stink was struck by the man's coolness. Then Gob got onto the kidnapping, how it was the chance the Knot had been waiting for. Stink found himself writhing inside. He listened more closely than he had ever listened to Gob before. So close that he heard through the words Gob spoke, clear through to where they were constructed in the throat and lips, then further still to where the words were inchoate in Gob's teeming bone-box. *This was the revolution!* The revolution Gob had promised him. The revolution his father had always talked about; freedom from all that was complicated in the world. Gob did not divulge the process by which the ransom money would be recovered, saying that would come later. He had called the meeting as a warning, and to prepare the Knot for what was to come. He announced another meeting at the same place in two days' time, on the eve of the day Muraskin was to pay up.

Stink was anxious to leave. His head threatened to explode. Confused emotions were at war in him, fear dominant. Again he felt transparent. Even in his shadowy corner he was sure the others would notice what raged inside him. He knew they mustn't see it. He must get out.

Just before the meeting adjourned Gob pulled a briefcase from under his wheelchair. With a great sense of ceremony he opened it and dramatically withdrew a small black revolver.

"A .22 magnum, Ivor Johnson Cadet," he announced. There was a hush in the room. Gob took two more of the dark little machines from his case. "A wonderful *first* gun," he said. "Such is the nature of this escapade that Gob has decided on a special guard of these premises on the night of the fourteenth. Who shall it be?" He eyed the expectant group, taking them all in with his gaze, even Stink this time, much to the boy's torment.

"My Ruffler," he said handing a pistol to Earnie. "My Rogue," he said and Arlo approached the dais. "And last but not least, my Angler." With this, Captain Hakum stepped forward and received his weapon. Gob leaned back in his chair with a smile like a grandad at Christmas. "You have three days to familiarize yourself with the workings of these toys. Be careful on whom you practise." He chuckled. It was meant to be a joke.

Then the meeting was over, or at least it was over for most of the gang. Stink heard his name called out and he stopped dead in his tracks. He wanted to run but that would have been suicide. He turned and approached Gob.

"Your little friend is missing," said Gob wheeling himself up to the very edge of his improvised stage.

There was a click and, snapping his head sideways, Stink noticed Captain Hakum examining his new toy.

Gob laughed at the look of fear on Stink's face. "My, my, but we're jumpy. Is there something we have to tell Gob?"

Stink tried to speak but couldn't. He shook his head.

Gob's smile diminished. "Where is she?" he demanded.

Stink shook his head again. From the corner of his eye he could still see the sleek black barrel of Hakum's revolver. "You needn't worry, Sly Boots, the Captain won't harm you." Stink turned his attention back to Gob. Gob leaned over him. "Do you mean you don't *know* where Teri is, or won't *say?*"

"Don't know," Stink managed. He didn't and Gob sensed as much.

"But you will let Gob know, won't you, when you *do* know?" Stink stared into Gob's eyes. They seemed deeper and blacker than he had ever known them to be.

"Yes," he said. Gob's smile widened.

❖

Stink had planned on going to the Mercers' directly after the meeting but not yet two blocks from the mews he changed his course and headed south towards his aunt's apartment. So did his shadow. There wasn't a member of the gang better at tailing someone than Stink; it didn't take him long to guess he was being tailed himself. He thought Gob hadn't believed him. So they wanted Teri, did they, and he was supposed to lead them to her?

Stink darted down an alley and up a flight of concrete stairs to another alley. The shadow followed. Wherever Stink went, he could not dodge him. Stink smiled to himself. The consequences of what he was doing were drastic but Stink could think no further than the exercise at hand. Consequences happened in the future and that was when he would deal with them. For the moment his perceptions were heightened and his strategy, skimpy though it might be, was razor sharp. He had caught a glimpse of his pursuer, it was Wagtail.

It was an insult; not just being tailed – everything. The revolution. It was just another scam; bigger than anything else Gob had conceived but no different in kind. Gob had forgotten his promise or never meant it. What surprised Stink more than anything else was that he was not really surprised. The moment of revelation passed through him and was gone but in so doing, it had sounded a quite different alarm. He was afraid for Teri but more than anything else he wanted to join her, wherever she was going. But first things first.

He had noticed the unused garage before. He had checked it out. The overhead door was badly warped. It would not go all the way up, but it was otherwise sturdy and the mechanism to open it was broken inside although it worked on the outside. There was no other entrance to the little garage, or exit.

Wagtail thought Stink had entered the ramshackle building. He had seemed to, made a noise as though he had. Stooping almost to his knees the boy passed under the broken door and as soon as he had done so, and had a chance to change his mind, Stink jumped from the bushes beside the garage and slammed the door down to the ground locking Wagtail inside. Stink could hear him banging his fists on the door even before he had left the alley.

Pausing to catch his breath, Stink considered his fate. What had been a raging impulse only half an hour earlier was now a cold certainty. It was all over. Locking Wagtail in the garage had been an act of revolt. There was no going back to the Knot. There were two things he must do now, escape and make certain Teri had done the same.

It was with the latter consideration in mind he set off towards the Mercers' house. Halfway there he was suddenly struck by another terrible certainty. Gob would not simply have sent Wagtail after him if he really suspected Teri of copping out on the gang. Someone would have been sent directly to the Mercers' and someone else to Teri's mother's place. No stone would be left unturned in finding the truant. He broke into a cold sweat, and began to canter. In his mind's eye he saw again his encounter with Gob and he heard the click of Hakum's gun which had frightened him as surely as if it had been levelled at his head. He felt that now it was.

Trembling inside, Stink stopped once more. From where he stood he could see the Mercers' house down the street. The lights were on, pale behind drawn curtains. It seemed so peaceful. With an effort Stink tried to calm his rampaging pulse. There was nowhere to hide directly in front of their house. Guards were stationed, no doubt, across the street. He had no idea how extensive the watch might be but, taking no chances, he slipped down a narrow path between two houses to the alley which passed behind the Mercers'. Checking that it was clear he made his way down towards the house. The Mercers' backyard, as he remembered it, was large, affording several places to hide. A large stone garage faced the alley and a four-foot-high stone fence surrounded the yard. Stink's approach to the house was painstakingly slow but at last he reached the corner of the stone wall. An ornamental wooden door was built into the fence and peering through the fretwork Stink surveyed the snow-covered garden. There was a grape arbour by the garage and crouched behind it peering up at the house was the lank figure of Captain Hakum. His head was bent back, his eyes rivetted to a second-storey window.

Digging silently with his bare fingers Stink extricated a rock from the frozen earth. He looked through the gate again; apparently he had not been heard for Hakum's eyes had not strayed from the lace-curtained window. Stink clutched the rock tightly. It was the size of a large fist.

The stories of Hakum came back to him; his victims seemed

to hang in the cold night air all around him. Stink ducked down again and leaned against the rock wall, scarcely able to believe what he was contemplating. Teri was safe as long as she was inside, he told himself. And why would she come out that late? Stink's mind raced. Perhaps he should call the police and they could round up Hakum. They at least would be armed. He was certain that he couldn't tackle Hakum himself.

He was still trying to think of what to do when suddenly he heard the crunch of footsteps in the snow on the other side of the fence. He froze – the steps seemed to be heading towards the gate – towards him. They stopped and after a moment Stink dared to look through the fretwork. Hakum had moved out from the arbour into the open. He was kneeling on one knee and with horror Stink realized he had his gun held steadily before him in both his hands. Glancing up, Stink received another shock, for the window on the second floor was no longer empty. Two silhouettes had appeared behind the lace curtain; Kate and Teri were facing each other and talking. Kate was crying, or seemed to be, for her chin was on her chest and her shoulders heaved now and then. Teri's head was perched as still as a stone on her long neck.

Hakum raised his gun.

All in one motion Stink reached through the gate and sprung the latch and threw open the gate. Hakum was fifteen feet away and so absorbed in his target that his reaction was slow. By the time he turned on his knee to face the intruder, Stink was ten feet from him with his own simple weapon raised high in the air. Hakum lost his balance just for an instant and Stink, with all the strength that he could muster, let the rock fly. The missile smashed down on Hakum's head, and he crumpled sideways into the snow. The gun, unfired, fell from his hand.

Stink stared at him, at what he had done. He looked up at the window. The two silhouettes had become one in an embrace. Stink dug the cold black revolver from the snow and slipped out of the yard, pulling the gate shut behind him.

33

Crawford was not surprised to find headquarters buzzing Wednesday morning. As predicted Skene had conducted his commando raid on Duranovitch's Montcalm Street residence.

They found only the vaguest of human remains; a record on a turntable that was not dusty. Skene said the place "smelled used," but he was referring to sensations perceived by the intuitive nose; there were no noticeable odours of habitation.

The raid had been disappointing, but controversial. A neighbour had phoned the police about the break-in and since no one had come to take her report, she phoned Winona Enterprises who in turn got in touch with Duranovitch's lawyers. It didn't take them long to guess what was going on and they were demanding an investigation into the break-in. Skene's excuse of having heard suspicious sounds did not wash. The "dustlessness" of the record on the turntable was explained by the attorney as being due to a housekeeper who came in once a week; a housekeeper who obviously listened to Duranovitch's records. Not one of the neighbours Crawford had spoken to mentioned a housekeeper.

Beryl English could still not track down Gabriel Duran and his elusiveness made him more and more interesting. Only one of his relatives even cared whether Duran was dead or alive, his uncle Yaroslav Duranovitch, Uncle Yogi, as he was called. But he hadn't seen his nephew in over a year and thought he might be in New York or Hollywood. Gabriel was an actor.

As it turned out, Duran, like his brother, had a criminal record dating from several years earlier, for burglary in Montreal. And to make everything nice and cozy, Duran figured, if only nominally, in an illegal business practice suit in Toronto which featured, among others, Anselmo Cannelli, Dato's partner in DurCan. Gabriel Duran must have been a very small fish for, in the end, he was not even arraigned. But small fish grew.

The day before, English had found out his former agent's name for Actors' Equity and was trying to locate the man who was apparently no longer in business. She had found at the equity office a list of Duran's most recent engagements and they were not all that recent. He had not acted under contract for two years and had not paid his union dues for one. English had dug up several photographs of the man from programs, an article in a theatre magazine and a handful of reviews in newspapers. The photographs were not very helpful for, in each case, he was heavily disguised in roles as diverse as Frankenstein and Martin Luther. He had done some film extra work and she was following up that lead. Nobody seemed to have his resumé pictures on file any longer. There were rumours that his agent was promoting freaks and animal acts.

There had been an interesting development concerning the silver trailer Boost said he had seen outside the Royal Hawk Mews the previous Saturday. Sergeant Reuter had discovered that none of the Airstream trailers which fit Boost's description belonging to Winona Enterprises should have been at the construction site the previous Saturday. The foreman was not on duty on the weekend so if any of the trailers had been used it had been used by someone with a key to the stockyard. Reuter had had a forensic expert look at the trailers. The man had taken samples of dirt from the trailer's tires comparing it to dirt at the site of the mews. It would take time to get the results, and they wouldn't be altogether helpful. If it was not one of the Winona trailers then it was an imposter. Then what? A crackdown on all Airstream trailers – a helicopter reconnaissance of the city?

Crawford's mind turned to the Our Town Body Shop behind Duranovitch's house. There might not have been anything there when he looked but it would be a great place to park a car or a trailer or both. For that matter, it would be a good place to park a thirteen-year-old boy who was worth a million plus. The shop wasn't owned by Duranovitch. That much had been ascertained. The property belonged to Centre Town Development, which was a subsidiary of a major investment firm. The owners flip-flopped on allowing a search of the building. At first they had said yes and then they changed their mind, demanding a search warrant. It seemed to be a manoeuvre for more time but within an hour after having said no, the company changed its mind again.

Crawford and Reuter arranged to meet a company representative at the shop, and arrived there before him. Crawford chuckled to himself when he saw Werner Boost duck out of sight further down Tepworth Lane. The Elmsley Court Irregulars on patrol.

At 2:00, a grey-suited, white-Corvetted employee squealed to a stop outside the shop. He was friendly enough if reluctant to take his expensive suit for a walk in such a grimy place. Crawford suspected that the man's discomfort was that of the fastidious in squalid surroundings, not of the guilty.

The large space was empty but for a small, walled office at the far end near the back door which led out into Montcalm Alley. The office was empty. There was a staircase beside it which led down to a partial basement. There was no basement under the shop's floor. There was a parts room now empty but for the shelving, a closet-sized room which housed the electrical boxes, and a filthy washroom which stunk of mildew. There certainly was no sign of any use.

The building had been empty for three years. They were "sitting on it," Grey Suit explained. He glanced at his watch a number of times and murmured something about a "liquid lunch that just wouldn't quit," which he had apparently left to open up the shop. He was obviously hoping to get back. Crawford was in no hurry. He stood for some time in the large grey cavity, like Jonah in an oil-stained whale, thinking and observing. The place intrigued him.

Holes capped with metal discs showed the places where pneumatic hoists had been. There were also several pits where mechanics could work under a car parked on ramps to either side of the pit. There was one pit that was wider than the rest and longer, presumably for working under a large truck. The construction seemed newer; the concrete was less stained than the other pits. Crawford walked down the ramp into the pit and looked around. There was nothing much. Reuter had taken a few Polaroids for the record but it was not possible to say if the place had been recently used.

Grey Suit left as soon as he had locked up. The Corvette's tires squealed in departing, and squealed again as the car turned the corner and vanished.

There was a call from headquarters almost as soon as the two detectives were back in the car. They were to make their way directly to the Muraskins'. A parcel had arrived, but was not delivered to the door. It had been left between the spokes on the Muraskins' wrought iron fence. It was ticking.

When Crawford and Reuter arrived, a bomb squad was already at work. It didn't make much sense to blow up someone from whom you were hoping to extort money; and not much to Crawford's surprise the bomb was a hoax. The hoax, however, was cruel; explosive in its own way. Not dangerous to life and limb but to the senses. The face of the clock had been replaced by David Muraskin's face. Where a trademark might have been was a message in transfer letters: "No funny stuff," it warned. It might have been a general reminder but Crawford couldn't help thinking it referred to the raid on Duranovitch's. Something the police had done had been too close for comfort.

McIlwane arrived at the scene. Although he had little input into the investigation anymore, he was following its progress closely, and Rum was glad to see him. "The same mind that conceived the B & E crap," he said after examining the clock.

Crawford nodded, frowning. "He won't quit fooling around, that's what gets me."

McIlwane almost smiled. "If we're lucky, maybe he'll fool around once too often."

�֍

That evening Crawford again found himself at the Muraskins'. The arrangement and conditions of the ransom drop-off had arrived by Special Delivery.

The plan for the ransom delivery was extensive, and for the first time the police were confronted with the possible proportions of the operation they were up against. There was not to be one drop-off point, but forty, located the length and breadth of the city. Analysis of the array of locations revealed no particular pattern and suggested no centre. Judging from the illogical locus of the joined points on the map, it seemed unlikely the pick-up was to be accomplished by one party alone, for it would take them a month. The locations were not always out-of-the-way spots; several public lockers were to be utilized in apparent defiance of the police. The conditions made it quite clear that any attempt at blocking any one of the pick-ups would be fatal to David Muraskin. Each individual making a pick-up would be under the constant protection of four armed guards, all of whom would be in radio contact with a central headquarters. Any ambush by the police would be unlikely to net all five individuals and if such interference occurred, a warning would be given. If it were not obeyed, David Muraskin would be "executed."

Furthermore, according to the plan, the individual making the pick-up was not going to be the same individual who delivered the parcel to its final destination, and would not even know where that final destination was, so it would be useless – and dangerous – to trap any one of the pick-up crew. Nor was it advised that the police attempt to follow any carrier since there would be a variety of check-points through which the carrier would pass under observation. The operation was to be conducted like an army manoeuvre and the investigative team had no reason to doubt this gang's ability to pull it off. The police were hamstrung.

The size of the operation was disheartening. It dwarfed the investigation, which seemed now only to have been nibbling away at one small corner of the case, or so Crawford felt. The cops were virtually helpless.

The police notified Muraskin Thursday morning that he might start preparing for the drop-off and he sounded fatalistic. The money didn't really concern him, only David's safety. He made it clear that he did not want any police interference on the pick-up. He was a shrewd businessman and recognized a shrewd opponent. He demanded only that proof of David's well-being be established at the time of the pick-up which was scheduled for any time after eight the following evening. This too was provided for in the plan: a phone call. A question from Connie, a one-word answer by David, just as in the previous call. According to the plan David would simply be dropped off somewhere downtown at midnight of the fourteenth.

34

Crawford breakfasted at a coffee shop near the precinct with Beryl English and Derrick Reuter at 6:30, after a night of empty planning. The sun would not rise for some time; it would think twice about doing so at all. The weather had turned unexpectedly cold, and it was not a lot warmer inside. The cook flipped pancakes, wearing his jacket and gloves. The three sergeants, all in civvies, were his only clientele. They took their time and drank lots of coffee.

Crawford sat across from Reuter, who had bought the morning *Sun*. There was a full-colour cartoon on the front page of a giant rope in a knot which was strangling several caricatures of policemen and detectives – himself prominently, dressed as Sherlock Holmes. The faces – choked and red – poked out from between thick strands of hemp, while two giant fists at the edge of the picture pulled the knot tighter. Underneath the knot, in its shadow, was the caption: "One More Day."

Back at headquarters, Skene and others were attempting to establish a strategy to follow up the boy's release. It was generally accepted that the collecting of the ransom could not be averted and so attention was turned to capturing the kidnappers after the fact.

Wearily Crawford checked out his desk. Lying there was a most surprising message. At 8:00 he phoned the number and found the party had long since been awake. She invited him to her hotel.

When Connie Scollard opened her hotel-room door, Crawford was immediately struck by her wariness. She was beautiful; suffering had not reduced her in appearance but there was a guardedness in her manner that he sensed was learned, not instinctive.

She had ordered coffee and croissants, which sat on a table by a window overlooking Nathan Philips Square. No one was skating on the rink. Civil servants with their hats battened down fought the cold wind and streamed into City Hall.

Crawford had called her once in Vancouver detailing the police's beliefs but since then she had heard no further word on whether or not her husband was implicated in the Muraskin kidnapping or, for that matter, whether anyone was still looking for him at all. She feared he had been lost in the shuffle and had decided to fly out and determine for herself exactly what was going on. Crawford apologized for not keeping her informed on the progress of the case. She was not indignant about this omission and thanked Crawford for his prompt attention to her call. These civilities taken care of, he briefly caught her up on the situation, making her aware that the police believed that if they found David Muraskin, they might find Ross Scollard as well.

"Do you think he is alive?" she asked.

"I can't say," Crawford answered. "We have heard his voice on tape only."

"This kind of trauma would kill an average person in his condition," said Connie after a moment's reflection. "It would bring on a massive stroke – that's what happens to a lot of Alzheimer patients, you know. But not Ross. He is a very spunky man." She smiled radiantly for a moment.

As she sipped at her coffee and stared across the street to City Hall, Crawford considered what must be going through her head as she stared at that edifice and recalled the office her husband had won and never had time to fill.

"I think I know how this started," she said at last. "Some of it anyway. If our child...if Amelia had been a boy, we were going to call him Ross after his father and his father's father. We were quite sure that I would have a son; it wasn't a question really of preference, just feeling. Scollard even had a silly business card printed up one day when I was still pregnant. It read: 'Ross Scollard, Baby' and there was an address and all. He was delighted with the birth of his daughter and never once showed the slightest disappointment that there was no 'Ross Jr.' but later when his health was failing, he would sometimes ask where his son was. I burned all the silly business cards, but Scollard asked anyway. It was the one thing he didn't forget. It's strange to say, but his son was never more than a memory."

She looked up at Crawford to see whether he could understand such an idea. He could. She continued. "As his condition worsened, he would have dreadful dreams that some awful fate had befallen his son. He would be depressed or horribly angry, sometimes blaming me, but more often than not blaming himself. I was having enough trouble looking after him physically without having to look after his fantasy life, but the final straw came one day when he took Mellie out in the stroller for a walk to the nearby bakery and came back without her. I eventually found her unharmed, the stroller still sitting in front of the bakery, but it was finally too much to put up with any longer."

She didn't expect sympathy. She lived with the decision she had had to make. "There's something else that might interest you," she said. "I visited him in the hospital for two years after he was admitted. Finally I accepted an offer to join my father's business in Vancouver; I was in no position to turn it down. I have a daughter to support and it was difficult to tell at that time whether or not Ross even recognized me or Amelia anymore. Some thought was given to having him moved out to Vancouver but there was no facility as good as the Dalton, and he seemed relatively happy there. I remember visiting him one day a few months before I left. He had remembered about the mayoralty race and wanted me to tell him about it. The following day I took in a scrapbook I had made with all the newspaper stories. I left it with him. He seemed to enjoy reading it. It was shortly after that he started calling himself Crunkscully. He insisted that everyone call him that, including me, and one day he showed me a picture in the scrapbook of himself at an all-candidates debate. The heading was 'Scollard Pulls Through in the Crunch.' He had pointed at it and smiled. Somehow he had made a name out of that heading – it was like a title he bestowed on himself. Crunkscully. I think he will pull through," she said wistfully. "I hope you'll find him."

They talked a while longer. Crawford thought to mention Elmsley Court and Frank and what care Scollard had received. Connie was touched. She hoped she would meet them, she told Crawford, to thank them in person.

Connie would stay in Toronto. Crawford left with a promise to keep in contact. Out on the street again the wind almost tore Crawford's coat away from him. The cold had frosted up his car locks. When he finally did get in, the car wouldn't start. The day was not beginning well.

35

Two days after the incidents which effectively terminated his membership in the Knot, Stink had collected his savings from his closet. In the obscurity of an abandoned warehouse where he had been holed up, he weighed his chances of survival. His thoughts turned again and again to Teri. He had only been able to sleep fitfully, when at all. His muscles twitched, his head burned.

There could be no escape; Gob had made that abundantly clear. Stink could not imagine a place in which Gob would not find him out. He did not think he had killed Hakum and by now, Hakum and Wagtail would have made their reports to Gob. Stink would be a marked man. But he did have two things in his favour; he was Sly Boots, the best sneak in the gang, and he had a gun.

On Thursday morning he phoned Teri. Reuben Mercer answered the phone and told him Teri was not in. "Stuart?" he asked and there was something in his tone of voice which stopped Stink from hanging up. "Teri told us last night she was part of some kind of gang and they were after her. Are you part of this?" There was more concern than accusation in the question.

"I was," said Stink. "Only I got out too. Like Teri."

"She seemed frightened," Mercer continued. "In fact, Mrs. Mercer has taken the girls out of town for a few days."

Two feelings collided in Stink at the news. Teri was gone. He wanted to cry and he wanted to scream for joy. "They got away?" he asked breathlessly.

"This morning at about eight," came the reply. "Stuart, if you need any help...." Mercer didn't finish his offer before Stink thanked him.

"You'll hear from me somewhere," he said and placed the receiver in its cradle. So half his wishes had come true. Teri had escaped. As for himself, incredible confidence began to brew in him. There was nowhere Gob would not find him. Unless, of course, Gob was dead.

✤

In a dilapidated garbage shed full of boxes behind a hardware store on Parliament Street, Stink made himself a new nest. Through a crack in the door he could see across Tepworth Lane to where the Royal Hawk Mews stood darkly. He had been in place early enough to watch the Knot arrive for the Thursday meeting Gob had told them of, early enough to watch the guards find novel ways to play Bo Peep in this less isolated venue. He had stayed all evening in his garbage shed, long enough to see Llaldhar Arnoldin let the gang out of a back door into Tepworth Lane, one at a time, like sky divers over enemy territory. Stink prepared himself.

Ever since he had talked to Reuben Mercer the idea had grown in him – a world without Gob. For the first time in his young life something like freedom seemed at least possible. *This was the revolution,* he had realized in a rare moment of clarity. Fear was the confusion, not the world but fear. Stink feared nothing so much as Gob and to end Gob would be to put an end to fear.

When the back door of number 6 Royal Hawk Mews had closed for the last time, and he felt sure the guards had dispersed for the night, Stink make his way to the basement window, through which he had made his entry Tuesday night. The board would be replaced soon, and he had no sooner shinnied into the basement than he had heard heavy footsteps on the basement stairs. Directly across the floor was an alcove in which a water heater and furnace stood, and it was wedged in between these two utilities that Stink listened as the window hole was covered up with its plywood shield. The man retreated once this was done and was soon on his way back upstairs. Stink waited. His rather simple-minded plan had not taken into account Llaldhar Arnoldin. It had been difficult enough to imagine killing Gob. He knew he must think fast for they could leave at any moment. No thoughts came to him. His idea seemed to evaporate before his eyes.

It was with great surprise that he heard footsteps descending the stairs again and with greater surprise still he saw that one of the men wielded a huge silver breakman's flash. Gob had come to him. Fate, for once, was on Stink's side. Gob was trapped there with him, a pig in a slip. All Stink had to do was pull the trigger. Gob was carrying his folded wheelchair under an arm. He was speaking and although it was not entirely Gob's voice, there was enough of Gob in it to make Stink's blood tingle.

"I never made it to Broadway, Llal," he said. "But perhaps I will after all. They say there are ten thousand runaways living within a few blocks of Times Square. What a show we could put on, eh? The big time."

Arnoldin responded too quietly for Stink to hear but Gob laughed loudly. By then the two stood fifteen feet from Stink at the north basement wall. He wanted to jump out and fire again and again but something stopped him. The two men were chatting about the pick-up the following night. Number 6 was to be their headquarters, he learned. So there could be another chance if he failed now. He knew already he was going to fail; Gob's voice was like a powerful drug on all Stink's senses. He doubted he could even draw his gun let alone fire it. He watched, hopelessly stupefied. Gob shone the flashlight up to where the floor joists met the sill on the top of the concrete wall. He must have moved some lever for a low rumbling was set up which vibrated the furnace next to Stink. The wall was scored with expansion joints at two-foot centres and to Stink's amazement one of these portions of concrete was opening now directly in front of Gob. The two men passed through the narrow space and then the thick slab slid back into place, leaving Stink staring into the dark at nothing. It was the final tyranny. He left.

36

Ransom day arrived cold; as bitterly cold as the day before. At 5:00 Crawford left a briefing session that had gone on since noon. He had been up until midnight the night before at another such session and had slept poorly. He was running now on a mixture of adrenalin and caffeine and felt neither tired nor anything else.

The final briefing had been to confirm the strategy set for that evening. A tactical squad was to be on the alert and a general warning was out to all patrol units in the city. Skene, as the senior detective on the investigative team, was to remain at headquarters in charge of operations. A unit under Sergeant Reuter was to stake-out the Winona stockyards and Beryl English would be in charge of another unit working undercover in the vicinity of Riverdale Park. Several plainclothes men were to patrol Cabbagetown, Crawford among them. Despite the evidence to the contrary, Crawford felt that Duranovitch's house and the auto body shop still warranted consideration. It was not an opinion shared by his peers.

The special units, the plainclothes men, indeed every division in the city, had been alerted to the stricture imposed upon the authorities by the terms of the ransom demand. Under no circumstances did the police mean to interfere with the procedure until David Muraskin's safety was certain. However, they did hope to observe as much of the pick-up as possible and get some idea of where the central drop-off might be located without raising the alarm.

Crawford planned on hitting the street by 7:00, leaving him just enough time to drop by Elmsley Court where Boost had some important information, or so his phone message had said. Something that would get Boost to a pay phone on such a cold day might just be genuinely important. Crawford's Duster was still out of service, so he took a cab.

"Sank goodness you are here," said the large man, breathlessly ushering Crawford into the house and slamming the door on the icy wind. He was wearing a coat and muffler, as was Frank, and the two men were beside themselves with excitement.

"Vee vas vatchingk zee D'ranowitch haus and zee enwirons."

"We seen this guy," added Frank. "Chas seen him."

"He ees ober zair now!" said Werner pointing in the direction of Montcalm Street.

"Someone is in the Duranovitch house?" asked Crawford, already pulling his radio from his belt.

"No, no," said Werner waving his hands in Crawford's face as if Crawford were an imbecile.

"Een zee body shop," said Werner.

Crawford snapped his radio back into place.

"He had no lips," said Frank, as if that cinched it.

"Wait a minute," said Crawford, his initial enthusiasm slipping away. "What are you telling me?"

Werner stamped his foot like a petulant child and swore in German.

Frank tried to explain. "We seen this guy, that is Chas seen this guy going down Tepworth Lane and damned if he don't just walk right into the old body shop there. It was around three o'clock and he ain't come out yet."

"Zee body shop you vas eenspectingk earlier zis week," Werner revived Crawford's memory.

Crawford was not suitably impressed by the news which the Neverlanders saw as earthshaking.

"He was real suspicious," said Frank. "No lips," he repeated. "Come on, vee show you," said Werner grabbing Crawford's elbow impatiently.

"It's freezing outside and besides, there's nothing in the place."

"There is now," said Frank at the door. "That guy."

Crawford still resisted. "Vee haf to go," said Werner.

"He's right," said Frank. "Chas is standing guard. He's going to stop the guy if he tries to leave and if the guy don't leave Chas'll turn into an icicle."

Crawford sighed wearily and was dragged from the house.

In a matter of minutes the three of them joined Chas at the Tepworth Lane entrance to the body shop. Chas had only a thin coat on but didn't seem particularly cold. His breath was heavy with the smell of liquor.

"Da bugger didn't come out," he said.

"You see!" said Werner turning expectantly to Crawford.

"No, I don't see," said Crawford a little unstably. "There are lots of reasons someone could be in there. It could be someone from the firm that owns the place, a planner of some kind, a city inspector."

"With no lips?" asked Frank incredulously.

"With a package of groceries?" said Chas.

Crawford swung around to face him. He had heard nothing so far about a package of groceries. The others nodded their heads excitedly. Crawford crossed the lane and tried the pedestrian door through which Boost indicated the man had entered. The door was locked. Werner smiled at him, took off his gloves, and pulled a ring of skeleton keys from his pocket.

"Uh, uh," said Crawford.

"Vee jus' take a peek, yah?" said Werner.

Crawford frowned and, crossing his arms, looked away while Werner went to work.

"They oughta trow you in the hoosegow for that," said Chas, flapping his arms to keep warm.

Werner looked at him quizzically. "Vhat ees zis hoosegow?"

"Jail," answered Crawford wryly. And he himself would join Boost there as an accomplice.

Boost laughed very lightly and went back to work. "Maybe zair ees some kind of secret tunnel, yah?"

Crawford grunted. But the comment sparked something in the back of his mind; a piece of information concerning Duranovitch. He was a contractor, after all, and he had equipment and men in the area – in his own backyard. But there was something else. Boost had opened the door. He stepped in and back out again, letting Crawford enter.

"I don' haf my gun," whispered Werner as if to explain his retreat.

Inside only dirty light, the dregs of the day, filtered through the skylights, dim and uneven. It was very quiet. Crawford looked behind him and noticed that the three men had all taken a look and pulled away from the door. He felt strangely deserted.

Crawford walked a few paces into the garage. A man had ostensibly entered the building with a bag of groceries. He was no longer there and that *was* suspicious.

The door through which he had entered clicked shut behind him and he startled. Then suddenly there was a low rumbling sound which echoed in the cavernous building. He didn't move for a full minute as he tried to place the sound. It stopped and he knew where it came from and simultaneously he remembered what it was he had been trying to recall. Duranovitch's army project on the DEW line – some kind of experimental hangar system. And what kind of hangar do you build in the far north? He edged closer to the source of the sound and peered down the ramp of the large bay, presumably built for working under trucks. The end of the bay stood open; the concrete had parted a foot or so and beyond it was a lighted room. What he could see was a car. It was a yellow Peugeot. A freshly painted yellow Peugeot. There was still masking tape on the car's front grill.

In one startling second, a hundred questions were answered. With his eyes trained on the opening at the foot of the ramp,

Crawford made his way on tiptoe to the doorway through which he had entered.

He was at the door when it opened. It was not Werner or either of the others as he half expected, but a tall handsome man with wavy black hair and a regiment of teeth too regular and bright to be quite real. The man was surprised but gained his composure almost instantaneously.

"Can I help you?" he said in a deep, well-modulated voice. Crawford did not answer quickly enough. "This *is* private property," said the man as he took off his leather gloves. Crawford's eyes rested on the man's huge unnaturally gnarled hands.

He reached into his pocket for his service automatic, unloaded though it was, and as he did so he heard steps behind him. He swung around but not in time. A heavy weight crashed down across his ear while the man facing him lashed out his arm and stripped Crawford of his gun. The last thing he heard was the useless weapon skittering across the floor.

✧

Crawford awoke slowly, opened his eyes gingerly, as if even that slight operation might disturb the delicate network of pain pulsing in his head. Having accomplished the act, he let the lids simply slide back down cancelling out his vision again. The lights intensified the aching in his skull. He pressed his eyes tightly shut, sending a fresh volley of red shot into his head; he twitched from the pain. Against the dark of not seeing he saw fire. The fire came after the recognition, after the crushing sick-making blow to his head. In some such way Crawford reconstructed conscious memory out of the rat's nest of virulent pain and confusion.

He recognized two of the faces in the room. One had to be Tommy Connacher, from Chas's description. The other was the man whom the Neverlanders had seen with the groceries. It was the third man, however, who caught and held Crawford's attention. The face was the same as the one which had confronted him in the body shop but from the neck down the image was transformed. He wore an old threadbare jacket, under which was a ratty sweater and several layers of shirts all of worn and faded fabric. From the neck down the man was the beggar Gob. He was sitting and smiling at Crawford. The lipless man trained a gun on Crawford and nothing in his flat doughy face led Crawford to believe he would refrain from shooting given the slightest excuse. Somewhere a clock chimed eight times.

The man with the dark hair spoke.

"We are in a basement, Sergeant Crawford, a very well-insulated basement playroom for Dato's dear little noisy Trudy."

"Gabby!" interrupted the lipless one and glared at the spokesman.

"Don't worry, Llaldhar, Mr. Crawford will not be in a position to pass on what he hears. Where was I – ah, yes – Trudy's playroom. You may scream if you wish to test just how insulated it is."

Crawford closed his eyes. Even the thought of screaming hurt.

"I doubt if the police will raid this house again since their previous attempt was such a dismal failure," said the man called Gabby. "And on the off chance that someone saw you entering the body shop we have covered our tracks, so to speak. Actually it is fortuitous that you have dropped in like this. I will be sure to warn my children to keep an eye out for your confederates this evening, and we have already taken precautions to divert their attention elsewhere, if need be."

There was nothing of Gob in the voice to make it recognizable. The man seemed more like Gob's antithesis; he was elegant with slightly effeminate or perhaps just grand gestures. But he clutched the arms of the armchair from which he proclaimed and he held his knees together, primly, as if they were confined to a far more narrow space.

"Tommy here tells me you are something of a hero; so much of one they gave you the year to recuperate from your heroics. Congratulations. I wonder what kind of rest you'll get when we've finished with you." The man with the red hair found this irresistibly funny and whinnied like a horse. The man called Llaldhar scrunched up his face, obviously irritated by the high-pitched laughter.

"Tommy reads all the headlines," added Gabby. "Crack detective indeed. What's the going rate on crack detectives?"

Again Tommy laughed; Llaldhar winced. Crawford shifted his weight slightly. He was bound with strands of thin but tough wire which cut into his legs and across his stomach, and most tightly of all around his wrists. The slightest move created tension somewhere else so that relief was impossible. Llaldhar, the one with the gun, was whispering to Gabby.

"Llaldhar here says one can't *redeem* cops. Llaldhar doesn't put it that way but that's what he infers. He may have a point. You may not be much use to us after all since you would only be dying in the line of duty. Cops are not for ransoming, I suspect, not even heroes."

Llaldhar would neither be pleased nor upset by the decision to spare or kill him, Crawford decided, looking at his lifeless face. Llaldhar didn't look like he necessarily enjoyed killing, it simply held no moral repugnance for him. In a way he was glad Tommy did not have the gun. He appeared to be in an advanced stage of derangement. His eyes would not stay still in his head and he flicked back a red lick of hair from across his eyes by jerking his neck like a neurotic stallion besieged by flies. Gabby contemplated his captive calmly.

He had just resumed his one-sided debate on the pros and cons of killing Crawford when Llaldhar spoke in a voice which may have just been irritated but in fact seemed imperious. "Hadn't you better get your face on?" he said.

Gabby glared at him and for an instant Crawford was not entirely sure who the boss was. Then Gabby grinned.

"My man here reminds me that there are far more important things to do than chat with you." He got to his feet and from his sweater coat pulled Crawford's 7.65 which he handed to Connacher. "By the way, we have made good use of your mitre set," he said and this time it was Llaldhar who laughed. He had a silver canine tooth in the upper left side of his lipless mouth.

To Crawford's surprise Gabby did not return, and after a few minutes spent longingly aiming his new toy at Crawford's head, Tommy grew bored and left the room.

The wires which encircled Crawford were wrapped several times around a stout pipe beside the wall. Inch by inch he was able to lower the strands far enough on the pipe that he could lie flat on the linoleum floor. He had no hope of escape. He lay his head back. Blood throbbed through his temples. The room was very still and dark. He tried to consider a reasonable argument he might present to Gabriel Duran to save his life but he was too tired.

There was a gaily painted rocking horse five feet from his head. He gazed at it. It seemed to rock almost imperceptibly. Slowly, Crawford fell into an uneasy sleep.

❖

Crunkscully had learned to read the sounds of the house. The comings and goings of its inhabitants – three for the most part. He knew for certain when they took Ross away. He called out in distress but no one answered him. The boy had struggled. The difficult reunion to which Crunkscully had come so close to accomplishing had slipped away from him. They would take Ross to that other place now. It seemed perfectly obvious.

The room he presently occupied represented no more to him than the moment at hand. It had no past, it existed only in the present and Crunkscully, while locked inside, found the past slipping away like his boy. The boy would be locked away from him in that long cluttered room with the passageway only wide enough for Gob. The room in the middle of the large weathered room in the middle of nowhere – no – somewhere, there was a car lot. Closing his eyes it was there. Not cars – wrecks, and off beyond the wrecking yard there was a stand of cedars. It was all shockingly clear again. The strange food, the tea that the man had called blood. It was in that room Ross was first promised to him. Crunkscully sat up suddenly in his cot. It was all very clear to him. He could never hope to find Ross here, but there, back in that teeming room. He tried the door of his cell but it was locked. Still there was hope in remembering.

It was some time later that he heard the report of a gun. There was a commotion outside of his room and then shouting and more shooting. He heard the roar of a car near at hand starting up and leaving. He waited. Then he heard a further disturbance. Feet were approaching heavily and he dared to hope they were coming for him for he recognized the voices. He called out: "I'm here!" as loudly as he could.

⊕

Stink had watched the mews most of Friday afternoon; by 6:15 the last of the construction workers had left, and he made his way into the basement of number 6. He replaced the board over the window socket, as had been done the previous night, and took up his spot between the water heater and the furnace. With a flashlight he searched the wall through which Gob had walked the previous night but could find no lever which would release the door. There was no sign of there being any door whatsoever in the wall and Stink wondered if he had imagined the whole thing. He shook the idea from his head and sat down on the cold concrete to wait for the evening to come. It was like the climax to a lifetime of waiting for something to happen.

Gob and Llaldhar Arnoldin had come through the moving concrete door at 8:40. They were arguing about something. Gob had been walking as he had the night before, carrying his useless wheelchair under his arm. Stink steeled himself but he couldn't pull the trigger. And in the moment of his indecision they passed by him and up the stairs. He sank to the floor. For the second time he had failed. He prayed for one more chance. Shortly before 11:00, the chance came. Two men made their way down the stairs. Stink breathed very deeply and held his breath. He felt strangely calm – cold all over. His legs were like pin cushions under him from his long night of crouched waiting. The door in the wall was opened and each man deposited several sacks in the mouth of the tunnel beyond. They were laughing and chatting. Stink raised himself silently to his feet, leaning against the cold wall in the shadows. He was ready to fire, but he had not really taken Arnoldin into consideration. Then Arnoldin suddenly made his way back through the basement with the flashlight, Stink guessed to pick up more of the money sacks left upstairs.

Gob was left standing in the lighted orifice of the tunnel and Stink watched while Gob chuckled to himself, and then suddenly started tugging at the skin around his collar. It came away: the face, the wet sandy hair, revealing the gummy face of a complete stranger.

Stink felt the strangest sense of elation, a series of thoughts flashed through his mind. Gob did not exist. To kill Gob was to kill no one. There was nothing to stop him.

He stepped from the shadows and before the man could say more than Stink's name, the little .22 magnum fired and he fell over clutching his left shoulder.

The coolness which had ruled Stink's mind deserted him. The man was whimpering horribly behind the hideously gummy mess of glue which had served to hold Gob's face implacably in place. Hearing Arnoldin respond upstairs, Stink made for the mouth of the tunnel, which the man lay across, for it seemed the only way out, and as he did, Gob curled away from him pleading, "No. Please – not *now*." He was clutching one of the money bags to him like a child a toy.

Arnoldin was on the stairs behind Stink. Stink rushed into the tunnel, swooping up the mask from the floor, and then he ran faster than he had ever run before.

The tunnel went due north from number 6. Lights were fixed in the wall every twenty feet or so. At best, he was a shadowy target. Arnoldin fired twice and the shots seemed to whirl around Stink in the circular conduit. It was as if he was in a dream, in the very belly of a rifle.

He was running under the vacant lot which separated the

mews from the auto body shop but before he reached the sub-basement of that building, the tunnel ended. A door was mercifully open and straight ahead there was a garage with a car in it. Beyond the car a door was open, wide enough for the car, but just when Stink was about to run towards it, a man with flaming red hair suddenly stepped out of the corner of his vision directly in his way. Stink skidded to a halt and dashed to his right down a narrow hallway with several doors off to the side. The redhead was carrying a gun but apparently had been too surprised to react.

At the end of the hallway a series of steps led to a door and through the door to a vestibule at the end of which darkness prevailed. Stink rushed into the darkness and found himself bound by coats on hangers and tripped up by winter galoshes. He fell and, in so doing, pushed yet another door open. He had fallen through a closet. Clambering to his feet, dragging half the closet's entrails with him, he ran towards a staircase. He seemed to be in the basement of someone's house but didn't bother to stop and consider if anyone was home. He could hear steps in the hallway he had just left. Seconds later Llaldhar barrelled through the closet, behind him, and fired at Stink's feet before they disappeared from view up the stairs. Two more shots followed him but by then he was in the hallway of a house, an elegant townhouse. Before another shot came, he was through the front door and out onto Montcalm Street. And, recognizing where he was, he knew he had escaped.

The rest was a blur. He did not slow down for half an hour. He shed the gun in a garbage can. He ran past his aunt's apartment and out of Cabbagetown down towards the lake. With every stride he grew more confident. He ran for so long nothing ached anymore. Still clutching the mask, he ran until speed deserted him and then like an animal, he just loped easily, for the joy of it. Eventually he came to the multitude of tracks which lead to and from Union Station. He hadn't ever been on a train, but he would now. The wind had dropped. The night warmed around him. Tomorrow night he would be somewhere else entirely. "You'll hear from me somewhere," he had told Mercer.

He looked at the mask. It was of an oily rubber, thickly padded through the cheeks and across the brow. He coiled several thin strands of sandy hair around his finger and tugged them, making the rubber face distort. Finally he held it up before his eyes and stared into the vacant slits, through which Gob's own eyes had winked and glared. Stink could see them there now and they were frightened. That was what he would remember. Solemnly he fitted the mask over a parking meter. The meter knob pushed the nose cavity preposterously out of shape; the face deformed to that of a malevolent clown.

37

The first shot had been distant like a memory. Crawford hadn't wanted to wake up; he fought off consciousness but other shots followed, growing closer and closer. Guns going off filled his senses, exploding time, and then imploding it into a second. He saw a man clearly through closed eyes. The man's neck was broken; he couldn't kill anyone. It was all a bad joke that had gone on far too long. Two more shots were fired at close range. He woke up in a darkened playroom wired to a pipe. The pain in his head was like a many-pointed stone.

The disturbance outside ended. Time passed.

Then through the blazing headache he heard footsteps. He lifted his head painfully as light spilled through a crack in the playroom door. It took a lumpish silhouette several minutes to find the light switch and Crawford several astonished seconds to blink out the glare and recognize Olga. What made the whole strange episode stranger still was that Olga did not see him immediately. She was fascinated with the light switch, a brightly painted plastic clown. To attract her attention Crawford groaned.

Olga approached him with her hands clasped to her bosom, delight disorienting her wildly focussed eyes. She watched him for another infinity of time until, at his suggestion, she finally knelt and attempted to find a knot on which to start to unravel him.

"The others?" Crawford inquired. Olga nodded vigorously.

"Chas put Tommy through the wall and Werner's got a large gun."

Crawford groaned again but this time with relief; it seemed only right that it would be Neverland's own Elmsley Court Irregulars who would come to his rescue. He could hear the other Neverlanders somewhere near at hand cheering. In another moment Chas poked his head around the door and came to help untangle Crawford's complicated bondage. He was drunken clumsy. Out in the basement Crawford heard Frank's voice. In the distance he heard sirens.

Olga meanwhile had left Chas to the task she had started and wandering off she found young Trudy Duranovitch's record player on which she placed a very scratchy version of Tchaikovsky's *Nutcracker Suite*.

The scene became more bizarre by the minute and Crawford began to seriously consider himself not rescued at all but merely delirious.

"Put him clear through the wall!" said Chas, grinning.

The others arrived, Werner first, Frank and Buck after and between them Crunkscully. He stood serenely between his rescuers while Tchaikovsky swelled brokenly into the playroom and the Neverlanders bustled about all talking at once. While Chas untied Crawford with painful slowness, Crawford tried to piece together a story out of the cat's concert of reports.

It seemed Chas, Frank, and Werner had cleared away from the auto shop unnoticed. When Crawford did not reappear, the two men had broken into the shop again, only to find it empty. They guessed there must be a secret tunnel. In the mysterious fantasy world in which Werner Boost carried out his investigations, underground tunnels were as reasonable a phenomenon as anything else.

"So you called the police," Crawford interjected.

"Hell, no!" came Frank's response.

The story continued. They had retired to Elmsley Court to consider their attack and also to get Werner's gun.

"It was dark by the time we got back," said Frank. "We start poking around when Werner sees this kid on a store roof. Then we see them everywhere, on roofs, in the trees, in garbage cans. We pulled back outa there real quick."

"Vonce beaten, tvice shy," said Werner pleased with the phrase, and tapping the wound under his eye.

Crawford shook his head; something was very wrong. "And there was *no* police around?"

"Oh sure," said Frank. "We seen a couple a old-clothes-men types, like yourself, but they didn't fool us one bit."

Crawford trembled slightly at the response. "But if you *knew* they were cops, you could have told them what had happened to me."

Frank was momentarily taken aback. "That's the last thing I'd a thought of first," he said.

Werner was shaking his head.

"Anyvay, vee vanted you for ourselves," he said.

Crawford had been about to remonstrate further but Boost's statement caught him up short.

Chas grinned and continued the story. "We looked around some more and when we didn't find you we went to the Winchester," he said.

"Vee vas vorkingk on an alternate solution," Werner explained.

"We drank the whole place under the table," Chas added.

"When we came back – no kids nowhere," said Frank. "Then *pow*, we hear this gun shot from the new development. We run down there and Chas finds the place just like that – he's got a nose for cordite. There was this loose board over a basement window and he kicks it in and is down the hole like a greased weasel." Chas's grin widened.

"Unt zat's vhen vee found zee tunnel leadingk to zee body shop, unt zat's vhere vee found Herr Crunkscully unt zat's vhen vee found you!" Werner laid his hand over his heart as if the exertion of his summary had overcome him.

At that moment the *Nutcracker* reached a crescendo and

Frank barked at Olga: "Turn that fairytale off!"

In the silence which ensued they all heard the sirens converging nearby.

Chas finally liberated Crawford's torso from the wire.

"How much of a tunnel is there?" asked Crawford leaning heavily against the playroom wall and rubbing life back into his chafed wrist.

"It goes to hell and back," said Frank expansively.

"And there was no one but Tommy?" Crawford asked.

"Nope. We seen this car – least we heard this car taking off out through the body shop there. It sounded like it was in one helluva hurry. Next thing you know we hear this Godalmighty yell, 'I'm here!' and damned if we don't find Scully – I mean The Honourable Mr. Scully – locked up in this little room down thataway." He flung his arm behind him indicating the direction from which Crawford had heard them arrive. It was from that direction that the sirens were loudest; in Tepworth Lane, he suspected. The sirens seemed to have perturbed the Neverlanders. They raced pell-mell through their tale fearing the imminent arrival of the forces of law and order, not to mention proportion.

"That's when Tommy came," said Chas, his eyes glistening.

"Through a door, a hidden door."

"Behind a closet in zee basement."

"Tommy had a gun," Frank continued, "but it wouldn't shoot."

"That's when I put the damn bastard through the wall."

"And I found you," said Olga.

Abruptly the story was over.

Several men could be heard entering the basement outside the playroom and by the sound of it, their entry was by means of the closet through which the rescue party claimed to have made their way.

Crawford shouted: "In here, don't shoot!"

In a moment the room filled with blue shirts.

✤

Reality had crashed in on the Neverlanders, yet again. Looking glum, they huddled around Crawford, who was passing on what information he could to be radioed back to headquarters. This done, he turned to his dispirited friends. "Why don't you guys show these cops where that tunnel goes?" he said.

Spirits revived instantly.

Frank led the way; back through the closet in the basement and down into a wing of the underground network leading west from Duranovitch's house under Montcalm Alley to the body shop. There were several rooms off the underground garage, small and empty except for the one in which Scollard had apparently been kept. In that room there was a cot, a card table, and chair. There was no David Muraskin. There was no one but Tommy Connacher, whom Chas had literally thrown through an unfinished wall of plasterboard. The Neverlanders watched with pride as their unconscious ex-housemate was extricated by two policemen and carried off.

Crawford found his service revolver on the floor and thanked whatever neurotic god it was who had convinced him not to load it. Bending to pick it up he almost fainted.

The police had made their way into the underground garage via the body shop for both the outer door and the sliding concrete door at the base of the ramp had been left open when the Peugeot had fled. Down that same ramp Crawford was pleased to see the familiar if slightly blurred figure of Beryl English approaching with reinforcements. While a squad was sent to explore the southern arm of the warren which led from the body shop down to the mews, she caught Crawford up on what had taken place.

She had responded to a call for back-up at around 9:00, she presumed from Crawford. The call had led her to an abandoned factory where nothing beyond his mitre set had been found. She decided to remain with some of her unit and had done so until a radio call summoned her to the auto body shop.

Fortunately the initial gun shot had been heard by a plain-clothes man. He had not been near enough to trace the shot to its source, but the subsequent shots had led him to radio for support.

It was now 12:05 and, according to the ransom demand, David was to be released at midnight. There was no word from headquarters and Crawford felt a sinking sensation in his stomach that was as painful as his crashing headache. From time to time he glanced at Scollard, who seemed remarkably well considering his imprisonment, and quite at ease amidst the noise and bustle of the investigation.

"Are you all right?" Crawford asked.

"Oh, fine," said Scollard.

It was a ridiculous answer, but no more so than the question, and Crawford suggested to Frank that he take the man home.

"Oh, he's fine," Frank said, parroting Scollard. The Neverlanders intended to stay until the bitter end. The bitter end seemed to be drawing unsatisfactorily near.

Then suddenly there was a break – a call from Skene indicated something was up at the Winona stockyard which Reuter had staked out. Leaving English in charge of the Duranovitch site, Crawford decided to go to the stockyard. He was about to collar a driver for that purpose, but when he tried to walk he found he grew quite dizzy, and stopped. A loud cough from Frank caught his attention.

"We can take you down," Frank offered timidly.

Crawford shook his head, a gesture he should have avoided for the pain made him feel faint again. Chas propped him up with a massive brown hand.

"It might be dangerous," Crawford muttered between gritted teeth.

Chas laughed. "Hell, we ain't afraid," he said.

"Only I am comingk viz him," said Werner boastfully.

"No," said Crawford. The debate was making him feel nauseated.

"But I am armed," whispered Boost in his ear. Through the folds of his old trenchcoat the blue polished butt of his Llama automatic glistened. Crawford glared at him, breathing deeply.

"The adventure is over boys." He looked at the Neverlanders one after the other."Over," he repeated and the words reverberated in his skull. No one would stay still in his vision. He pulled his arm away from Chas's support only to find his knees buckle under him. He fell forward into Frank's arms. Unconscious.

Beryl English called to one of her officers for help but Frank winked at her. "It's okay," he said. "We'll look after him – hell – we saved his life."

The clock on the dashboard said 12:27 when next Crawford came to. He was too disoriented to question where he was – only the time registered.

Then a voice said softly: "Now ain't that smooth as silk. You're on the wings of a Golden Hawk, Mr. Crawford." Turning his head very slightly Crawford could see the dim figure of Frank Qualtrough draped over the steering wheel and squinting terribly. "Ain't driven at night for years," he admitted in a whisper. Then he swore quietly and held a bleeding palm up to his lips. Crawford noticed that the gear shift was a naked pole.

It was a fairytale, Crawford concluded. The Neverlanders had successfully sloughed off the real world again, "on the wings of a Golden Hawk."

Crawford turned his head just enough to make out the compressed figures of Chas and Scollard and Werner stuffed into the back seat.

"You can't do this," said Crawford in a lack-lustre voice.

The others chuckled. "So you srow us all een zee whadyacallit – hoosegow. So vhat?"

"It's obstruction of justice," Crawford argued.

"So was rescuing you," said Frank.

Crawford shut his mouth and his eyes. His tongue was stinging slightly, his mouth tasted of liquor. Opening his eyes again he saw Frank guzzle from a flask. "Where are you taking me?"

"Where you want to go," said Frank cheerfully.

"I want my son," said Scollard from the back seat.

Crawford's head was still spinning but not quite as badly and the nausea had passed. Some of the disorientation was beginning to pass as well. Ahead of him up the road there was a blaze of lights: patrol cars, an ambulance, fire trucks. In another moment Frank pulled the Studebaker through a chain-link gate in a four-wheel drift. It was the entrance to the Winona stockyard. Frank slammed on the brakes and skidded 180 degrees.

Several police sharpshooters had rifles trained on the car by the time Crawford climbed out into plain view. The other passengers didn't need a second warning to stay put. From a cruiser across the noisy, brightly lit yard Reuter approached Crawford who stood breathing in the cold air and letting the snow splash some sense into his aching head. Reuter apologized for the greeting. He had received no word from English that Crawford was coming. He led him to the smouldering wreck of a once yellow, once black Peugeot.

"There were two of them," said Reuter. "Both dead. Wheeled in here at midnight – tried to pull out again when they saw us. We hit a tire. There was return fire so we opened up. The Peugeot careened into a lumber shed and burst into flames. We got them out in time," said Reuter. "There was some money in the boot but only twenty-five Gs, no more. And no boy."

Reuter supplied all the right answers for the time being except the big one. Where was David Muraskin?

Crawford was led to the ambulance. He pointed at one of the corpses. "Someone named Llaldhar," he said. And then to the other. "Unless I'm mistaken, that's Gabriel Duran."

Reuter raised his eyebrows when he heard the name then he frowned and nodded towards Crawford's right temple. "Who did that?" he asked.

Crawford nodded at the dead man. Reuter winced in sympathy. He turned and looked back at the Studebaker.

"Who are the kooks in the chariot?" he said, indicating the Golden Hawk.

Crawford looked across the yard to where Frank's car stood. Momentarily it caught the light and seemed on fire, its golden side splashed with red. "The Neverlanders," he murmured.

"Who?"

"One of them's Scollard," Crawford said loudly.

"You found him!" said Reuter.

"No, he found me...it's a long story," he added to put off further questioning. "Any idea where they were heading?" he asked, gesturing at the two dead men.

The air began to pulse with light and across the snow-filled night sky Crawford saw helicopters, with spotlights hanging from their bellies, approaching the stockyard. It was an impressive, eerie sight.

Reuter did have an idea and had acted on it. He had been quite certain that the stockyard had not been Duran's final destination since there was no indication that the yard, despite its enormity, held any secret spots. This had made Reuter curious about the gate at the back of the yard. He had gotten hold of the foreman to come and unlock the old padlock with which the gate was chained shut. It wouldn't open. The foreman discovered that it was not the original lock at all nor any lock for which he had the key. What was more, Reuter realized that it would be impossible to see the gate from the foreman's shed. Crawford was piecing together the rest of the story.

"It's a long shot," said Reuter. As the helicopters pounded nearer, he had to raise his voice to be heard. "Somewhere out there he must have some kind of hideout." He waved his hand towards the hilly wooded land beyond the stockyard. "It's worth a try," he added without a great deal of hope.

Crawford was thinking about Connie and Bernard Muraskin and telling them the news. His headache was a dull throbbing now in sync with the helicopter engines. He watched three shafts of light wavering back and forth over the ragged face of the hillside, lighting up the tops of trees.

Reuter was called over to a patrol car for a message from headquarters. After a moment Crawford saw Reuter shaking his head. Still no David. Crawford walked towards the back fence, his hands in his pockets. The chain which had held the gates shut had been broken. The gates hung open and a police four-wheel-drive truck was having a spotlight fitted on its roof to join the manhunt in the woodland. The copters were moving away up the valley. The snow was thick, a blanket across the already impenetrable night.

"Quite a sight, ain't it."

Crawford turned to see Frank had joined him. Frank offered Crawford the mickey and Crawford swigged deeply from it and handed it back.

"He's talking," said Frank, a perplexed look on his face.

"Who?" said Crawford.

"Scully. Weird stuff – keeps saying something about a wrecking yard and drinking blood and his boy Ross."

Crawford turned to look at Frank. Everything seemed suddenly to stop. His headache, the thrumming of the whirlybirds, all the sounds of authority in the stockyard behind them.

"A wrecking yard?" said Crawford more to himself than to Frank. "Does he say where?",

Frank shook his head. "Just a wrecking yard." Frank tapped his head as if to suggest the wrecking yard might be in Scollard's mind. Crawford wasn't so sure. He turned and raced back to Reuter still talking over the radio.

He looked up as Crawford approached. "What's up?" he asked.

"Have you got contact with the copters?" Crawford asked. Reuter nodded. "Tell them to look for a wrecking yard of some kind." Reuter looked only momentarily perplexed before passing on the message.

Frank had caught up to Crawford now. "You think he knows something?" he asked. Crawford turned and looked towards the helicopters perched on their moving pedestals of light. He spoke to both Reuter and Frank. "Scollard was abducted once before, in the Peugeot...." There was nothing further he could add.

A crackled response came back from one of the pilots of the helicopters. He had passed over what might be some kind of abandoned car lot although it was too snow-covered to really tell.

Another closer pass did not reveal any structure standing in the vicinity.

In desperation Crawford barked at Reuter. "Tell them to look *really* hard. Tell them to land." Reuter passed on the command.

Crawford watched the three dark machines circle closer together so that for a minute their lights mingled over a rise of land not a quarter of a mile away up the valley. Even through the snow he could see their bellies lit up red as rust. Then one of the helicopters started to descend. Its pedestal of light grew shorter and the trees below seemed to fill with a pale glow. The other two helicopters descended onto the hill until the hill seemed to spill fire down its snow-covered sides. Then it came, the radio message as excited as a landing party on the moon itself. "There's some kind of old barn – hidden in the trees on the side of the hill above the wrecking yard. There's an Airstream trailer inside." Another few moments of waiting and then: "We got him! We got him! He looks…he's okay. It's our boy, all right. We got him! Over and out."

Crawford turned and Scollard and the Neverlanders were behind him. They had heard the crackling report, and all but Scollard were whooping with joy.

Crawford found himself staring at Scollard. "We found the boy," he said.

Scollard smiled at the sky, at the spot where the three helicopters were now rising with their precious cargo. He nodded his head slowly up and down and then looked squarely into Crawford's eyes. There was relief, huge relief, in Scollard's eyes. His very strange and difficult ordeal was over.

38

It snowed all night. Deeply, evenly, without wind. Without tracks. Safe at 14 Elmsley Court Scollard woke as slowly as a worm out of a deep tunnel of sleep. He was having a mild argument with himself, the gist of which went that if holes were buried in the ground one would have to dig to find them. He was awake just enough to realize how far he had come up from under. He was asleep enough to feel whole.

Crawford had stayed at the stockyard until David Muraskin was landed and he had accompanied the boy to his parents' home. With remarkable wisdom or discretion Frank Qualtrough had taken Scollard back to Elmsley Court before the helicopters had arrived. The illusory reunion was over for Scollard. His son's redemption was completed in his mind.

At Baseball Park Road Crawford slept more deeply than he had in a year.

The following day Crawford was taken to the site of the hideout. There had once been a road, Green Road, which had run down through the valley. It had fallen into disrepair since the Bayview Extension had been completed. All access had effectively been cut off by the construction of a water main across the Green Road's north end and it had been left to the slow traffic of weeds and rain. The car lot once serviced by Green Road seemed, at first, to be utterly inaccessible, except by the air, but in fact there was a way, as Sergeant Reuter and his men discovered.

The dry river bed behind the Winona stockyards proved as hard as rock and as flat as a tarmac. The river way meandered southwest until it passed within a few hundred yards of the abandoned car lot. At one point the banks were not steep and deep ruts in the side of the hill indicated the recent passage of more than one vehicle. The Peugeot, apparently, and a half-ton truck used to pull the Airstream. The half-ton was found among the wrecked and dilapidated cars covered over with a canvas which in turn was crusted over with snow. The Airstream itself sat snugly in the old barn out of the elements and out of sight. Snow, deep winter snow, would no doubt render the approach to the lot impractical but for the rest of the year it had offered an irresistible hideout.

A Winona Enterprises sign was found in Duran's trailer. When the need arose to move from his lair he could simply drive back "up river" and when no one was around drive up the ramp into the stockyard and from there out onto the Bayview Extension. It would take a certain amount of gall on Duran's part but there was nothing to indicate he was lacking in that. In the gullet of the river, bouncing along in the police four-wheel, Crawford noticed that he could not see traffic on the more conventional valley roadway, the Bayview Extension, although it was not a hundred yards away. The forgotten river had etched itself deeply into the land.

When Crawford was led into the trailer a couple of disgruntled officers were taking inventory. No more of the ransom money had been found but the contents of the trailer indicated a thousand other petty crimes might now be solved. Amidst the plunder the men had found four B & E uniforms complete from cap to shining shoes.

The trailer reeked. The smell of decaying food subtly turned the disorder into derangement, in Crawford's eyes. He hoped Doctor Wenzel, the forensic psychiatrist, would see it for it represented a mind turned inside out. The officers were too busy to notice Crawford slip something into his pocket, nor would they have cared since it made their horrendous task one item lighter. He found it on a ledge above the sink amongst a clutter of knick-knacks, belt buckles, watches and the like. It was a small wooden ball with a stylized golden hawk emblazoned on its surface.

❖

Later that day Crawford picked up his car from the service station and the following morning he picked up Connie Scollard from her hotel. They had been invited to Elmsley Court. She had not yet seen her husband although Crawford had contacted her to say he was safe.

Connie was introduced around the room and last of all to her husband who kissed her on the cheek and said, much to everyone's surprise: "Hello Connie, how are you?"

Connie bit her lip and said: "Fine," and sat down beside him on the davenport.

Crawford could see how awkward she felt but she handled the whole thing remarkably well.

She and Crawford had arrived in the middle of Frank's recounting of Friday night's adventure, this time for the benefit of Monsieur Calmette who had been released from Wellesley Hospital that morning.

"I feel like Christ," said Frank holding out his scarified hand for Calmette's inspection. "Well half a Christ anyway," he added, beaming.

"A th-th-a third of Christ," corrected Buck and pointed a shaky finger at his crossed feet to make his meaning clear.

Frank nodded agreeably. "A flight on the wings of the Hawk," he said.

"Vee vere zee Luftwaffe, yah?" Werner Boost loudly proclaimed. Frank's expression soured a little at the suggestion. Werner tittered.

Crawford took the opportunity to present Frank with the gearshift knob he had found the day before in Duran's trailer. It was the fitting end to the fairytale. To Frank it was the story's punchline – its moral and its essence. There was new cause for celebration and a bottle of fine sherry was brought forth by Werner, as befitting the company.

In the middle of a protracted toast offered by Frank, Olga made her appearance. She clambered down the steps and stood before everyone at the entrance to the room. She was wearing a cherry-red sweater over her crazy-quilt print shift. The sweater was held discreetly closed across her bosom with a sweater clip and she wore matching red socks inside her patent pumps. Her lank grey-blonde hair was held back on one side of her face with a hair clip adorned with five prancing white lambs. She looked as if she were about to cry. She cleared her throat loudly. "I let the cat out of his room! I'm sorry now. Maybe none of this would have happened but it couldn't be helped. It was making such a racket. Chas didn't know I done it," she added, unnecessarily absolving him from her guilt. "Now if Mr. Crunkscully wants, I'm prepared to go and find him another cat. I seen one prowling around here just the other day." Then, without waiting for Crunkscully's reaction, she left the house, without coat or boots.

From the window they watched her traipsing through the snow, on the unshovelled street.

"She von't find her vay back," said Boost.

"She don't even know where she's goin'," said Chas.

"I-I-I'll catch her up in-in the ca-caddy!" exclaimed Buck. Without a word he grabbed his plaid jacket and hobbled out the back door, his eyes bright with anticipation.

Crunkscully sat on the davenport next to Connie. In a blissful stupor, he was satisfied to gaze out the window to where birds picked at shadows on a drift of snow.

Connie Scollard at last was called on to tell Crunkscully's story, for only she could supply the background. She started falteringly, looking at her husband for support. He smiled encouragingly.

It had all begun with an idea about recovering a lost son, but there was no son and hadn't ever been. She related the incident with the lost baby pram. Her audience listened with rapt attention.

Then Frank spoke up enthusiastically: "It's like in the book," he said. "In *Peter Pan*. Only boys fall out of their prams – girls are too smart."

"And the boys end up here," Crawford thought to himself.

"Goddammit," whispered Chas, "it's the first I heard of it."

Connie Scollard smiled weakly and took her husband's hand in hers. "His feelings of guilt confused the imaginary son and his real daughter. You see, it's strange, but for the nine months I was pregnant he loved a son without knowing him."

"It's like that, I guess. I mean about children," said Frank. "Now I'm kind of a strange case. You see, I got two boys both in Africa, but they are foster kids. I seen their pictures and read their letters but I never really knowed them. I always hoped one day I'd go and visit them but I ain't never going to get that kinda money together. It's funny though, in one way I know them better than Scully knew his son but in another way he was a lot closer to his son than I ever was to mine, if you get my meaning. I mean, for nine months he was just that close, a belly away from him and here I am six trillion miles from my boys."

Distant waves of conversation lapped over Crunkscully's consciousness. He was trying to concentrate on something else. He had been waiting for Tinker Bell the whole morning. It was in this room he had first seen her and the sun, which was at least part of her nature, was out and shining on the crisp drifts of snow between the shadows of branches. Birds as light as shadows pecked away in dappled peace in the front yard. He watched them, resting his head on the back of the davenport. He had turned his attention briefly back to those in the room, perhaps at the moment when Connie had taken his hand.

Then to his surprise he saw her. The sprite was back darting around the walls. It was extraordinary because he hadn't a knife or anything shiny to tip the sun into that ecstatic dance. She must – he conceded – be there of her own accord, without his connivance. Some precious ineluctable trick of perception. A mystery.

39

The case would be closed in time but never completely solved. Apart from the $25,000 found in the Peugeot's trunk, Muraskin's ransom was not recovered.

The Neverlanders had said they had heard a car drive off from the body shop after they heard the shot in the mews. By the time they had reached Crawford it was shortly after 11:00 and the Peugeot didn't arrive at the stockyard until just after midnight. It was at most a twenty-five-minute drive from the body shop to the stockyard so a drop-off could have been made.

It was suggested by the media that the ransom might simply have been stashed, a suggestion which caused a flurry of excitement and launched a treasure hunt through the ash cans of Cabbagetown and along the route through the valley. If anyone was successful he made himself scarce.

Bernard K. Muraskin was happy enough to have his son back. He and his wife packed David off with them to Jamaica to recuperate. No comment was forthcoming on what school their son would next attend. Having heard the story of Ross Scollard's strange odyssey, Muraskin very generously donated what money had been recovered to the Alzheimer Society for research purposes. A cure must be found for people with diseased memories.

It was assumed the money left in the car was simply Duran's cut in the venture and therefore that he had been working for some underground organization. But by the time the pathology report was filed this opinion was subtly changed: the report indicated a double-cross. Duran had picked up only superficial fire in the police ambush. What had killed him was a slug from Llaldhar Arnoldin's gun, delivered execution style in the side of the head. There was also a .22 slug removed from Duran's shoulder, which suggested the man had a variety of enemies.

Tommy Connacher was not dead but he was deluded beyond hope of an early recovery. He supplied little in the way of hard facts. He said the operation was supported by funds from someone called the Grand Vizier. He also claimed that someone called Stink had double-crossed Gob. The allegations were disregarded as the metaphorical wanderings of a sick mind.

Tommy had been loyal to Gob. Gob, he told anyone who would listen, was going to lead a holy war against the rich and, in Tommy's demented mind, he had died a martyr to the cause. Tommy Connacher was commited to a hospital for the criminally insane where he proposed to start a cult around Gob the Martyr.

Gabriel Duran's uncle came forward to claim his nephew's body once the pathology lab had finished with it. From Uncle Yogi many things came to light about Duran, not the least of which was his difficult relationship with his brother Dato.

Gabriel Duranovitch, who had shortened his name for the stage to Duran, had been brought up by his Uncle Yogi and by his grandmother Marichka. Dato, Gabriel's older brother by a year, was brought up by his real parents. Gabriel was dumped on the relatives at birth for the simple reason that his mother didn't want him. Apparently she had developed allergies after the birth of her first son and some fool of a doctor had recommended she have another child right away. Twelve months later, Gabriel was born. The allergies didn't go.

Yogi, now in his sixties, remembered what a yoke around his neck Gabby had been. Gabby had been brilliant in school but could not afford a university education. Dato had only a pedestrian mind but had stumbled through an engineering degree and joined his father's company, filling his shoes when the old man died. As soon as their mother passed away, Dato made an attempt to redress the balance for by that time he was a successful contractor. Gabriel had grown bitter and took whatever Dato gave him. He considered it his due, though there would never be enough of it to make up the injustice done him. He started coming up with schemes and getting Dato to bankroll them. Dato invariably did. The emotional blackmail continued. Gabby had imagination and talent but no head for business and no patience. His schemes all fell through and Dato grew tired of feeling guilty for the sins of his parents. In time, he started to reject Gabby and to the latter, it was like adding insult to injury.

Uncle Yogi had seen trouble coming for a long time but he always hoped Gabby's acting career would take him out of himself. He hoped he would achieve success on his own and leave the past behind. Yogi wasn't surprised when fame eluded his nephew.

"He got into theatre for all the wrong reasons," Yogi had told Sergeant English. "Ever since high school it was not enough to be a big shot, to show off. What Gabby wanted was to shock. He liked only to shock."

At what point in time Gabby had become Gob was not difficult to guess once his former agent Bimbo Gallant had been located.

"Gabby was one in a million," he said very easily as if everyone was one in a million to Bimbo Gallant. "Could have made it to the top of his class as a character actor but he was too damned irresponsible. It got so his reputation beat him to the audition. That's when he got outa acting and into the movies. B horror flicks for the most part. Gabby was the perfect monster," Gallant said with affection. "What he couldn't do with his face! I swear if someone hadda gave him the chance he coulda had Viv Leigh's part in *Gone With The Wind,* but he stuck to monsters. Then he got in some kinda shady business deal, scuttled everything. Then he split. He owed me too!"

According to Bimbo, this incident had occurred two years earlier, which coincided with Gob's first appearance on the streets of Cabbagetown, police discovered.

It was Gallant who informed the police that the Airstream had been Gabby's living quarters and a means of getting to out of town jobs. "Wouldn't fly," said Gallant. "Scared of flying."

The trailer had once belonged to Winona Enterprises but had been auctioned off some years earlier along with other equipment when the company had been in bad straits. Duranovitch's secretary, Swaantje Bremane, now recalled that Gabby had taken to parking it on Winona construction sites to avoid paying for parking elsewhere.

As the file on Duran grew over the weeks and the depth of his rejection complex came to light, the outlandish "Gob" came to light as well. Wenzel's report to the coroner was lengthy but it was to begin laconically enough. "Schizophrenic, paranoid type. Psychotic."

Dato Duranovitch's underground warren interested the authorities as much as his brother's attempted kidnapping. There were two laboratories in the process of being set up and all the indications suggested the manufacture of synthetic drugs.

The elusive Dato Duranovitch did finally put into port in Florida, but had no comments to make concerning his brother's doings and was in no hurry to return to Toronto. Extradition was applied for and his legal counsel flew to his side in Florida ostensibly to help him come up with an explanation for his underground facilities. Dato was apparently unaware of the use to which Gabriel had put the underground sanctum in his absence.

There was only the Knot left unaccounted for, and so completely did that entity elude detection, let alone capture, that Crawford found himself wondering if it had died with its maker. There was little enough proof that the gang had existed at all. There was the signature on Sally Paza's backside, although Crawford had only her word for it. He had of course seen something in the park on Hallowe'en, but what exactly had he seen? Many darting shadows dispersing into the streets of Cabbagetown. A mock rape. A ritual-like death?

The Police Commission were asking for a comprehensive

report, but Ewart and the men at 51 Division, could only watch and wait while McIlwane scanned the monthly statistics.

The idea was vexatious and yet compelling – street-wise children operating below the law. An elite army of thieves and con artists under the eye of a gifted lunatic. For a few moments in a basement playroom Crawford had seen such a man between states of being: an actor wearing Gob's shabby clothes or Gob wearing the mask of an actor. It was difficult to say, in retrospect, which was the role, which the man.

Crawford mused to himself that the Knot may have been no more than a figment of a disturbed mind. Gob's, that is. Or perhaps his own.

Epilogue

The shot Crawford had been waiting for had come at last. It hadn't killed him, but, rather like a kiss in a fairytale, it had revived him. The trauma of a year began to loosen. Crawford could close his eyes again and dare the dead to appear. They could no longer hurt him. He let slip the ties which connected him to the past. It wasn't exactly like forgetting, but it was a start.

Jeff Brothers wanted to write a profile of the hero but instead Crawford granted him a confession.

"I don't solve cases," Crawford admitted. "They resolve around me while I take a bullet in the leg or a smack across the back of the head. It's like some kind of a passport stamp – 'I was here.' I am part of each case, not above it or outside it. Cops are not outside the law; they, and the criminals they chase and the victims of those criminals, are all lashed together," he said. "In a knot."

✦

Over the Christmas holidays he finished renovating his house with the help of the Neverlanders. They all came for Christmas supper – all of them except Crunkscully, of course. Crawford heard from Connie that she had arranged to have him moved to Vancouver to be near his daughter. Scollard had no further illusions about a missing boy.

276

McIlwane dropped by for dessert and Crawford revelled at the chance of introducing him to Werner Boost. They almost got along. McIlwane left after a while for he had a family at home, but the others, Crawford included, had no family and they caroused until all hours. At some point before dawn Frank gathered his troupe and piled them into the Golden Hawk and took them home.

Crawford waved from the front door until the car had driven off. The air was cool and anise-scented. It was very calm.